Dragon Dreams

Muses of Mythology Anthology

Edited By Draco Amethystus

Storm Dragon Publishing

Dragon Dreams: Muses of Mythology Anthology
Edited By Draco Amethystus

Published by Storm Dragon Publishing, LLC.

Copyright © 2024 by Draco Amethystus.

Cover design by Damonza.

Printed in the United States.

Cataloging-in-Publication Date on file with the Library of Congress.

www.dracoamethystus.com

To all those who dare to dream of dragons.

Introduction

Dragons have been my favorite mythical creature since I was a little boy. It began for me with tales of Saint George and the Dragon as well as Bruce Coville's *Jeremy Thatcher, Dragon Hatcher* and carrying on to Tracy Hickman and Margaret Weis' original *DragonLance* books and beyond. As my love of reading also morphed into a love of writing, I began to weave tales of these magical monsters of myth.

Monsters…that's what much of Western culture collectively has seen dragons as, although that has shifted in more modern times. As I conceptualized the Muses of Mythology Anthology series, I knew that I wanted to begin with dragons. And I knew that I wanted to share tales where they were seen not as monsters, but rather for the majestic, glorious beings they are. So, *Dragon Dreams* was hatched.

In this beautiful collection of both poetry and short stories, you will be regaled with tales of dragons in various historical settings from the 1700s to our current time and even into the future of science fiction renown. You will meet dragons both great and small. Tears will be shed and laughter shared. But magic will also always be wielded.

Featuring the famous dragon author, Maria Grace, and many other authors both established and new to the fantasy world of writing, *Dragon Dreams* holds a story for anyone who loves dragons.

Draco Amethystus
August 1, 2024 – Thursday

Table of Contents

Maria Grace

Sweeping up was not usually the part of the day people looked forward to, but—not for the first time in her life—Maud Garston was content to be different. In the tiny village of Mordiford, it took little to earn the distinction. Being a twin would have been enough. But running the local dry goods shop with her twin brother, Mattias, only added to her notoriety.

Then there was the dragon. The Mordiford Dragon. Carrying both the names of the girl who cared for the dragon and the family credited with slaying it, someone always has something clever—at least in their own minds—to say on the matter.

Though it still bothered her, she had grown more adept at handling the remarks. A quick gesture toward the painting on the shop wall, a copy of the dragon's painting that decorated the nearby Holy Rood church, and the delivery of one of three or four well-rehearsed remarks distracted all but the most determined from talking about that dragon.

No one was ever to talk about the other one.

The shop door swung open, thumping against the plain wooden wall behind it. A fat, rusty-brown blur carrying something white and muddy scrambled in, as fast as his four legs could waddle past Maud and into the back room. Mr. Harrison Rundgut—yes, that was both his name and his description; a man about whom everything was round and either bald, red, or bulging—but it was best not to ever remind him of that—staggered in after, panting and clutching his side.

"That mutt of yours dun got into me wife's laundry. Again." He braced his hands against the long counter and gasped for breath. "Stole her best petticoat he did, and she will have it back. The damned thing is brand new and iff'n it be damaged—"

"Yes, of course. We will make it right with you. Give me a moment and I will get it from him. With any luck, all it will need is the charwoman's attention—"

"You best hope so, girl, the fabric to sew it cost—"

"Excuse me a moment." Maud set aside her broom and stomped past Mr. Rundgut and through the doorway into the back room. "Per-ci-val! Percival! Come here right now!" She drew the curtain across the doorway and peered into the dimly lit room. "Don't make me get down on my hands and knees to come after you, you little scamp."

Not that such talk had ever worked before. And Percival utterly predictable. He always stole fresh laundry. He always ran back here with it. And he always hid in the corner where the two sets of shelves did not quite meet, leaving a dark, narrow cubby for him to duck into.

And yes, there he was, huddling in the shadows, the white petticoat in his mouth, wrapped back across the wing nubs on his shoulders.

Maud squatted in front of the shelves. "What do you have to say for yourself? How many times have we been through this?"

"I can't help myself." Percival muttered around his mouthful. "It is my quest, my holy grail!"

"No, it is no holy grail. I understand, dragons hoard, and it is simply in their nature. You are helpless against it. You tell me that every time we are in this position. And yet, you are very specific about the laundry you steal. I wonder why that is."

"Because I am a dragon."

"No, it is not that. Now, come out here, and give me the bloody petticoat."

"No, it is mine. I need it for my hoard." His taloned front feet scraped little gouges in the worn floorboards.

"No, you don't. Your hoard is full."

"A dragon's hoard is never full."

"You have filled the closed bed upstairs to overflowing with your hoard." Not to mention the pile under the bed, and the one growing on top of it. "Mattias has no place to sleep."

"That isn't true. Your closed bed has two levels. He sleeps above you."

"Only because he is still enamoured with having the only dragon in England living with us and allowed you to take over his closed bed when you overflowed the trunk that we gave you to store your hoard." Now might not be the time to inform Percival that Mattias regretting that decision daily. "Come out here right now, or I will drag you out by your useless little wing-nubbins."

"Don't insult my wings!" Percival poked his nose out.

She reached for him, but he ducked under her hand and scuttled out from his hidey-hole.

"My wings are wonderful. If I met another of my kind, I know they would be admired. But you are right, meeting another dragon, a mate, not this rumpled old laundry, is my holy grail." Percival dropped the petticoat, raised his head frill, and lifted the little boney stubs to spread the fragile hand's width of webbing underneath.

He would never fly, much less meet another dragon. She would never say it aloud, but compared to the image of the Mordiford Dragon, he looked unfinished. More than anything else, Percival looked like a fat little pug dog, if a pug was a lizard, not a dog. With short pudgy legs, long claws on his toes, a short snout, and a red brown scaley hide, it wasn't hard for him to persuade those who could not hear his thin little voice—which was everyone else in Mordiford village—that he was a badly behaved little pug.

How exactly the persuasion worked, neither of them knew. But it kept his secret safe, and that was all that mattered.

"I'll take this." Maud snatched the petticoat and shook it out. "At least you haven't torn this one. Just a bit of dirt. That'll be easy enough to make right with Mr. Rundgut. I'll get this back to him—"

"No, I'll take care of that." Mattias slipped in behind the curtain.

Even after twenty-one years, looking at her twin felt like looking in a warped mirror. Red hair, hazel eyes, narrow freckled nose on a slightly too-round face. They favoured one another enough that the villagers always did a double-take to ensure they knew which one was walking by.

Checking for dress or pants should have been enough. They had stopped playing that sort of trick more than a decade ago. But people had long memories.

"What's wrong?" she asked.

Mattias shook his head. "Keep Percival inside. I'll settle matters with Rundgut. Then we are going to close shop for the afternoon."

"I didn't do it! I swear, I only took that petticoat, which is what everyone in the village expects I will do." Percival skittered back toward his hiding place.

Mattias took the bedraggled white linen petticoat and slipped through the curtain.

"No one has accused you of anything, at least not yet." Maud crouched by Percival and scratched under his chin. Poor little creature. Despite his proclivity for stealing small clothes, he really was a dear little fellow. Everyone in the village had a soft spot for him, believing him a silly little dog who brought no harm to anyone.

If they had known he was a dragon, though, things would have been different. Since he was such a wee thing, it was hard to guess whether they would want to kill him or slap him in a cage and put him on display to draw paying visitors to Mordiford. *Come see the real Mordiford Dragon!*—what an attraction what would be.

They had promised that would never happen when they first befriended the lonely little dragon.

The only dragon in England.

Mattias returned, scowling. "You cannot steal from the Rundguts anymore, Percival."

"But you know I can't…" Percival's front feet danced on the scarred wooden floor.

"He came by to warn me they got a dog. A real dog. A large dog that likes to chase and eat smaller animals." He dropped to the floor beside Maud. "You see, they actually regard you as endearing, despite regularly chasing their laundry through the village. And, as such, they do not want to watch their new dog tear you into little pieces and snack on your bones. Nor do I want to explain whatever it is they might see when you can no longer persuade them you are a spoilt pug!" Mattias slapped the floorboards.

"They would do no such thing." Percival tossed his head and stuck his stubby nose up as high as he could. "They respect me. I am named after a brave and revered knight."

Mattias scooped up the diminutive dragon and marched to the front of the shop, right up to the open door. Maud trotted behind.

"Ho there, Mr. Rundgut. Would you and your son wait a moment? I thought it might be best to show little Percival here what guards your laundry now." He tucked Percival firmly under his arm and stepped out into the street.

Percival's tail lashed and his feet churned through the air, looking for purchase. He hated to be carried like a sack of flour.

"What are you doing? Are you trying to get your dog kilt?" Mr. Rundgut's nearly grown son, his very spit and image, struggled to keep the snapping, snarling monster at the end of a thick rope from running at them.

Was it possible the dog saw Percival for what he really was?

"I warned you. He'll eat that damned dog of yours for dinner if'n you doesn't keep it away." Mr. Rundgut laid a hand on the black-masked, brindled mastiff's head and it settled down.

Percival yelped, scrambled over Mattias' shoulder, landed hard, and streaked back into the shop.

Good heavens! It was almost as tall as Maud herself and likely weighed more. "Pray tell me you did not get that enormous beast to protect you from our little Percy. He is not enough of a nuisance as to warrant that.”

“Much as I’d like to have him skinned and spitted at times, nah, Copper here ain’t ta protect us ag’in that mutt. I got much bigger concerns. Don’t want to go spreading no alarm now, ta be sure. But I’ve had several o’ me sheep go missing.”

“You said Sufton Court dogs got them, and Mr. Hereford himself paid you fair price for every head.” Mattias crossed his arms and pursed his lips.

“I did indeed. But it don’t mean I want ta keep losing me flock to whatever lousy mongrels Hereford’s breeding. I has a right to protect meself and me livestock. Copper here kin do that.” Mr. Rundgut took several steps closer and leaned into Mattias’ face. “Besides, I don’t believe it were dogs what dun it, ya know.”

“Don’t tell me you think poachers are after your sheep.” Mattias rolled his eyes, but his posture seemed worried.

“Nah, something much worse.”

“Wolves, then? Wild boars?” Maud asked. None of those had been seen in their woods for years, though.

“We are in Mordiford, lass.” Mr. Rundgut raised a knowing brow and glanced church at the end of the lane, the sun glinting off the picture of the dragon above the church door.

Mattias snorted. “That story is a myth, a legend, not a lick of truth to it.”

“That’s what the magistrate would have you believe, ain’t it? But why would the tale ‘ave hung ‘round so long if there weren’t a speck of truth involved?” He nudged Mattias with his meaty elbow.

“You believe there’s a grain of truth in the story of a little girl who raised a dragon?”

“That part’s poppycock. But a dread beast in the woods capable of destroying me flocks? That’s the sort of thing a man needs to take serious. You might do well to be concerned, too. You mayn’t have a flock to worry about, but ya gots your sister. Everyone knows about dragons and pretty maidens."

Maud blushed. It was nice to be called pretty, even if it was not true.

"I will take your advice to heart. Thank you, Mr. Rundgut." Mattias tipped his head and waved Maud back toward the shop.

"Remember to keep your scrap of a dog away, though. You been warned, I ain't takin' no responsibility for anything what happens to the little fellow, ye?"

Copper the dog barked as if to agree.

"We will ensure Percival stays away. Good day." Mattias stalked back inside the shop, turned the door sign to read *'Please knock'*, shut the door and turned the bolt. He shuttered the windows and stormed to the backroom. "Percival! Percy, out here right now! You don't want to make me come find you."

Percival scuttled out from between the shelves. "I didn't hurt those sheep!"

"You have an easy life here with us and are too smart to jeopardize it by doing something so incredibly stupid as killing sheep. But …" Mattias parked his hands on his hips. "you've been staying out of the woods. You know something."

Percival shuffled his feet and stared at the dusty floor. "I have seen no traces of any warm-blooded predators capable of taking down a sheep."

"Prevarication if I have ever heard it," Mattias muttered. "What do you think is in the woods?"

Maud crouched beside the little dragon. Every bit of him shook—with fear? She sat down and gathered him into her lap, stroking his back, between his wing numbs, a spot that always helped calm him. "Mattias is full of bluster, but no one and nothing is going to hurt you. Just tell us what you suspect, and you shall have a treat."

Percival pressed into her and looked up into her face. "What kind of treat?"

"I shall fix you a bowl of bread and milk, with a touch of cream on top." Food was the fastest way to gain Percy's attention.

"And a fresh egg?"

"If you are correct, you shall have the egg as well."

"You are spoiling him." Mattias's eyes approved despite his grumbly tone.

"Be a clever little fellow and tell us now." She scratched his back and under his chin.

"I haven't seen it, mind you, but I am certain there is something big in the woods. Much bigger than any wolf or boar." Percival ducked his head under her arm. "As tall as two men, maybe more."

"What could be that size?" Maud whispered.

"We are in Mordiford." Percival wrapped his tail around her waist.

"You cannot be serious. You told us there were no other dragons in England," Maud said.

"Your nest-mates and parents were all eaten by cats in the spring, before we found you, starving and fighting off the cat for its food, claiming to be the last of your kind." Mattias tapped his foot rapidly, his face pulling into an angry scowl.

"It is true! I was absolutely convinced there were no other dragons in England, large or small. How could big ones possibly keep themselves from our notice, especially with what they must eat? You are forever complaining about how much I eat—how might an enormous dragon go unnoticed?" Percival peeked over his shoulder at Mattias. "But there might be one in the woods, near Sufton Court."

Mattias paced, footfalls solid and heavy as he muttered and mumbled.

"Do you suppose a great dragon might be like Percival, though?" Maud asked.

"What do you mean, Maud?"

"If Percy can talk to us, is it possible that a bigger dragon can as well? And if such a dragon is intelligent, like Percy, then …"

"No! Absolutely not!" Mattias waved his hand. "You think we could simply take it in like we did with Percival? Look how he has turned our lives upside down as it is. Can you imagine—"

"But if it can talk and reason, then we owe it the opportunity to speak for itself, explain itself." Maud bit her lower lip. "We don't know that it killed those sheep."

"You are as bad as the Maud of the Mordiford legend! According to Percival, we are the only ones in the village who can hear him speak. If the villagers cannot hear him, how will they be able to hear a gigantic, terrifying dragon? Would they even take time to listen before they attack it?" Mattias stopped and hunkered down beside Maud. "Besides, if a big dragon is like Percival, then it can persuade the village of whatever it likes, like Percy does. Maybe we are already persuaded it is a huge buck in the woods."

"But what if it cannot? We owe it to Percival—"

"But nothing, Maud. We are not going into the woods looking for a dragon."

Two days later, Mattias was off to Sufton Court to deliver a substantial order. Mr. Hereford, master of the estate, did not need to patronize their little village shop. In fact, there was every reason for him not to bother, since he had the means to purchase his items at larger, more prestigious shops in Hereford, less than five miles away. And yet, he opted to buy whatever he could from the village shops. He called it his "civic duty". Whatever he called it, it went a long way toward keeping a roof over their heads and food on the table.

Around midday, Percival dashed into the shop, running so fast his back legs outpaced his forelegs. He tried to stop at Maud's feet, near the counter, but failed and he rolled several times before regaining control of his limbs.

"Have you gone and bothered the Rundgut's dog? We warned you about that?" Maud gathered Percival into her arms.

"No, no, not that."

"Then why are you running in like a monster was chasing you?"

"Because there are monster-hunters gathering in the village, preparing to search the woods."

"For a … dragon?"

Percival pressed his cold, scaly head to her neck, sending chills chasing down her back. "Old Rundgut lost another sheep, and this time he is convinced that no dog killed it. He is whipping the villagers into a frenzy."

"Mattias told us to stay away from anything Mr. Rundgut stirred up. They are more likely to hurt one another than to find anything in the woods. Just stay out of their way and let them be." Maud stroked between Percival's wing nubs.

"What about this?" Percival chittered. "Rundgut found it in the woods by the remains of his dead sheep." He twitched his wing nub and something green and oblong fell to the floor. "I snuck it out of his bag."

"I am not even going to ask how you accomplished that." Maud picked it up. Hard like a fingernail, rough and scaly, with the barest bit of sheen in the light. "I've never seen anything like it. What is … it looks like one of your—" She leaned hard against the counter behind her.

Percival leapt onto the counter. "Even Rundgut recognized a dragon's scale when he saw one."

"There really is a Mordiford dragon?" Maud stared at the crude painting of a long, serpent-like creature, with four legs and wings. Could the scale she held have come from such a creature?

"What other explanation can there be? That scale is fresh, too."

"I thought you said there were no such things as huge scaly dragons."

"Well, yes, but now that I have seen the scale, I am a big enough creature to admit my own error." Percival stood on his back legs and looked into her eyes, his tail sweeping across the countertop. "Now that I have, we must do something about that mob forming to hunt down and kill the only other dragon in England! I must meet the creature. It is my sacred quest!"

"How am I to do that? On the best of days, Mr. Rundgut hardly listens to anyone, let alone me. And now he's stirred a pack of men into action? There is no chance."

"But a dragon! Another one of my kind! We...I... can't let—" It was hard to blame Percy for his urgency. To find out one might not be the last of their kind...

"If he is like you, the other dragon will persuade them away, like you do. What could you or I possibly do to help such a creature?"

Percival snorted and bared his fangs. "To be effective at persuasion, one must have a well-thought-out plan. I cannot simply blurt out any old thing and expect those who only hear my persuasive voice to go along with it. I cannot tell a man he can fly and expect him to jump off a roof, flapping about like a goose."

"I never considered that. What can you persuade people of?"

"Mostly what they would already like to believe. No warm-blood really wants to see a dragon. It is far too inconvenient and would complicate their lives. They would rather perceive me as something ordinary, and what is more ordinary that a fat little dog?" Percival yipped like a pug.

"I suppose that makes sense."

"The trouble is, that mob out there very much wants to see a dragon. So, if they actually do, it will be difficult to persuade them otherwise. A compelling story will be necessary, and that takes time. Which that poor dragon out there might not have if we do not help."

Maud peeked out the window and shuddered. What chance did even a dragon have against the angry mob Mr. Rundgut commanded? "Why would such a creature will listen to me?"

"I listen to you." Percival jumped to the floor. "I am leaving right now, whether you come with me or not."

"The woods are dangerous! Dogs and badgers, and cats—"

"Whom you rescued me from. If you did that for one dragon, surely you can—" Such huge pleading eyes!

"Very well, but you are going to explain this to Mattias." Madness! This was absolutely insane.

Percival hopped back and forth. "Hurry! Hurry!"

Maud closed the door and shuttered the windows. A moment later, they were out the backdoor and down the footpath heading into the woods. The roar of the gathering mob swelled in the air behind them.

"Where do we even look for this creature?" Maud asked.

"Rundgut grazes his sheep on the estate whenever he thinks he can get away with it. I know the place. I say we start there." Percival broke into a trot.

"That sounds like something he would do. I suppose that's why he would have thought Sufton's dogs took the others." Maud struggled to keep up.

The manor house was a mile off, but they crossed the boundary stones of the estate after just five minutes.

"This way, toward the hill, that's where they found the most recent carcass." Percival pointed.

Naturally he chose the direction where the woods turned thick and ominous, with branches interlacing above them in a dark, heavy canopy. Maud shuddered. "Oh, what is that odor? Dust and must and sheep … and a bit like you."

"Are you suggesting that I smell bad?" Percy glanced back at her.

"Not bad. Distinct. Could that mean—"

"That the dragon is that way? Yes. Come!" Percival darted off toward the hill.

Maud followed, trepidation growing with each step.

Percival yipped—a foreboding opening in the hillside? Heaven's above, was that a dragon's lair? Her scalp prickled.

"Oy, there? Is anyone there? Are you at home?" Percival called.

"Who is calling?" A rumbling voice she felt in her bones as much as heard boomed from within the hill.

"I am Percival, and my friend Maud is with me." He sat back on his haunches and puffed out his chest. "I am the dragon of Mordiford."

"Mordiford dragon? No, I think not." Thundering steps approached from the darkness. "I am Mordiford, the dragon of this territory."

A square, grey-green scaly head scraped the top of the hillside opening, raking loose clods of dirt and small stones. A neck and body appeared, at least twelve, maybe fifteen feet tall. Lizard shaped, with broad, flight-worthy wings, it had only two back legs and a powerful tail ending in three spikes.

Great merciful heavens! That—she gulped—was a dragon! A huge, living, breathing dragon!

Percival squealed and leapt into her shaking arms. Her legs trembled, ready to run.

But the creature had spoken intelligently and made no threats. At least not yet. Perhaps she could talk to it. What would be the point of trying to run away? It could pounce on them as surely as a cat caught a mouse.

"What are you doing here, trespassing in my territory?" Mordiford, the dragon, asked.

"We meant no harm, good dragon, sir, but there are those coming behind us who mean harm. They have found a scale of yours, and they are hunting the killer of their sheep."

"The creature was in my territory. It was mine to eat as I willed." The dragon peered over Maud's shoulder into the woods.

"It did not belong to the Sufton flocks, but to Mr. Rundgut."

"What is in my territory belongs to me."

"The shepherd does not see it that way and is bringing a band of armed men prepared to dispose of the dread creature that has been stealing and eating his sheep." Pray let the dragon not take his ire out on the messenger.

"Dragon's fire! What a bloody nuisance." Mordiford stomped hard enough to shake the ground beneath her feet.

"Do you have the same power to persuade that Percival does, good dragon?" Maud asked.

"Laird Mordiford. That is my name. Call me that. Or simply Mordiford, that will do. And, yes, I can persuade, when necessary, but there is no need."

"Will you hide in your cave? If we found you, then I am certain they will as well."

Laird Mordiford turned and beckoned them toward the lair with his wing. "Come inside. Do not fear. The Pendragon Accords forbid any harm coming to you unless I am acting in self-defence, and since you are here to defend me, I have no grounds. Quickly, now."

"Pendragon Accords?" It might be the stupidest thing she would ever do, but Maud followed.

"The founding documents of the Blue Order. You cannot have forgotten that." Mordiford edged behind her and shoved several boulders into the lair entrance. An effective disguise.

"Why would I know anything about Pendragon or an Order?"

"I thought all dragon-hearers were part of the Blue Order. Interesting. Hush now, though, the villagers coming. Follow me. I will take you back to the manor, and my Keeper Hereford can explain." Mordiford ducked his head and trundled deeper into the hillside. "The tunnel is not long and leads into the cellar of the manor."

"It is getting too dark for me to see." And she could hardly breathe in the confined space that smelt of stale air, dirt, and, apparently, dragon.

"Put your hand on my tail, and I will lead the way. Don't be afraid. Even if you aren't familiar with the Pendragon Accords, I am. And I abide by them."

All good sense told her to run.

"Do what he asks," Percival said. "I trust him."

Daft, as it was, Maud listened to the dragons.

The narrow tunnel widened, and Maud stumbled on the suddenly smooth floor.

"The cellars, as promised. Wait here a moment." Mordiford took several steps without her. "Hereford! Hereford, come here immediately!" He turned back to Maud. "He will be along in a moment and will explain everything, I am sure."

A few minutes later, a door creaked open and the glimmer of candlelight penetrated the darkness. A well-dressed man stood at the top of a plain wooden staircase staring into a fully stocked cellar. "Miss Garston? What are you doing here—with Mordiford?"

"She and her little Friend came to deliver me from that mob Rundgut rounded up to bring about my demise."

"Friend? Rundgut? Demise?"

"You must find it in you to speak in complete sentences or Miss Garston, as you called her, will think you an imbecile." Mordiford turned to Maud and Percival. "Perhaps one or both of you can explain and help him find his tongue once more."

Maud quickly told their story while Percival interrupted as often as he could.

"So, there you have it. They are unaware of the Order. You need to do something about that. I will leave you to it. Do come by and visit me sometime, puck. You seem an interesting little dragon." Mordiford lumbered into the darkness of the tunnels and disappeared.

"Nothing of the Order?" Mr. Hereford stroked his chin. "Well, that is a problem. Come upstairs with me. Your brother is already here. It appears there is much more than my dry goods order needing discussion." Hereford beckoned them to follow.

"What did Mordiford call me?" Percival trotted up the stairs beside her.

"A puck, the name of your species of dragon. It is no insult." They stepped into the kitchen, and Hereford closed the door behind them.

"Forgive us, sir, but his family was killed by cats when he was quite young. We've done the best we could by him, but neither of us knew what sort of dragon he was, much less that there were any other dragons in England or anyone else who could hear them."

Mr. Hereford seemed contemplative as he led them through the house. "I suppose I can understand how a tiny village like Mordiford might give one that impression. But it is still irregular."

Percival's claws tick-tick-ticked on the polished floor tiles of the corridor. Paneled with polished wood and hung with old portraits. It was the finest place Maud had ever seen. No doubt the rest of the house was as grand. What must it be like to live in such a place?

Mr. Hereford pushed open a door to a sunny room filled with bookcases, a massive desk and chairs and — "Ah, Mr. Garston, look who I have found!"

Mattias jumped up from a massive leather chair. "Maud? Percy? What are you doing here? You didn't—"

"Have a seat, all of you. No need for remonstrations, Garston. Your sister and your Friend did us a great service. They warned Mordiford of Rundgut and his lot and helped avoid a rather tricky situation. I had been ignoring the sheep he was grazing on my land, but this trespass and threat to my dragon, I cannot ignore."

"Your what?" Mattias' jaw gaped as stared at Percival and Maud.

"Pray, sit down, Miss Garston. What I am going to tell you will be difficult to accept, I am sure."

"Me, too?" Percival stood on hind legs like a dog begging.

"Of course. You might find that footstool comfortable." Mr. Hereford pointed to a plain, pillow topped stool near the fireplace screen.

"You can hear him?" Mattias whispered.

"Like you, I am a dragon-hearer."

Mattias pressed the back of his hand to his mouth. "Stars above! I had no idea there were others."

"I am a Dragon Keeper. Mordiford, with whom your sister recently became acquainted, is the dragon I Keep. Of course, ours is only a modest estate, as far as the dragon estates of England go."

"There are many dragon estates in England?" Maud barely choked out the words.

"Several hundred estate territories belong to major dragons, if I remember correctly. I am not sure we have an accurate census of England's minor dragons like Percival."

"There are more like me?" Percival stood on the stool, wing nubs extended.

"Many more. Dragons and dragon-hearers, pledged to work together for the sake of England's dragons. We are called the Blue Order, founded centuries ago by Uther Pendragon."

"Can we meet them?" Maud asked.

"More than that—you must join us! This afternoon, I must deal with Rundgut, but tomorrow I will take you into Hereford to meet the Blue Order regional undersecretary. Pray stay with me tonight, and I will begin your introduction to the Blue Order."

"I am sure we could not impose upon your like that. Percival is not—"

"He is very welcome…" a sweet voice spoke from under the desk. A dainty red dragon who looked much like Percival crept out from under the desk. "My name is Grail."

"I cannot believe it!" Percival leapt off the stool, wing numbs extended. Was his leap that powerful, or did he glide to her side?

"I never believed it would happen." Mattias' jaw dropped. "Percival actually found his Grail."

Six-time BRAG Medallion Honoree, #1 Best-selling Historical Fantasy author Maria Grace has her PhD in Educational Psychology and is a 16-year veteran of the university classroom where she taught courses in human growth and development, learning, test development and counseling. None of which have anything to do with her undergraduate studies in economics/sociology/managerial studies/behavior sciences. She pretends to be a mild-mannered writer/cat-lady, but most of her vacations require helmets and waivers or historical costumes, usually not at the same time.

She writes gaslamp fantasy, historical romance and non-fiction to help justify her research addiction.

Her books are available at all major online booksellers.

She can be contacted at:
author.MariaGrace@gmail.com | Facebook | Random Bits of Fascination

Notice from the Pond Princess

Emma T. Elias

In a way, I envy the princesses who sit there, waiting in their dragon guarded castles.

I can see them from my little spot by the pond, see them mope and grumble, and cast angry glares at the beast that prowls the path that leads to them.

I think we would be good friends – the dragon and I, that is – if I were to have one of my own.

I would not see her as my jailor or adversary, but rather as my protectress.

No man dares approach the princess in the tower lest his intentions be true – for who would risk facing the dragon if he did not sincerely believe what it was guarding to hold immense value.

No half-hearted suitor would step foot on the banks of my pond.

I would name my dragon – if I were to have one of my own – and every morning I would assure her of my gratitude, I would thank her for sparing me the cheats, and the liars, and the men of ill-will, not even to mention the wimps and losers and creeps.

If I had a dragon of my own, I would not be wasting my time discerning deadbeat from daydream.

My dragon would do that for me, and one day a knight would come to face my mighty monster. He would stand before her with his chin up and his weapons ready, prepared to risk his very life so as to make it to my door.

He who my dragon deems worthy of me, would be given leave to pass.

I watch those princesses, with their princes who face dragons for them.

But alas, I am not up there in the tower to be earned in feats of valour and heroism.

I am here, by the pond… kissing frogs.

There are a great many frogs who claim to be princes.

"Poor me," they'll croak, in a speech that always sounds so very much like every other speech given by a frog trying to win the heart of a princess.

"You'll not believe the misfortunes of my past.

"I've been cursed and mistreated, neglected and scorned. My life's been naught but tears and sorrows.

"But I am a prince, I assure you, despite my wicked form. Just one kiss from you, dear princess, and I will be restored.

"I'll give you diamonds and castles, anything your sweet heart desires. Just one kiss is all it takes."

And every time I squeeze my eyes shut, wish with all my heart for this frog to be true, and plant a kiss on its slimy puckered lips.

For all the different frogs I have kissed, there has never been any transformation.

They take their kiss with a triumphant grin, and off they hop – slimier and froggier than ever – leaving me by the pond, trying to wipe the bitter taste of frog off my lips.

I have no dragon to ward off the frogs.

"But why on earth do you keep kissing these frogs?"

That's a good question, and many have asked it.

I suppose I am a fool, for listening to the fairytales and believing they'll come true.

I suppose I am a fool, for seeing a glimmer of earnestness in their orblike eyes.

I suppose I am a fool, for wishing for my own happy ever after.

And perhaps they're right.

But it gets cold here by the pond,

and if truth be told,

I am deathly afraid of sitting here alone… forever.

How I envy the princesses, guarded by beast and burning.

I know they have their reasons for despising their dragons, but I am so tired of kissing frogs.

So, I will take matters into my own hands, make a dragon of my own – of a sort.

I will build a creature to stand before me, what a vicious winged thing it will be.

With swords for talons, and razors for teeth,
and with broad steel feet, designed for squashing frogs flat.

I will boarder up my pond with nets, and salt, and traps,
and no frog or prince will present himself before my pondside throne
lest his intentions be true.

It is cold by the pond, yes, but my dragon's fire will suffice for now.

Let this notice be read throughout all the kingdoms and beyond,
I, the Pond Princess, will not be kissing any more frogs.

Emma T. Elias is an Australian writer of Lebanese decent. She has been writing stories, poems and scripts, for as long as she could hold a pen and has never lost her passion for it. She has had a number of short stories and poems published in anthologies and literary magazines but is working on a novel that she is looking forward to publishing. When she's not at work or writing, she's probably doing some other random hobby such as archery.

Learn more about Emma at: Instagram

<u>*Picnic Thief*</u>

Kyle O'Kane

Brigham turned the fine silverwork about in the palm of his hand and smiled a secret smile. It wasn't the best work, but it was *his* work. The tiny oval sapphire might be a shoddy cut, and the band might have been a bit wonky, but the stone caught the fading summer light just like her eyes did. It was a solid year's worth of work on a prentice wage, and after all the effort he was giddy about the prospect it embodied.

It was just as he was ruminating if it would be well received, that a familiar and pleasant voice called out from behind him.

"There you are! I was looking all over for you!"

And just like that, he was raised from his reverie like an anchor. The din of festival revelry crashed about him, the smell of cider and sweet cheese assaulted his senses pleasantly, and Brigham hastily pocketed the ring before Wyn embraced him from behind.

"What you got there? Found a shiny beetle?" Wyn giggled softly. The loose leaves in her long blond curls tickled the back of Brigham's neck.

"It's nothing. Have you got twigs in your hair again?" He asked, managing to wriggle about to face her. He returned her buck toothed grin with his own tired smirk.

"Maybe~" she pouted. "Me and Smoke were picking some apples and well… you know how he is…"

As if on cue, the tender moment was shattered by a sudden weight landing upon Brigham's head. The sharp pain of tiny claws danced over his scalp, and after he had done flinching, he was greeted by a pair of beady golden eyes peering upside down at him.

"Smoke! You pesky thing!" said Wyn, taking the small house dragon in her arms. He didn't go without digging his claws in a little bit though.

"Your pet hates me, I swear," Brigham winced, rubbing the tender spots atop his head.

"Rubbish! He likes you! Don't you, you little rascal!" Smoke was half draped and half perched about Wyn's shoulders now, and as she scratched the scales under his gaunt chin, his head bobbed up and down as if in agreement. "See?" Wyn smiled as her dragon whipped his tail   about.

Despite the soreness, and Smoke's inquisitive look, Brigham blushed. He lived for that smile, and the twinkle in those sapphire eyes. "I don't know, I mean… I think I'm bleeding from those claws," he joked.

"Honestly, when will you two get along!" Wyn giggled. "Anyway, come on, the festival's in full swing! Let's go and eat cheese and drink lots!" As if he found the choice rather agreeable, the little house dragon aptly blew out a smoke ring and wagged his tail, long stiletto horns getting tangled in his master's golden locks.

Brigham got up to follow her but stopped. Should he do it now? Before they both got too distracted by the day? "Wyn…"

"Mm?" She wheeled about, bare feet almost losing balance on an uneven tree root.

"Um…" No, the moment had passed, he was sure of it. "Meet me under this tree after the festival. I thought it would be nice if we could have a moment? Just the two of us."

Wyn raised her eyebrows in a sort of expectant smirk.

"...The three of us," Brigham corrected. Smoke simply tilted his head like a curious puppy.

"How lovely! Pastries and jams?" She asked.

"Pastries and jams," he answered.

"You're so thoughtful Brigham. Now let's go!" With that, they both set off at a brisk pace down the hill to the revelries of Applehorn's harvest festival.

The village below was overflowing with life. Stalls piled with dairy products, country wines and ciders littered the square. People of all social castes danced, drank and joked with one another like time weathered friends. And all about, perched on shoulders, bathing in fountains, and eating from the many vast platters of fruit, dragons!

Dragons of all shapes and colours were a common sight within Applehorn, so named for the sweet toothed little creatures skewering apples upon their horns to save for later.

Their temperament was of a grouchy feline mixed with an overexcited hound. Not only that, but they are guided by a mercurial cunning that could only be right for a creature of such wonder. To Brigham's mind, none of them embodied such a thing half so well as Smoke. The pesky draconid insisted on stealing cheese out of his hand, jumping on his head whenever he tried to kiss Wyn, and flicking more than one glass of his drink off a table whilst pretending to snooze.

Every time Brigham was about to snap or lash out to bop the little fiend on his snout, Wyn disarmed him with a smile. The three of them spent many satisfied hours speaking to locals, family and even a few travelers from afar, all aglow with the buzz of alcohol and hopes of what the year would bring.

Before long, the day culminated in a glorious feast, and Wyn, Brigham and Smoke came away from it satiated and eager for a restful evening.

They were just heading up to the old tree on the outskirts of the village, when someone called after Wyn. It was a deep, booming voice that could only be that of the innkeeper Walden, the girl's garrulous father.

"Oh bugger, I'll have to catch up with you Brigham, Smoke got into one of the cider barrels earlier and I hoped Da wouldn't notice! Meet you there!" She gave him a quick kiss, one that the little dragon didn't have time to ruin and set off at a jog to her father.

Brigham didn't mind so much, with every step up to that tree his stomach nearly did a somersault. This way, he would have time to settle his fraying nerves.

He put out a blanket on the ground and nestled a wicker hamper between twisted roots. The sun was hanging fairly low in the sky, setting the scene for his plans. He agonized a lot over the little details. The angle of the wine bottle nestled amongst the tree roots, the board of pastries, jams, glasses and cutlery. And of course, the final and finest of touches: the ring. It was nestled safely at the bottom of the hamper in between two apple turnovers.

Brigham sat for a little while watching the sun go down, pleasantly distracted by the rippling oranges and yellows. His body ached, and his mind was ever so tired. Though, just as he was closing his eyes for a well-earned power nap, he heard a rustling and a clatter beside him.

Looking over, albeit groggily, the hamper was jostling about from side to side, wicker frame bulging at odd angles. After a moment, the movement stopped, and a small grey draconic head poked up out of the hamper's lid.

"No you don't! You little-" Brigham scrambled to get closer, but stopped dead when he noticed something.

As Smoke shook his head to flick away a lump of apple turnover from his chops, Brigham noticed a distinct blue twinkling on one of the little dragon's horns.

"...Smoke…"

Smoke fixed him with a beady golden eye, the movement of his head causing the ring to spin loosely about his knife point horns. He had at this point, perched delicately atop the basket's handle, wings extended and wobbling to maintain balance.

"Don't you do it," Brigham readied himself at a snail's pace to pounce. If he lunged for it, he might be able to get a hold of the little bastard.

The dragon cocked his head as if to say, *"I don't know what you mean you silly man."*
Smoke twitched. Maybe it was just that he lost balance, but Brigham was dancing on a knife's edge, and so he made a snap decision to spring forward.

The little house dragon remained still for a moment, eyes widening in perturbance, but at the last moment he bounced deftly upward.

Brigham, conversely, crashed down hard, all but destroying the hamper and what remained of the apple turnovers. For the second time in the day, the pinprick pain of tiny dragon claws lanced through his scalp, as Smoke used his head as a stepping stone.

"You little sod!" Whirling about in a fit of cold rage, Brigham swiped for the scamp.

It was no use though, the dragon was gracefully gliding away back to town, horn twinkling in the falling summer light.

"No No! *NO!*" Brigham sprinted down the hill back to Applehorn, the reality of the situation dawning on him. There was every chance that Smoke would squirrel that away to his personal hoard, and not even Wyn knew where that was. There was also a chance that the little fiend could eat it, or worse, present it to his mistress like a cat presenting a dead bird.

Those things, Brigham resolved, would *not* come to pass. He ran arrow-straight to the dragon's meandering path, and his ruthlessness took him barreling through several gardens on his way down the uneven hill.

"Sorry Mrs. Greenbury!" He yelled behind him, stamping through a purple squash. "I'll pay for that, Mister Muldoon!" He shouted as he accidentally brushed a garden ornament off of a stump. "Bloody dragon!" He screamed as he ran through a laundry line, snagging all sorts of frilly garments as he went.

Smoke was flying toward the Inn, where a tired looking Walden was stacking up a small mountain of spent cider barrels against the building's backwall.

"Brigham! What brings you running down the hill?" said Walden, wiping sticky cider off of his hands with a yellowed cloth.

"Evening Walden! I um…" Brigham's eyes drifted to Smoke, who had now perched atop one of the inn's chimney stacks and was peering down at him. "I came to see where Wyn was?"

"Hah!" Walden stroked his dirty blond moustache. "You sound like you're not so sure boy. I just told her to keep an eye on that dragon of hers, then she galivanted off. Troublesome thing."

"The Dragon? Or-"

"Why not both!" Walden interrupted with a chuckle. "But we do tolerate the inconveniences for those we love! Don't we, Brigham." He finished, staring Brigham down with a look that made the boy gulp.

"Uh, absolutely Sir... I-"

"Still! You're here now! Might as well help me stack these barrels. I'll roll them out and you put 'em on the pile. You can get started with this one!" Walden tapped a small wooden keg with his boot, turning about without even waiting for an answer.

Brigham looked up at the roof of the inn. Smoke was still perched atop the clay flue, eyeing up Walden as the man made his way back around. When he was out of sight, the dragon peered down at Brigham, and blew a little smoke ring as if to say. *Well come on then, I haven't got all evening!"*

That was all the impetus that Brigham required, and with a grumble he clambered up the pile of barrels like a rage-stricken acrobat. The kegs wobbled with every uncertain step, and more than once he nearly lost it. After many close calls, he finally reached the top. Gracelessly, he pulled himself onto the slate tiles and grimaced, noticing the sticky patina of wine, cider and fruit flies on his clothes and hands.

"Smoke, give it back. You come here and give it *back* you little *scamp!"* Brigham tottered up the incline of the roof, never taking his eyes off the dragon.

In response, Smoke hopped to one of the other flues, and playfully started basking in the plume of woodsmoke being belched from it.

"*You rascal,*" said Brigham through clenched teeth. Just a few more steps now and he could dive for it, whilst Smoke was distracted.

He took a wide step, and the dragon stopped basking for a moment to fix him with a mildly perplexed upside-down stare.

He took another step, and Smoke started to scrabble up into a seated position. Now was his chance! Brigham lunged, and several things happened.

First, one of the slate tiles that he was standing on couldn't take the force of a grown man pushing off from it, and so it shot out like a skimming stone. Instead of lunging, Brigham got a mouthful of slate and moss and a bruised face.

Secondly, Smoke, startled by the sudden motion and realizing he didn't have time to take flight, darted down the chimney flue like a panicked mouse.

Lastly, with the dread of realizing the whole exercise had been for nothing, Brigham slid down the slope of the roof and tumbled off the edge, crashing down into the mountain of kegs.

Barrels shot and rolled hither and thither, and anytime Brigham tried to grab hold of one to steady his fall, he managed only to upend a load of dregs all over himself.

Finally, he came to rest on the dirty floor of the inn's back alley, groaning in agony.

"What's all that racket!" a voice bellowed.

Brigham was going to get thrashed. He knew it.

Walden barreled round the corner, two more empty cider kegs under each arm. Surveying the carnage, his face steadily grew redder. By the time he fixed Brigham, lying there amid the mess, he was the colour of a radish.

"Brigham."

"Um. Yes?"

"You mind telling me what happened here?"

"I… slipped." Brigham didn't feel like the specifics would help.

"Well," Walden said in a hushed voice "You best slip away, before you *slip* again, Ey?"

"Aye. Sorry…"

The big man sighed and placed his keg's on the floor. "Accidents happen, lad. Now, go on inside and help Wendy with the cleaning."

Brigham didn't stick around and took off at a spurred jog to the inn.

The festivities had wound down by this point, but the inn was still very much alive with a heady buzz.

Brigham got a few funny looks, coated as he was in a film of dregs. As he surveyed the place in return, he noticed a few people gathered around one of the many fireplaces. Getting a bit closer, he caught a snippet of conversation from someone holding a broom, half-heartedly tickling a trail of ash and soot on the floor.

"Can't wrap my head around it, Dale. Thing shot down the chimney and nearly set the place ablaze the way it scrabbled about on the logs."

"Must have been startled. You reckon it's alright?"

"Aye, it's a dragon ain't it?"

Instead of joining the conversation, Brigham looked at the trail of debris along the floor. It struck a winding path through several table and chair legs, but eventually it led to the kitchens, from where a pleasant singing could be heard. Passing through onto the slightly uneven black and white tiles, the tune abruptly stopped.

"Hello trouble!" said a woman wearing a stained baker's garb. "What was that awful racket outside?"

"You heard that?" Brigham asked, looking around to find out where the little nuisance had gotten to.

"Oh sweetie I think the whole village heard it!" Wendy laughed, face flushed and ruddy.

"I don't think I'm that good at climbing…"

"Climbing? What?" Wendy shook her head. "You aren't making sense at all. Here." She stopped kneading at a lump of dough and took a swig from a flour coated bottle. "You wouldn't give us a hand with this floor, would you?"

"Oh, yes. Where's the mop?"

"In the corner, I'm heating up some water on the augur too." Wendy headed for a door into one of the inn's many pantries. Her voice was somewhat muffled, but Brigham could still make it out. "Buckets are about! I need to get more flour. Thanks!"

And with that, Brigham was left in an empty kitchen, the sound of a large pot steadily coming to a simmer.

He looked about nervously, and spent a cautious minute flinging open cupboard doors, opening draws, looking under worktops like a man who… well, like a man who had lost his wedding ring. What would Wyn think! She was probably up on the hill already! And he was here. Helping clean the floor.

Brigham snatched the mop from its resting place and went over to the pot upon the augur. Kicking a bucket into place, he peered down at a strange murky water bubbling away on the hob.

"What sort of cleaning salts are those?" he mused.

It was just as he lifted the pot up ready to upend it into the bucket, that he noticed something that made his heart leap. Deep within the inky palette of the water, a muted twinkle of blue could be seen.

Brigham couldn't believe it. The little rascal had the nerve to dump his treasure in a pot of murky water! Frowning, he grabbed a metal spoon to fish it out.

However, with the utensil at the ready, Brigham noticed something else, and this time his heart sank. Beside the sapphire twinkle, two flecks of gold suddenly appeared.

"Oh… You wouldn't *dare*!"

With a sudden thrashing, Smoke erupted from the pot. Brigham yelped as it smashed down and cracked one of the tiles, spraying a fountain of murky water across the floor and near scalding his legs.

"Right! I've had it!" And with a yell, Brigham threw the spoon like a hurling axe, only to miss Smoke by a shameful distance and burst the bottle of wine on the table. With Wendy's dough garnished with broken glass and sodden with spilt drink, Brigham took up the mop like a polearm. Cursing, he brought it down onto the spot where Smoke had been with a wet slap. The little dragon, however, didn't feel like getting bopped. Half scrabbling and half flying, he bounced off Brigham's head with an infuriating agility and started zooming about the room.

Brigham whirled the mop about like a knight, spattering a good deal of the wall with sooty water. "*Come here*!"

Smoke did not in fact, comply, choosing instead to frolic about the countertops, weaving skillfully amongst the clutter.

"Give!-" A pot of sugar went spinning into oblivion. "It!-" The mophead snapped and hurtled into the fireplace. "Back!" Brigham lunged, and the door to the pantry shot open.

"What's going-!" Wendy didn't have time to finish. As Smoke darted between her legs, Brigham tried desperately to stop himself but slipped on a patch of murky water.

"*No!*" Was all he managed to say, reaching out to stop himself on the only thing he could reach, none other than a big bowl of flour carried by Wendy.

She tried to pull it out of reach, but far too late. The bowl tipped, and nearly all of the flour poured over Brigham like a sad dusty waterfall.

"Sorry! Sorry! By the crown I'm sorry!" Brigham coughed and thrashed about to get the flour off of him. But, with all the sticky cider that had drenched his clothes… To say his shirt was done for was an understatement, let alone his hair.

"Ohhhh Brigham! This'll take me an age to sort! You and that dragon, you're as bad as Wyn I swear!" Wendy tutted.

"I- I will help in a moment. Smoke took something important from me!"

"You what? You ain't going anywhere young man, not looking like that!" But it was no use. Brigham ran through the pantry, through the open back door and onto the tight cobbled lane beyond.

"You've pulled my chain you little bastard." Brigham scowled, seeing that Smoke was now flying away. That was bad enough, but it was where he was flying that really took the cake. The tall old tree on the hill. No doubt about it. His feet ached as he followed.

By the time Brigham got to the top of the hill, the state he was in was beyond pitiable. His hair was a sweat-caked mess of flour, his once fine shirt looked like a dusted sweet loaf with dead flies instead of currants, and his trousers and boots were a sodden disaster.

There was absolutely no way Wyn would say yes. She had probably already come and gone!

As he trudged over to the tree in the dimming twilight, he noticed the unmistakable glow of a candle dancing across the roots and branches, and a soft giggling over a shallow breeze.

"Brigham? Is that you? I've been waiting here forever!" said a playful voice.

Like that, Brigham's anger melted away.

Wyn stepped around the tree to face him. She looked wonderful, clad in a flowing green dress complete with beads and sequins, long curls adorned with an odd and well-placed flower. A smile was spread widely across her face, though it did take a bit of a confused wobble when she finally saw him.

"Brigham? Did you get attacked by a flour monster?"

"...yes." He flashed back a smile, and Wyn giggled.

The two came closer, and despite his sorry state, Wyn embraced him with an earnest passion that warmed him to the core. She smelled like lavender and her eyes glinted with a daytime blue. They stayed there for a time, swaying gently in the candlelight.

"Oh! I nearly forgot! Smoke found something!" Wyn wriggled out of Brigham's arms and went over to the blanket Brigham had laid out earlier. There, wrapped about the candlestick and snoozing without a care in the world, was Smoke.

Brigham's stomach did a half-hearted flip when he recognized the telltale sapphire glimmer on the dragon's horn. Deftly, Wyn slid the band off and waved him over. "Look at this! He pilfered a pretty ring! I'm so proud of him."

"How lovely," Brigham forced through gritted teeth.

"Do you think I can keep it? I mean, it probably belongs to someone right?" Wyn looked up at him, turning the jewelry about in her hands.

"Wyn…" Brigham stepped closer, heart pounding. He took her hands in his. "It… belongs to me," he began, struggling to find the words. "I made it…"

"No way, it's so beautiful!" Wyn beamed, giving it back to him.

"Aye, but…"

"Sorry he took it from you! He likes sapphires… you're not mad, are you?" Her wide eyes took on an expression of concern, and Brigham worked quickly to put it right.

"No. Never." Brigham took the ring, and before she could take her hands away, he gently stopped her. "It belongs to me… but I want you to have it, Wyn."

"What?" She said, a little dumbstruck.

"I… Wyn. Will you?" His voice was barely a whisper from the nerves, and he stilled his hands, holding the band steady just at the end of her finger.

Wyn looked down at the ring, and then at Brigham.

"Oh Brigham… Of course I will, you silly man."

She pushed her finger forward, and the ring fit perfectly. With a deft movement, and a glint of sapphire, she wiped away the flour from his face and kissed him.

Down by the candle, Smoke opened one groggy golden eye to survey the tender scene. After a moment, he emitted a contended purr that seemed to say: *"You'll do."* And with that, he fell asleep. Satisfied with a hard day's work.

Nothing but an itinerant racounteur! Through my inspired ramblings of the chartered provinces, and even a few of the uncharted and better-left-alone ones, I have gathered a colourful plethora of fables! Despite my foibles I believe that good, or at the very least passable, stories should be shared. I can't promise that there won't be any embellishment, but I'm certain these accounts will entertain at least one of you!

Learn more about Kyle at: Instagram

Reptile Narratives

Addison J. Fulton

"Here is your treasure hoard?"

    Asks the Dragon to the Gecko

    As the Dragon holds its eye to the window

    Eyes roving over the room

    Logs and dead crickets and a porcelain frog

    And a water bowl and a lid with holes

    "This is it"

    Says the Gecko to the Dragon

    As it presses itself to the wall of the tank

    Eyes roving over the little girl

    With her gentle hands and her books

    On reptile keeping

"Here is your home?"

    Asks the Gecko to the Dragon

    As it swings its head to-and-fro across the jagged cave

    With its cold stone floor

    And its dark walls

And the lonely shadows crossing the floor

It shivers

"This is it"

Says the Dragon to the Gecko

Gleaming eyes eyeing the gleaming

Golden and silver and stones

Shining through the darkness

Rubies and sapphires reflecting

The dragon back to itself and itself and itself

"Here is my tongue"

Says the Dragon

As its tongue rolls out of its mouth

Past bone-white teeth

"Here is my tongue"

Says the Gecko

As its tongue flicks in and out
Quick as a light switch

"Here is my story,"

Says the Dragon to the Gecko

"I capture a beautiful maiden to add to my hoard

And then I am slain by a Knight on horseback

With his sharp and bitter steel blade"

"Here is my story,"
	Says the Gecko to the Dragon

"I am taken home from the petshop by a girl

And I lie on rocks under heat lamps, and sometimes

She lets me ride on her shoulder around the house"

"I do not understand you, creature"

	Says the Dragon to the Gecko

	And the Gecko to the Dragon

"Do you not want to be free?"

"Do you not want to be loved?"

And when rises the sun

It will come first through the window

Then the mouth of the cave

And the Dragon will wait for a human to feed it

And the Gecko will wait for a human to feed it

Addison Fulton was born and raised in Albuquerque, New Mexico on the most beautiful sunsets. She has deep roots, like everything that grows in the desert. She believes all of life can be sorted into the following categories: the beautiful, the grotesque, and the mundane. In her work, she seeks to create art that exists at the intersection of all three. She has previously been published in the literary magazines, *Homer Humanities*, *Scribendi* and in the short story anthology *Pretty Obscure*. She has a series of urban-fantasy thriller novels titled Social Animals, debuting in 2024 with Far West Press.

Learn more about Addison at: Author Website| Instagram

Charles Ta

TALES FROM THE DRAGONING

ONE: TERRA DRACONIS

January 22nd, 1774

To His Majesty King George III,

It is with great trepidation and excitement that I inform you I have made a marvelous yet fearsome discovery in the southernmost extremities of the Pacific Ocean. The importance of this finding behooves me to address you with utmost haste, for its implications could shatter the very foundations of our nascent scientific civilization, and our most venerable Empire.

Our crew reached the latitude and longitude of 58° south, 123° west on the late evening of January 21st on our way to the Antarctic Circle, in search of Terra Australis, as your secret instructions so charged us, whereupon we fell victim to a great gyre and a tempest that blew us off course S.W. within telescopic sight of a collection of large, unexplored islands and icy promontories rising out of the boundless sea. We decided to land ashore and set our anchors upon the nearest isle for safety until the storm subsided, so that we could continue on our glorious and righteous enterprise the following day, Providence willing.

Scarcely did we land on the islet, disembark upon its craggy banks, and claim it for Britain when we felt the very earth shake beneath us and our sloop. The ship proceeded to rock from side to side as mighty waves crashed upon and battered the vessel, and nearly drenched us in salty seawater. Murmurs of panic began to arise from the nervous and unsettled crew, though Lt. Cooper and Lt. Clerke strove to maintain calm and order amidst their ranks to the best of their abilities as we cautiously tread further inland.

Suddenly all the members of our expedition heard what sounded like many deafening roars and cries coming from all around us, which pierced the cold air and the wild winds of the tumultuous squall. At this moment, I saw the faces of my fellow soldiers grow pallid as they gazed about the island in all directions, muskets aimed this way and that, and I confess to your Majesty that my heart was stricken with the most primeval of all fears, like none I had ever felt before, despite my worldly travels. The renowned naturalists Sir Forster and his son, Georg, who were staring at a tall, lengthy, and steep cliffside that towered above us with awe and terror in their eyes, then began to shout for our attention, and point their fingers at something they said was emerging from the topmost region of those stony precipices.

Incredulous yet nonetheless deeply perturbed, I looked up in their direction, as did the crew, and in the flashes of lightning and raging ice of the powerful storm, I glimpsed what appeared to be a massive yet hideous beast with crimson scales fully reveal itself perched like a gargoyle on the highest summit of the cliffside, and spread its ghastly chiropteran wings wide, before letting out a cry akin to that of a mangled cacophony. The beast, imposing, vile, and grotesque with its smoldering body and many rows of teeth, was soon joined afterwards from behind by about a dozen creatures of similar size and appearance. Some were more feathered, while others were covered in horns, spikes, quills, or reptilian frills, and still more possessed serpentine bodies that faintly glowed in the dead of night like shining gems—but all of them stared at us with crocodilian eyes that burned like xanthic sulfur.

A feeling of extreme dread rose up from my once proud chest that I attempted to conceal behind my stoic countenance, and I ordered my men to ready their muskets and open fire upon the foul creatures, who appeared ready to attack us. Soon they flew down to the ground like bloodthirsty birds of prey, and began to approach us, enraged and hungry for our flesh. In mere moments, the demoniac lizard creatures surrounded us on all sides, except behind us, where the Resolution and our rowboats sat at the mercy of the tides.

I was about to give the order for my men to fire as they backed away slowly, just as the scarlet winged creature and its companions endeavored to assault us, when, to the right of us, we all heard another loud cry in the distance resembling the high-pitched screeching of rusty metal. Turning towards the cry, we soon beheld a beast as white as ivory larger than the crimson one, whose gorgeous plumage shimmered like gold, silver, and platinum as it descended like a flying snake from the island's mountains flanked by others of its kind, and landed in between us and the crimson winged lizard, shielding us with its gigantic body.

The crew and I made suitable distance between the saurian and avian animals for our protection, and witnessed the white beast thrash its tail and flap its wings aggressively as its cohorts neared, then encircled the crimson beast and its compatriots. The crimson beast, in turn, gradually stepped backwards as it too, assumed an aggressive stance with its cohorts. What occurred next, my Lord, made even my most hardened marines gasp in confusion as they trembled with their guns, and were I not there to personally witness the events that transpired, I would have dismissed them as fairy tales from a bygone era.

In short, my liege, I heard the beasts speak to one another, not in the language of grunts and roars, but in the language of men and women. The white beast—a female—stared down her foe with eyes of brilliant turquoise, and bade him in a soothing voice not to hurt us, and return to his lair with his allies, calling him by the name "Torburn". Torburn responded in anger that "this world was not for men to rule", and that "the dragons of old would one day return to reclaim their place on Earth" after the heroes of yore hunted them down to near extinction. He also labeled the white beast called "Palatia" a "traitor to dragonkind".

The confrontation between the two monsters—who we now understood in disbelief, but knew deep in our hearts to be dragons— soon settled down as Torburn let out one final thunderous roar before flying away into the stormy sky with his followers, leaving myself and my crew still in shock with Palatia and her companions in our proximity.

The majestic creature then turned to us and regarded us with an unusual tenderness and benevolence, informing us she "meant no harm" to my crew, and that we could "lay down [our] weapons in the interests of peace and harmony". I was the first person to speak, as Captain of the Resolution, for my crew had fallen silent out of fright, and from our brief interaction, I had ascertained the history of the dragons, and how they had gone into hiding centuries ago after the last of them had been slain in Europe, Africa, and Asia during the Middle Ages. This, I deduced, was the source of Torburn's vengeful fury, and hatred of humanity.

Knowing the magnificence of the alabaster beast I was dealing with, I was humble in my affairs with Palatia, who introduced herself as Queen of the Dragons, of which there were only ten thousand in number. The two of us soon came to an agreement for the benefit of all parties: Palatia led my crew to the refuge of a nearby island cave that the dragons knew well, where we spent the night. Then, the following morning, when the weather had improved, she bestowed upon us dozens of dragon eggs from a large dragon nest to take with us to England as a sign of our newfound friendship, while also ensuring the survival of her race.

We departed thereafter from the islands, which we christened Terra Draconis—Land of the Dragons—and swore as sailors to maintain the secrecy of the place we had discovered (but not the existence of dragons), so that they could live in peace. I write to you now asking your Highness to engage in similar measures for the good of all, and to ensure all the necessary preparations are made for our immediate return to England, so that the infant dragons may be taken care of in the best manner possible. William Hodges, my painter, has provided sketches of what I saw in my travels, as their historical significance cannot be ignored. I hope you will reply to my letter without delay—our dominion over the world depends on it.

Sincerely,
Captain James Cook

December 26th, 1776: This diary was presented to me as a Christmas gift by my mother, Evelyn Elizabeth Hachette, so that I may record my deepest thoughts and feelings within it, as she thought befitting of a young lady suffering from a lack of friendships and a certain timidity of character. Grateful as I am for this journal, I hope that, in time, I may come to appreciate what it will do for me. Otherwise, I think my lonely heart will wilt like a dying rose from sorrow, and my affliction of the soul shall worsen until the end of my days. Poor me!

April 2nd, 1777: My parents and I traveled by stagecoach from Tours to Aunt Mallory's dragon emporium in Lyon to purchase for me a pet dragon in order to keep me company. I could hardly contain my wonder and excitement on the way there, as is typical of a child who just turned fifteen. Father was very stern with me as we journeyed through the countryside, however. He said that dragons and their evolutionary cousins, being "exotic creatures of extreme rarity, were prohibitively expensive", only accessible to the gentry, and the nobles of the royal court, and that he was spending a fortune acquiring one for me for my own sake.

Father knew, of course, that I was a bookish and demure girl that liked to read volumes from his study, yet one who was resistant to the manners and social pleasantries of the times, which he respected (unlike Mother, who has grown more disappointed in me by the day), but he still thought it appropriate for me to have something approaching a companion. He also knew that when I attended my first dragon show last month in Nice, and read Georges Buffon's new treatise on dragonology, I was enamored with the creatures, and had been begging him to get me one for weeks. Oh, how wonderful it is that dragons are truly real and alive! How happy am I as a child living in this world—a world that has changed forever, and for the better!

April 5th, 1777: In recent days I have been filled with nothing but joy and amazement. Father bought me a gorgeous green hatchling—called a Jadeskin—from Aunt Mallory, who had received it from my Uncle Bettencourt in his travels as a Colonel abroad. He didn't tell me its exact origins, but he did claim that he had obtained it from an Indian merchant, who himself had received it as an egg from a sailor in Macau, who himself asserted he was once on the crew of Captain James Cook. Aunt Mallory, who called herself the "greatest dragon breeder in Lyon", then told me that Karl von Ehrlich, a student of Linnaeus, had begun to classify the various kinds of dragons known to Europe since their re-discovery, after the news had spread like wildfire, even to the New World. "We're in the middle of a Revolution," she said with a smile to us over dinner at Uncle's estate. "A Draconian Revolution."

On my first night with my hatchling, the two of us immediately befriended one another with a bond few could count themselves fortunate enough to have, and he slept at the foot of the bed reserved for me at Uncle's manor like a dog that had found a new owner. After some thinking, I decided to name the dragon Leon, after his beautiful mane, which reminded me of a lion's mane. The next day, I fed him some tender mutton like Uncle recommended (for dragon-rearing is still very much a new science) and was surprised to see him cook it with his fire breath before swallowing it whole! I've since experimented with giving him different kinds of meat, and he seems to like bacon, poultry, and fish the best. I cannot wait to see my cherished Leon grow into a beautiful adult one day–he is already like a brother to me!

June 22nd, 1777: Leon has grown exceptionally quickly, both in size and in intellect! He seemingly understands my words and responds to my calls. Yesterday, I could have sworn that he said his first word—my first name "Celine". He can speak! He can speak!

October 14th, 1777: I flew on Leon for the first time this morning! He's three times the size of Father's horses now, and he offered to let me ride on his back all around Tours! At first I was scared of being so high off the ground, but as I ascended up into the sky, holding tightly onto his long whiskers like horse reins, and saw my home city like the angels from Heaven would see it, I felt as light as the air, and as free as a bird! Mother was livid with me when I eventually landed back down on the ground, and threatened to punish me for my little excursion, which she described as very "unladylike". When Father found out, however, he laughed and admonished Mother. "Let her live a little," he said with a hint of sadness, I noticed, in his voice. "You were once a child, as was I, yearning for freedom. The world is miserable enough."

January 6th, 1778: I celebrated my sixteenth birthday today near Bordeaux with Father, Mother, Leon, Uncle, and Aunt Mallory! They took me to a dragon race—the Dragon Prix—held in the countryside in the afternoon, and I saw dragoneers from all over Europe performing daring stunts and death-defying acrobatics while they flew their dragons in loops across the sky. There was a Spaniard riding a rainbow-colored Brazilian Quetzalcoatl, a Prussian with a Coaldrake, a Swede with an Arrowhead, an Ottoman soldier showing off his Desert Wyvern, an English boy flaunting his Crown-Horned Goldwing, and a Frenchman with a Speckled Stonemouth! There was even a woman I met who had come from the Russian Empire, at the behest of Catherine the Great! She won the race and stunned the crowds with her Great Eastern Snowfur, whose icy breath cast the sky in a white fog. Leon adored the exhibition, too—when I spoke to the Russian lady, who was called Natasha, and revealed she was a Countess, I saw her Snowfur talk with my Jadeskin. Later, she invited my family to a ball held that night in the city, and I danced with the Countess! Oh, what fun I had! I shall never forget this glorious day!

February 3rd, 1778: Father had to leave home early this morning in a rush. Something about a business meeting he had with someone very important, upon receiving a letter sent by messenger dragon. He didn't say where he would go to or who he would meet, at least not at first, but when I had woken up with Leon from the noise he was making, he told me to inform Mother that he would be meeting with an emissary on behalf of an overseas client, but did not know how long he would be gone. Worried, I pressed him to reveal more, telling him I knew he was hiding something from me, while Leon stood beside me for support. Eventually, he relented, but I only understood some of the things we discussed, and was left wanting more:

"What I am about to tell you, Celine, is top secret", he said gravely. "You must listen to me very carefully and tell absolutely no one of what I am doing. Understand?"

"Yes, Father," I replied to him, worried. Leon nodded in agreement too.

Father then gazed around our living room to ensure that nobody, not even Ms. Rochelle, our kind handmaiden slumbering soundly in the next room over, could listen in on our private conversation. Afterwards, he sat me down and spoke. "I am going to Paris," he said to me in a whisper, "to rendezvous with a delegate from the English Colonies. You know, as I'm sure you do by now, that England is currently at war with them, correct?"

I looked at Leon, who stared back at me, then turned my attention again to Father before nodding. Yes, I remembered I once eavesdropped on Uncle discussing the war with Father over a bottle of champagne, but I had not heard from him or Aunt Mallory since January. Suddenly, my heart sank as I came to an awful realization, and I began to cry.

"Is Uncle fighting in the war?" I asked tearfully. "Are you in danger?"

"He is awaiting deployment under the orders of Louis XVI, my dear," Father said, wiping my tears, "but he is alive and well, and wrote to me inquiring about you and Leon."

Leon then came close to me and wrapped his warm tail around my waist for comfort. I immediately felt safer closer to him. He was always protective of me.

"And no, I am not in danger—not yet anyways," Father continued softly. "Not as long as I ensure the Colonies achieve victory in the war by financing their activities—a possibility that is, unfortunately, growing less likely by the day the more aid is delayed."

"I don't understand what you mean," I said, heartbroken, confused and disoriented. "What about Aunt Mallory? And why is this war happening? Can't the British Crown and the Colonies make peace? What does our family have to do with this?"

Father said nothing initially, then took a deep breath before standing up, adjusting his tricorn hat, and turning his back to me as he advanced towards the entrance of the Hachette Chateau. Just before he left, he stopped and said: "It would take me too much time to explain to you the details of what I know now to be true, but in case I do not return for a long time, I will leave you with this, my daughter: I once thought for many years that all wars were folly, and that those who started them were no better than rats who feasted upon the filth of their own depravity. But I have come to realize recently that there are times in which the risk of not fighting a war, or remaining neutral far exceeds the risk of sacrificing tens of thousands of men on the battlefield. This moment in history is one of those times, my dear, and it is because the Colonial rebels, whom I support, are being crushed. Worse, some of their French patrons, now fearful of what horrors England is capable of, have begun to withdraw their support for the war effort, and instead pour their funds into… bolstering the national defense."

"Why? Oh, why Father?" I asked, disturbed and afraid of his words.

"Because England wishes to rule not only the Earth's lands, and the waves of the azure main, but now the open skies, through the dragons they have trained for war."

February 19th, 1778: Ever since Father left, my days have been consumed by agony, despair, and melancholy. Leon has learned much from me, and has been trying his best to be my greatest confidant through the difficult times I have experienced as of late. He can now speak to me in short sentences, and through his words I can sense his undying devotion to his fair lady, his unconditional love for his sister. Mother, on the other hand, has grown distant and bitter, frustrated over the fact Father had entrusted his housekeeper with stewarding the Hachette estate while away, alongside his butlers, servants, and maids. There has still been no news from Uncle or Aunt, and I am deathly frightened something has happened to them.

May 2nd, 1778: The American Revolution has failed, according to the papers. George Washington's Continental Army, already ravaged by disease and food shortages, was massacred in Valley Forge following a dragon raid by the Royal Dragon Force, and Washington and his allies were arrested, then executed for treason. Accounts of the attack said the winter camp was set ablaze and afflicted with poison, and the revolutionaries and their allies were routed and overwhelmed in the dead of night, with little time to prepare. The war is lost, and so is all hope of American Independence from King George, that brute.

May 5th, 1778: I am weeping as I write this. A soldier came to our manor this morning with horrible news. Uncle passed away in prison at the hands of British Redcoats, having served in the Continental Army under General Lafayette, who himself was also imprisoned before he too, died. Aunt Mallory, we were informed, was transferred to Corsica, and her dragons were now the property of the French government. I fear that war with England is on the horizon. War with England, and with innocent dragons! How wicked!

June 16th, 1778: The papers this morning said the Colonies submitted to the Carlisle Peace Commission and agreed to remain an English colony in perpetuity! Worst of all, King George has crowned himself "World Emperor" and sworn revenge on France and Spain for attempting to undermine his American colonies, vowing to "pursue British interests in all the known world" in order to "secure the dominance of Britain". He has gone mad and grown too powerful with his legions of dragons. I can barely sleep at night.

I've heard rumors, too, that King Louis has supposedly formed a coalition with Spain, Portugal, the Dutch Republic, Denmark, Norway, Sweden, Prussia, the Habsburgs, the Papal States, Sicily, and Naples. A confrontation with all of Europe seems inevitable. War is coming. Danger is coming. Even Leon knows it, which has made my heart swell with dread.

"Celine, we cannot stay here much longer," he warned me. "Come with me, far away, and we shall be safe." I retorted by asking him about Mother, and Father's housekeeper, and his butlers and maids. "I can't just leave them behind," I said to him, because they're still family, to which Leon remained silent. Oh, how I wish none of this was real.

June 28th, 1778: France is at war with Britain. I saw large flocks of dragons and their riders flying across the dawnlit sky, draped with French flags, and fitted with armor, harnesses, and reins. Mother said she heard from one of Uncle's friends that the French and Spanish navies were fighting with the British in the English Channel. Soldiers have been called to the front lines from all across the country. King Louis and Queen Antoinette are nowhere to be seen.

July 1st, 1778: Our navy has been sunken. Calais and Cherbourg have fallen to Britain. Crops have been burnt and people are dying of famine. It is beyond horrible.

July 14th, 1778: Mother found me crying in my room, with Leon consoling me by my side. I begged her to make preparations to leave with me, for the British were firebombing Paris, overpowering the French and allied forces amassed to the north of us. Leon concurred and asked Mother to consider leaving. She ignored us, saying she had faith in the French Army, denying the truth that stares at us right in the face. She is gone from my room as I put this to paper, thankfully. I am full of doubt and panic, but I know now what must be done.

July 15th, 1778: Paris has fallen. I am finally leaving tonight on Leon with my most precious belongings, without telling Mother or anyone at home. Leon said I was "doing the right thing" after I began sobbing again. Forgive me, Mother, but I have no choice. Goodbye.

July 28th, 1778: From the outskirts of Tours, I saw the smoke and flames engulfing the ruined city, and dragons murdering each other in the sky. It is evil and unforgivable. My Father is missing. My Uncle is dead. My Aunt is in hiding. Now my Mother has vanished to who knows where, and my manor—my country—is no more. But now is no time for weeping. I must be strong for my own sake and flee to some place where I know I will have protection, to ask for aid for France. I will first go to Corsica, for Aunt Mallory might still be there, and if not, I will fly to Russia. Perhaps Natasha remembers me and will take pity on me.

November 7th, 1779: The war has spread throughout Europe, Asia, and the Colonies. Thousands—no, millions have died. I could not find Aunt Mallory in Corsica, now annexed by Britain, so I was forced to fly east. I am currently in Russia, searching for Natasha, who I hope will agree to speak to Catherine the Great on my behalf. May freedom prevail.

THREE: A DRAGON'S PLACE

"...Regarding the nature of that once mythical species called *Draconicus*, it is doubtless that they possess reasoning and intelligence comparable to that of humans. Indeed, if they were truly of inferior breed and of lesser mind, they would not have devised their own government in the formerly clandestine isles of Terra Draconis, nor recognized their right to democratic self-governance, nor fought for that right in their civil war with Torburn, the Georgian Wars, the Qing Crisis, the Second American Revolution, the World Revolution (1789), the Great Dragon Rebellion, and the Siege of London that killed Emperor George III.

Therefore, on the question of the rights of dragons, it can only be concluded that there exists no reason nor justification for their present treatment as members of a servile underclass deprived entirely of their natural liberties, or worse, as mere tools of war and aggression. And this having been settled, shall we not ask ourselves the same question of those unfortunate peoples shackled under the barbarity of the slave trade, or of women who for too long have been ensnared, oppressed, and silenced by men, or of soldiers misled, sacrificed, and discarded in blood-soaked battlefields for the benefit of black-hearted monarchs and emperors? Do these downtrodden peoples not deserve as much equal representation under the law as the dragons who, while nonhuman in appearance, are nonetheless humans in spirit?

Never across all of history has the principal social cause of the times been so manifestly obvious: that of the liberation of dragons and all subservient peoples from enslavement and oppression, and the recognition of their natural equality as free, sovereign citizens. Any civilization that retains its old ways of Empire, therefore, is not really a civilization at all, but rather an offense against life, beauty, and morality itself."

—Mary Wollstonecraft, A Vindication of the Rights of Dragons (1794).

THE LEXINGTON LINDWORM

Containing News of All Things Draconian
THURSDAY, OCTOBER 20TH, 1825

DRAGONS LIBERATED!

The newly elected Supreme President of the UNITED REPUBLIC OF COLUMBIA, William Crawford, assembled today in New York City with the leaders of the world's Great Powers, alongside Palatia, Queen of the Dragons, and Empress Celine of the Russian-controlled French Protectorate, to sign the historic Treaty of Eternal Friendship Between Humanity and Dragonkind.

This aforementioned Treaty has established the independent sovereignty and autonomy of the Draconian Isles, enshrined peaceful trade between the Powers and the Isles, forced Britain to relinquish its last territorial claims in Oceania since the downfall of its World Empire, and redefined dragons as sentient beings deserving of equal rights.

Such a momentous occasion in history has divided the Nation, and led to mixed reactions amongst various members of the Public. Abolitionists allied with Palatia and Empress Celine have rejoiced at the triumph of their movement to free dragons from the servitude of their human masters, following their victories in fighting for the liberation of colored people and women from slavery. Anti-abolitionists, however, have expressed fury, disgust, and outrage towards the Treaty, citing its terms as deleterious to the Nation's economy, health, transportation and communication systems, and industrial as well as agricultural sectors.

"If this Treaty comes into effect, Columbia shall be ruined, and people shall be plunged into poverty, hunger, and despair," said Elijah B. Montgomery, a rising Senator from Tennessee. "Should the tyrannical and vile Crawford Administration not revoke its approval of the highest corruption and theft our Nation has seen since its inception, a Government independent from Columbia and its regulatory schemes must be formed without delay," he added.

President Crawford could not be reached for comment…

Charles Ta is a writer, illustrator, and educator based in Union City, NJ. His short story "Tough Luck, Kid" was previously published as part of a short story anthology in the book BLAST by author Robert Blake Whitehill, the latest entry in his Ben Blackshaw action/thriller series. He has also had stories published in Sci-Phi Journal ("Xenogram: A Chronology Of The Global Erasure Of Vowel Number Three, And The Merger Of Man"), and 365 Tomorrows ("To the Bitter End"), as well as written freelance nonfiction pieces for clients on LinkedIn. When not immersed in a good book or traveling to strange, often alien worlds, Charles teaches special education students in West New York, NJ.

Learn more about Charles at: **Instagram** | **Author Website**

<u>*Dreamscape*</u>

Karin Eaton

You came to me again
last night while I slept
fanning flames of wonder

what do you want I asked
you don't speak
just hover
warming me with a glow
of comfort and kindness
and then you are gone
I am left to ponder

In the morning light
I watch the clouds
for signs

Is that your trail
the smoky arc that loops
with perfect symmetry
amongst the clouds
that shimmers while I watch
then disappears, like you?

Tonight, I will look for you
in my dreamscape
ready to be guided
ready to follow your lead

Will you let me fly with you?
Will you lift me
above the daily grind
beyond the stress of doubt
that hobbles my momentum
that clouds my judgement?

I wait through daylight hours
and watch the sun dip
coloring the sky with radiance
and then I see your wings
brilliant in the setting sun
fanning flames
that send a spark of wisdom
in that instant
I get your message

open your eyes
see the good that surrounds you
believe in yourself

I am no longer left to wonder

You will be my guide to
abandon self-doubt
to find my inner strength
that will break my bonds
of indecision.

And when I am ready
you will let me fly with you.

Karin Eaton is a writer, traveler and student of Ancient Egypt. Since retirement as an Arts Manager in Toronto, Ontario, she is enjoying the tranquility of country living, where she delights in observing the changing seasons. She particularly appreciates the metamorphosis of monarch butterflies in her garden and the migration of birds across the lake. When she is not indulging her love of travel and adventure, she spends her time experimenting with memoir, travel and poetry writing. She has won awards for her poetry and her work has been featured in a variety of publications including Common Tread – an online motorcycle magazine, the Persimmon Tree Short Takes and six Quillkeepers Press Anthologies.

Learn more about Karin at: Author Website | Instagram

<u>*Drakaina*</u>

Caolán Mac an Aircinn

ἀγχοῦ δὲ κρήνη καλλίρροος, ἔνθα δράκαιναν

κτεῖνεν ἄναξ, Διὸς υἱός, ἀπὸ κρατεροῖο βιοῖο,

ζατρεφέα, μεγάλην, τέρας ἄγριον, ἣ κακὰ πολλὰ

ἀνθρώπους ἔρδεσκεν ἐπὶ χθονί, πολλὰ μὲν αὐτούς,

πολλὰ δὲ μῆλα ταναύποδ', ἐπεὶ πέλε πῆμα δαφοινόν.

Nearby there was a sweet-flowing spring, and there with his mighty bow

he killed the she-dragon, the lord, the son of Zeus;

she was well-fed, great, a savage monster, who

inflicted many evils on the humans on earth; many evils on them,

many on their long-shanked sheep, for she was a horror who reeked of blood.

(Homeric Hymn to Apollo, lines 300-304; translation by author)

The trouble with the Europeans, Zakridis decided over his coffee one June morning, was that they didn't listen.

"Dangerous?" Fauvelet had scoffed, when they had spoken, a week ago or so. "My dear Zakridis, it is 1879. Our ancient sources tell us all we need to excavate the site. Our modern technology can abrogate any dangers. Please, Zakridis—I know the villagers put you up to this. Your concern for them is very noble, but it is unwarranted and unwelcome. If you wish to assist in the excavations, you are more than welcome, but if you continue to fling around fairytales and nonsense, then I shall have to consider you simply a foolish old man. Besides, the Hymn is quite clear. Apollo slew the beast."

Yes, thought Zakridis, sipping his coffee, looking out over the slopes of Mount Parnassus as the rising sun gilded the porcelain edge of his coffee cup and threw the scrubby olive trees on the harsh mountainside into sharp relief; that was just the issue. It was 1879, and the scouring light of European enlightenment had reached Zakridis' village of Kastri, high on Greece's Mount Parnassus, at last. The problem was that the Europeans were sure that Kastri was on top of Delphi, the ancient oracle of the gods, and nothing would stop them digging through to find it— not the villagers, not the village.

Not even a dragon.

The Irishwoman, Louisa—now she might be saved, thought Zakridis. She wasn't so arrogant as the rest of them; a lifetime of men and British telling her that her opinions counted for less no doubt predisposed her favourably to listen to those whom others might ignore. She hadn't believed either, but she had at least listened.

"Antonis, what do you mean, a dragon?" Louisa had said. "I thought Monsieur Fauvelet asked you to stop with this nonsense."

"It is not nonsense, madam," Zakridis had explained patiently. "I saw it with my own two eyes."

"When? How?"

Zakridis had told her his story. Did she know that Greece was a young country, and that he, Antonis Zakridis, had fought to make her free? He had come from his homeland of Crete—still sadly under the Ottoman yoke—to the mainland to fight when he was barely more than a boy—was he fifteen? If even that. Well, one thing had led to another, and he had found himself fighting with a band of *klepht*s, anti-Ottoman bandits, in Thessaly; and when news came that a detachment of Egyptians was moving up from Larissa, the leader of the band, one Mavroyiannis Stamatopoulos, had decided they must break for the hills.

"The Egyptians chased us," Zakridis told Louisa, "As far as Kastri— and that is a big thing, you know, it shows how much trouble we caused them. Well, they holed us up in Kastri, and they were coming up the mountain for us; if they reached the village, you know, they would have burnt it down around us, the people be damned. 'Well,' said Mavroyiannis, 'I saw a cave a little way down. We'll hole up in there.'"

"Not—"

"Yes, Madam Louisa, the very cave Monsieur Fauvelet intends to explore in just under a week, searching for remnants of the old oracle. We took enough supplies to last us a week and rested inside the mouth of the cave while the Egyptians scoured Parnassus for us. But it is a big cave, and we had time, so some of us took to exploring. One man, Kirillos, did not come back, so we went as a band to find him.

In a cavern, deep in the bowels of the mountain, where the light of the sun only barely reached, we found her—the *drakaina*, the she-dragon. She was terrible and beautiful; she was curled around a spire of stone, as long as a ship, and in the flickering light of our torches her scales glinted like gold. We were all rooted to the spot with terror, and when she saw us, she spat a great gout of poison—Greek dragons spit poison, you know; not fire. I saw it take Mavroyiannis, my friend; saw how it stripped the flesh from his bones. I ran, and did not stop till I reached the sunlight."

"How is such a thing possible?"

"You know that in the ancient stories of my land, they say the sun-god, Apollo, slew the dragon Python here, on this very site. Well, the earliest version of the story, the Homeric Hymn to Apollo, it says it was a she-dragon—later stories call her Delphyne. I cannot say surely, but I think maybe it was a *drakaina* that the sun-god killed, and she left a brood; and when the Roman emperors closed the oracle and throttled the power of Apollo, I think a new *drakaina* hatched."

She had looked worried, and Zakridis thought he had warned her off; but Fauvelet was not one to be denied easily, or at all. Zakridis found out later that she had agreed to go with him to the cave after all, to search for the ruins of ancient Delphi.

Today was the day. Today was the day the Europeans were marching off to die, and only Zakridis could save them. He groaned, finished his coffee, cursed the hubris of man, and then set off down the mountainside, taking care to bring one thing.

The *drakaina* was finishing up by the time Zakridis made his way down to the cavern. Most of the Europeans were lying in a pool of poison by the door, their yellowing flesh peeling in strips away from their skeletons. Fauvelet himself had earned the honour of being the starter; though his legs were recognisable by their leather boots, the ragged red thing at which the *drakaina* was tearing with vulture-like motions was recognisable as his chest only by context. Zakridis positioned himself in the last ray of sunlight by the cavern entrance and admired her. She was monstrous, yes, with her massive serpentine body and ivory fangs and her saurian eyes that held the cold knowledge of aeons—but she was sublime too, a force of nature without malice, but to whom respect was due.

With a surreptitious glance around the cavern, Zakridis spotted Louisa, hiding wide-eyed behind a boulder. So she'd listened to him just enough to know what was coming, and get out of the way. He had saved one, at least.

With a ripping noise, the *drakaina* finished what was left of Fauvelet and turned to face Zakridis. Her reptilian eyes narrowed.

"Do you think I'm an old man who hasn't learned his lesson?" Zakridis said, and now there was a merry glimmer in his eye. The dragon did not answer, but pulled back to spit another glob of poison.

"Mr. Zakridis!" Louisa cried.

But Zakridis had taken out of his pocket the item he had brought from his house. It was a cheap, cracked little mirror. He caught the little sunlight which filtered into the cavern with it and shone it on the *drakaina*. With a hiss, then a screech like tearing metal, she slithered backwards into the darkness: not dead, not even wounded, but afraid nonetheless.

Louisa scrambled out of her hiding place.

"How did you...?"

"Apollo, the sun god, vanquished the dragon once," said Zakridis. "He is not so strong as he once was, but she still fears her old enemy. I was safe, back in the war, when I reached the sunlight. Come, we have not much time, and we are still in her cave."

Louisa scrambled up alongside Zakridis and they began to retreat towards the light of day.

"To think, in 1879, that men could be killed by a dragon!"

"Don't blame the dragon, Madam Louisa, for the Europeans pushed into her home and it was her right to keep them out. To think, for all the ancient Greek works Monsieur Fauvelet read, and yet he did not pick up the most important message of all—the foolishness of hubris!"

Caolán Mac An Aircinn is a classicist, archaeologist, translator, editor and opportunistic zookeeper who writes primarily in his native Irish. *Dragon Dreams* represents Caolán's first work published in English.

Prince Imugi

Kimberly McAfee

I am an imugi.

I am filled with

dreams and hopes;

they crash within my heart,

like wild ocean waves

upon silken shores.

My greatest wish,

my truest desire,

is to leave this

serpentine prison behind

and grow to be

the yong I am

on the inside.

I need only a chance,

I need only one gift from

the benevolent heavens -

a yeouiju -

and then my destiny

will be fulfilled.

I will be as powerful

as the East Sea.

I will be as loved

as the Han River.

I will be the greatest

dragon this world

has ever seen.

An Imugi becomes a Yong.

A Prince becomes a King.

The Great Dragon becomes a God.

Kimberly McAfee is a writer and poet residing in the US. She has authored/co-authored works in a variety of formats, such as websites, e-magazines, anthologies, and even a peer-reviewed scholarly journal. Ms. McAfee has published the poetry collection, 'The Savior and the Shadow Queen: A Fantastical Tale Told Through Sequential Poems,' and the chapbook, 'AmerAsian: My Journey to Becoming Whole as a Mixed Korean-American,' with Quillkeepers Press; she has also self-published three chapbooks, available on Amazon. You can find more of her poetry on her Instagram page @writerpoetkim.

Learn more about Kimberly at: Instagram | LinkTree

<u>Baby Dragon's Nursery Rhyme</u>

Natalie Cooper

Baby dragons with their sweet little features

Are the busiest of magical creatures

But now is time for hatchlings to curl up tight

The sun is rising and it's much too bright

Baby dragons need a lot of rest

If they're going to be their best

So fold in your little wings and rest your weary head

Get cozy and snuggle down in your soft little bed

Baby dragon your dreams are spun with love

Shining down on you from the heavens above

So close your charming little eyes and breathe in deep

Letting your sweet little body fall gently to sleep

Baby dragon the world will wait

While you get your six to eight

Then tonight you will awaken ready to go

To fly amongst the stars watching the galaxy glow

<u>*A Trio of Dragon Tanka*</u>

Natalie Cooper

Ka Rui

Scarlet scales flash by

Glinting in the navy night

Ka Rui blazes bright

Though small in size he may be

Ka Rui enlivens the dark

Fuku Rui

Fuku Rui ascends

Bringing forth good luck to those

Who bow graciously

Gifting success in love and

Strong health to mind and body

Ryūjin

The ocean's vigour

Derives from sea god Ryūjin

King of the dragons

With tide jewels and vast strength

His waves touch the stars

Natalie Cooper is a Child and Family Educator who spends her days working with families and her nights writing poetry and creating digital art. Natalie's writing has appeared in Monash University's 2023 Verge, Mudgee Valley Writers 2022 Anthology, Paper Road magazine and Positive Words magazine. Natalie's photography has been included in exhibitions at the Museum of Australian Photography (STAGES: Life in Lockdown) and the Queen Victoria Women's Centre (Make A Fuss). Currently Natalie resides on Wurundjeri Woi Wurrung and Bunurong country (Victoria, Australia) with her trio of mischief making children and partner in crime husband.

Learn more about Natalie at: Instagram

Dragon Brother

Shea'Mia Harrell

Cynthia fell over backward in surprise when the speck in the distance she had taken to be a bird—then a very big bird—turned out to be a real, live dragon. Cynthia and James' mothers were still in the house, but Cynthia expected any moment that they would look out, see the dragon, and come running out to the yard screaming for their children to get away.

"They won't see her," James said with a laugh as Cynthia looked back at the house for the fourth time. "Adults don't look at the world in the right way to see creatures from Trynoria. I think most are too busy being adults."

"Trynoria?" Cynthia asked, picking herself up and brushing off her floral leggings. "Is that a country?"

James gave the little girl a wink. "It's a whole world; a magical world. You'll love it."

As stunning as James clearly considered FireStorm, his description did not do the red-orange dragon justice.

FireStorm's scales were as big as the little girl's hand, and those eyes that scrutinized with such interest were almost as big as Cynthia's face. The name FireStorm was apt, for red and orange mingled on the shining scales, catching the light in varying patterns as the dragon moved, giving the vague impression that her powerful form was created out of dancing flames.

"So, this is the little one you have spoken of so often," FireStorm said, her voice rumbling deep in her throat. "She does seem to have a powerful imagination. I can feel it from here. I'd love to see which creature chooses to meld with her. There might be some competition."

"How is she speaking?" Cynthia whispered behind James' shoulder. "Her lips barely move."

James laughed and led Cynthia directly in front of the imposing dragon.

"Place your ear right where her throat meets her chest."

Cynthia obeyed, and James spoke to FireStorm. "Could you only speak through your throat?"

The dragon smiled and Cynthia leapt back with a squeal of alarm. Both FireStorm and James then spent several minutes convincing the little girl that it was only a smile, and the giant teeth were nothing to fear. Cynthia blushed when FireStorm explained, with another smile, how dragons preferred to eat certain kinds of fruits. It was rare that they ever ate other living creatures and if they were forced to, they would never eat those with imagination.

"As a matter of fact, there's a fruit that's poisonous to humans but like catnip for dragons," James said, his smile gone. "Word among dragon-riders is that it's becoming a problem. Some dragons can't stop eating it. It makes them act weird, and sometimes dangerous. Thankfully, it only grows on the peaks of the Cloud Mountains and isn't easy to get."

When Cynthia's confidence was great enough to rest her cheek on the dragon's throat once more, her eyes were filled with wonder. FireStorm's voice was there, muffled and a bit garbled, but if Cynthia listened carefully, she could just make out the words.

"Most of the vocal sounds originate at the base of the throat. The rest of the journey out of the mouth serves to amplify the voice so it can be heard properly. Very little movement of tongue and lips is needed to enunciate."

Then, FireStorm spoke normally, her voice coming out powerful and clear. "Unicorns have even better voice centers. All they have to do is open and close their mouths a little."

"There's unicorns, too?" Cynthia jumped up and down, clapping and giggling.

James sighed and flopped his hands down by his sides. "What is it with girls and unicorns?"

Folding her arms over her chest with a humph, Cynthia stuck out her tongue.

"FireStorm needs to collect some flamestone for her cousin," James said, ignoring the girl's reaction, which seemed to annoy her even more. "Her cousin is expecting a clutch of eggs soon, and the flamestone will keep them at the right temperature during their early growth."

It took FireStorm opening a portal to Trynoria for Cynthia to forget that she was supposed to be indignant but forget she did. Through that shimmering circle was a whole different place, verdant, with all sorts of plants that she had never seen before; trees full of blooms like daffodils, ready-to-pick fruit growing off of single stalks like flowers, and what type of fruit they were she could not have said, for each time she tasted one the flavor was different.

"Are there supplies at the flamestone caves?" James asked.

"Yes," Firestorm said as she lay down and lowered her neck to the ground. "I tended to that this morning. Get on. It will be faster if you both ride."

"Cynthia hasn't flown before," James objected. "I'd rather wait a while."

"Then, I won't fly. I'll just climb. It will still be faster, and she can get used to riding."

At the base of FireStorm's neck was what appeared to be a saddle, just the right size for the thirteen-year-old boy with room for another rider. With some coaxing from both FireStorm and James, Cynthia found herself sitting on a dragon's neck as one would a horse. It felt so strange. Yet, FireStorm seemed content, as though this was as it should be.

"Isn't it undignified for a dragon to wear a saddle like a horse?" Cynthia asked, her voice quiet and timid.

FireStorm laughed, with a rumbling sound that gave the riders a slight shaking. "How else would a human ride a dragon? They'd just slip right off. Some might say we are proud creatures, but I think we should be able to make some effort to accommodate our humans."

"Your humans?" Cynthia asked, batting a strand of her light-brown hair out of her olive face. "Does that have something to do with that 'meld' thing, you said before? What does that mean?"

The sound FireStorm made could only have been considered a purr. "Dragons and unicorns can pick a human to 'meld,' or in other words, make a very strong connection with. We usually feel when we meet the right human, but logic plays a role in our choice, as well. Our humans' moods can physically affect us. We can also help guide them, which is important because human imagination affects Trynoria. James and I share a meld and the idea of living without him, or him being harmed, is almost unbearable. We can get very fierce when our human is in danger of any kind."

"That sounds amazing," Cynthia murmured. "Will I meld?"

James gave her a little squeeze. "It's possible."

The ride was not exactly smooth. As gentle as FireStorm tried to keep her movements, there were boulders and crags to traverse. Yet, despite the jostling, and the fact that the saddle was uncomfortably wide for Cynthia, James was right there, his arms cradling her on either side, holding her as stable as humanly possible.

After what seemed like ages of navigating grey rock face after grey rock face and crevasses that plunged farther than Cynthia cared to know, FireStorm clambered up onto a ledge. What greeted them was a cave spacious enough to allow a dragon to pass through, with just sufficient room not to be cramped. FireStorm allowed the humans to dismount and took a look inside. Cynthia was about to follow FireStorm when James took her by the shoulders and turned her around to look back.

Rich shades of green stretched almost as far as the eye could see until gently rolling hills grew into distant snow-capped mountains. Patches of pink, purple, orange, yellow, and blue dappled the scene, where flowers and trees proudly displayed their full bloom. Off in the distance, Cynthia could see a group of dragons gallivanting around the sky, chasing each other this way and that, performing somersaults and barrel-rolls. Her mouth hanging open, Cynthia marveled how such a dreary climb could end in such delights.

"Now," James said, crouching and turning Cynthia to face him. "Pay attention. I'll never be able to explain what happened if you go missing or get hurt in some that we can't pass off as just roughhousing in the yard. The adults can't know about this place."

"That's only half true," FireStorm said over her shoulder. "Some adults can learn about Trynoria, but if they didn't learn about it as children, the odds aren't good."

James cleared his throat and the ridges above FireStorm's eyes rose as she looked away. Cynthia marveled at the possibility of a dragon looking sheepish. It was a strange sight, indeed.

"Yes," James continued, "it isn't a good idea to tell adults about Trynoria. So, listen. Rule number 1: Always stay where one of us can see you. If you can't see us, we can't see you. I can't have you getting lost. Rule number 2: If you hear me yell 'Marco,' you yell 'Polo.' That means I can't see you and want to know where you are. Rule number 3: If you don't know where you are, yell 'Polo.' Don't move. Don't try to find me. I will respond and come find you. Rule number 4: and this is the most important … don't touch the flamestone. It burns. Call me for the little pieces and FireStorm for the big pieces. Four rules … not much. Understand?"

Cynthia heaved a heavy sigh and looked over one shoulder. Then, she nodded. When James turned away, she muttered under her breath. "Bossy butt."

James knelt by the supplies which FireStorm had brought to the cave beforehand. Removing items from the dragon-sized metal basket lined with what looked like dragon scales, James lit a lantern for himself and one for Cynthia. Then, James took a set of clothes and, as the other two waited at the entrance, he went inside and changed. When he returned in tunic, breeches, and knee-high boots, Cynthia couldn't help clapping her pleasure.

James took a set of clothes and, as the other two waited at the entrance, he went inside and changed. When he returned in tunic, breeches, and knee-high boots, Cynthia couldn't help clapping her pleasure.

"You look like you belong in an adventure story!"

James chuckled. "It's a bit more practical than that. If I wear these here," he indicated his neatly folded jeans, T-shirt, socks, and sneakers he held in his hands, "they will get damaged as sure as a dragon sneezes fire. My mom would kill me if she had to buy me new clothes over and over because of random burns and tears. I don't even know how I would explain it!" He, then, strapped a dagger to his leg and a set of dragon scale tongs to his hip.

Once they entered the cave and started their search, it was Cynthia who first found a piece of flamestone. She cried out at the beauty of the rock, which shimmered almost as though gentle flames crackled in its core.

Cynthia had become quite the rock collector over the last two years since her parents had moved to Montana. Many stones of various sizes and colors decorated her nightstand. Her favorite was what her father called "pyrite," but they all paled in comparison to flamestone.

"Just because you're older doesn't mean you get to make up stupid rules," she muttered under her breath.

"Stop!"

Before she knew what had happened, James's hand clasped tight around her wrist, flinging her hand away from the lump of flamestone.

"I told you not to touch it!" Just short of a shout, James' voice echoed around the cave, scolding her from every direction. "It was a simple instruction."

Cynthia had never seen him so angry. His kind features took on hard lines and creases. Somehow, his blue-green eyes seemed to narrow and widen at the same time, the color deepening with his emotions. She shrank away, holding her wrist.

At first, the shock of his transformation left her little capacity for her own indignation, but she quickly rallied.

"You're always making rules!" she shouted, then flinched as her own voice was echoed booming back to her.

James was shaking now, and Cynthia wondered if the echoes had startled him, also. FireStorm touched her chin to James' head, and Cynthia waited for the dragon to do something else, but all FireStorm did was look right back at her. James still shook, as he closed his eyes and clenched his fists, his jaw tight.

"You don't …" Cynthia began in a yell, then cut herself short as the echo began again. She began to shake with the effort of controlling her anger and her desire to scream it out of her.

"You don't get to make a bunch of stupid rules just because you're older." Settling on a whispered shout, she continued, "You're always bossing me around. 'Don't do that.' 'You're doing it wrong.' 'Do it this way.' Your way isn't the only way!"

James caught himself just before he bellowed his words. Instead, he spoke in low, controlled tones. "That's not an excuse. Sometimes, you have to do what you're told. Don't you understand that you almost got really badly hurt? I told you it burns. That's why it's called flamestone. Dragons eat it to keep their flame hot and put it in their nurseries to keep the eggs warm. Dragons can touch it because flames don't hurt them so much, but for humans, it's like putting your hand in a fire. That's what would have happened to you because you wouldn't listen to me!" His voice rose in abject frustration.

Cynthia looked at the flamestone, still seeming to flicker with an inner light, and then her eyes lifted to FireStorm who lowered her head to Cynthia's level.

"Once, when I was a little dracling, years before I met James, some young humans—
just a little older than you are now, Cynthia—were helping to find flamestone." The dragon's voice took on a solemn tone. "One boy was timid about being in the flamestone caves, but he tried to be brave and help. It's good to be alert in the caves, but he was easily startled, jumping at every sound. I went over to him to suggest that we leave and find some other way to assist …" Firestorm's voice trailed off and her head drooped.

"It wasn't your fault, FireStorm." James stepped up to the dragon and stroked her neck. "He was probably going to get hurt even if you didn't do anything. The other dragons weren't paying attention because they were busy and thinking of the humans from dragon standards. They know better now."

FireStorm took a breath and attempted a smile before continuing, "I made the mistake of coming up from behind. I spoke and he jumped. He tripped over a rock, and when he fell, his arm brushed a chunk of flamestone. I remember his cries of pain as though it was just yesterday. His sleeve was burned through, and a great strip of his skin blistered almost instantly. He wanted to go home, but there was no way to explain his injury to those in his world ..."

"What about the unicorns?" Cynthia asked. "Everyone knows that they can heal anything with just a touch of their horns."

James spoke up, seeing that FireStorm would continue rather than giving herself time to gather her composure. "Unicorns are, perhaps, one of the most magical beings of Trynoria. It's true, they can heal horrible injuries, but it takes time. Every now and then, as it did that day, time matters more than magic. If an injury is too extreme, we can die even if a unicorn is right next to us. I've heard the boy was in great pain for days, and he only brushed flamestone. If you had held it, it would have burned you much worse."

Cynthia looked wide-eyed at the rock and side-stepped away. "But it's so pretty. It looks like a decoration."

James sighed and knelt in front of Cynthia, placing his hands on her arms.

"I'm sorry," he said, "but many beautiful things in this world are dangerous, just like in ours."

Cynthia hung her head and nodded.

"Okay then," James said, giving his hands a little clap. "Now that we have that figured out ..." He reviewed the rules again with Cynthia, who meekly repeated them when he prompted.

They walked the winding tunnels and caverns together. In the walls at either end of each tunnel were arrows pointing back the way the trio had come.

Cynthia tugged at James' sleeve. "The arrows keep telling us to go back. Why do we keep going if the arrows are warning us not to go?"

"Those aren't warnings," James said with a laugh. "They were cut into the stone by dragons who came through here before so that we always know the way out and don't get lost."

Sure enough, not long after, the arrows stopped, and FireStorm began carving out new arrows with her claws.

At first, there wasn't much flamestone to find, it having been collected by those who gathered it before. What little they came across, FireStorm, or James with the tongs, would place in a metal bucket, also lined with dragon scales.

"The scales keep it from getting hot on the outside, or even melting the metal if the flamestone stays in too long," the dragon explained. "Humans can move the bucket that way."

"What is it?" Cynthia asked. "It's not a rock. It's not coals. It burns, but it doesn't burn out."

FireStorm smiled, and Cynthia fought not to cringe at the glint of the lantern light on the dragon's teeth. "There are little creatures inside. It's actually a cocoon. The creatures are like tadpoles ..." FireStorm used her tail to block Cynthia, who moved to get a closer look at a chunk of flamestone. "A dragon can see them, but human eyes get dazzled if they look too closely. You wouldn't be able to see properly for hours."

"So, you eat tadpoles in the flamestone," Cynthia said, before sticking her tongue out in disgust, as the group continued on their way.

After FireStorm and James stopped laughing, FireStorm explained.

"Yes, but that's a good thing. We have a second stomach, called a kiln and there's something in our kilns that allows the flamestone larva to mature. As the creature matures, it feeds the fire in the kiln.

"We dragons try to feed our kilns on the same day so that the creatures mature and can be released at the same time. You'll never guess what they turn into …"

FireStorm paused to chuckle, and before she could continue, Cynthia blurted out, "Fire frogs?"

James laughed so hard he doubled over, holding his sides, while FireStorm's eyes widened.

"Actually, that's very close," she said. "They're froglike with dragonfly wings. We call them pyr-sprites because we open our mouths and release them with bursts of dragon fire. Then, they glow like stars as they fly away. It's a whole celebration and quite a sight to behold."

"I'd love to see one!" Cynthia said, her voice almost shrill with glee.

"Maybe another time," James said. "There isn't another for several months."

"The sprites are a bit comical with their wings high up on their shoulders and their hips dangling." FireStorm laughed, as she tried to mimic the sprites, but her wings bumped the sides of the cave. She cleared her throat to continue on a more serious vein. "They warm the land and feed the energy of Trynoria."

When the bucket was full, FireStorm took it to the entrance to empty it into the basket while Cynthia and James continued their search a little farther in.

Following a faint glow from around a corner, they entered another chamber. There in the walls and strewn on the floor were chunks of flamestone. Such was the quantity that the lanterns the two carried were hardly necessary.

"Be careful, Cynthia," James said as he set to work with the tongs, moving the fallen stones into a pile for when FireStorm returned. "This is a perfect environment for an accident."

Cynthia soon understood the extent of FireStorm's previous words. As she looked around in wonder at the flamestone in the walls, she found that her eyes started to hurt. So, retrieving her discarded lantern, she made her way to the darker end of the tunnel at the other side.

"Don't get lost," James reminded her.

"I won't," she said, her voice drawn out in exasperation. "My eyes want the dark."

James laughed. "You've been looking at it too hard, haven't you?"

Cynthia didn't reply. It sounded like one of those questions that adults called rhetorical, and she had learned not to answer those. Answering would only get her into trouble or laughed at.

With a start and a little gasp, Cynthia lifted her lantern to see more clearly. She was almost certain she heard some sort of scratching sound, like a dog's nails on rock. Taking a couple of steps forward, she held the light a little higher. Two points of multicolored light shone back at her. She gave a little yelp.

"What are you doing?" James' voice sounded tense. "Are you messing with the flamestone?"

"No," Cynthia called back. "I think eyes are looking at me."

"What?" Now, James sounded almost as afraid as she was, though she was trying to be brave.

The eyes moved closer even as she heard James crossing the large chamber. Her light glinted on a row of long sharp teeth.

"James!" she cried out as she jumped back.

As James caught her under one arm and pulled her into the flamestone chamber, Cynthia screamed again. The creature that came into view was something out of a nightmare. Its teeth were so long that its mouth was unable to close and its eyes so large they filled up the rest of the face. The head looked like an apple on a stick of a neck. The rest of the body was just as skeletal. James pulled Cynthia behind him as he brandished his dagger.

As the creature swayed back and forth, seeming to contemplate its next move, James sheathed the dagger. Being certain to keep Cynthia behind him, James chucked his lantern at the beast, which leapt upon the metal case surrounding the now extinguished candle.

James took the opportunity to guide Cynthia backwards, away from the monstrosity.

With a whimper, Cynthia clutched at James' arm. "Look!"

There, in the tunnel, movement could be seen. The light from the chamber glinted off giant eyes and ever-bared teeth, but that wasn't the worst of it. Several more gleaming gazes joined the other.

Cynthia started to scream, but James clapped his hand over her mouth.

"Keep backing away," he whispered. "And don't scream. They'll consider you prey if you do. You've already drawn their attention. We have to hope they aren't in a playful mood."

"Playful?" Cynthia whispered back, her voice breaking.

James let out a slow breath. "For them, to play is to hunt."

The creatures crept into the light, first one at a time, then all at once, each tracking the two humans. Cynthia lost count at ten as the creatures began to jostle each other. James returned his hand to his dagger hilt.

"What are they?" The words barely squeaked through Cynthia's tight throat.

Then, one of the creatures lunged.

"Run!" James shouted, giving Cynthia a push. "Don't look back. FireStorm! Ember imps!"

Direction meant little to Cynthia as she ran. Where she ended up didn't even cross her mind. Escaping those horrible things was paramount. It wasn't until FireStorm nearly ran her down that Cynthia stopped.

"James?" Cynthia asked, looking around. He was nowhere to be seen.

With a sharp snarl, FireStorm raced past in the direction from which a strange chattering, almost like maniacal laughter could be heard.

The fear of those creatures was soon overshadowed by the horror of what might have happened to James. Cynthia pushed herself to run just as fast toward the danger as she had to escape it. How could she have not noticed he wasn't with her?

As it turned out, she had not made it so far away as she had originally thought, and she soon came upon the scene of battle. FireStorm, growling and snarling, swept the ember imps aside with her talons, but the creatures kept coming, jumping on her, biting and clawing. James' back was inches from a wall veined with flamestone, and every attack he deflected brought him closer to being burned.

Cynthia hesitated only a moment before reaching for the only weapons at hand. With a cry of pain, she threw two chunks of flamestone, one thumping hard against an ember imp's ribs while the other struck with a sickening crack against its head. The creature fell with a shriek that mingled with those of its companions, which were beginning to retreat from FireStorm's onslaught. Cynthia squealed with delight despite her pain. Several of the boys at school said she threw like a girl; little did they know what throwing like a girl really meant.

The other imp that had been attacking James now looked to the source of this new attack. That was its mistake. James' dagger slashed hard against the creature's chest with a ringing sound as sparks flew.

Clutching its chest, the imp retreated, having already been abandoned by its partner in crime. All the other imps routed, the dragon and humans drew a shared breath of relief.

Cynthia ran to James' side with a cry of dismay. "You're bleeding!"

Indeed, his tunic and trousers were shredded and wet with blood in several places.

"Worry about that later," he said, turning her around and pushing her out of the chamber. "Let's get out of here before they bring reinforcements."

The delivery of flamestone to Amber, FireStorm's cousin, was far smaller than all concerned had hoped for, but under the circumstances, they were more than content. Meanwhile, the humans nursed their wounds in Amber's home, a cave much cozier than Cynthia would have ever expected a cave could be. Two unicorns showed up shortly after. They said they were close enough to sense there were wounds which needed healing and so came forthwith. Cynthia would have barely been able to contain her awe and giddiness were it not for the pain in her hands. Now, that the excitement of a life and death situation had passed, the persistent stinging refused to be ignored.

"We will form a group to drive the imps out, and remove more flamestone so it doesn't draw them," said one unicorn called DiamondHorn.

Her mate, SilverMane nickered and shook his head. "They are getting more bold and more numerous. These are ominous tidings."

"Are we going to discuss how Cynthia was able to pick up and throw flamestone, and only be blistered?" James asked. "Wouldn't that cause her hands to be burned black? Can she use magic or something?"

"Since I've known you, you keep using the term magic," SilverMane said slowly. "I'm not sure that's the best way to describe it. Take us unicorns for example. We aren't magical as you might understand it. We use the energy that flows through Trynoria. Some creatures are more able to do this than others.

"Humans aren't usually able, except with a very powerful imagination, but to answer your question, James, I sense Cynthia has exactly that. She could have a strong inner fire which would counteract that of the flamestone. Combined, these two forces could tap into and shift the energies of this world, bending the natural order of things slightly, but not enough to truly break the natural laws of our world. This could explain how her hands are not as burned as they should be. Only time will tell, but I feel we can expect great things from her."

Over the course of several days, Cynthia's burns were tended along with James' cuts, and she was visited by several old dragons and unicorns. All the attention embarrassed her, but James seemed excited about the matter, though he never said why.

Ever since James had told her that he had always returned home not long after he had left, no matter how many hours or days he stayed in Trynoria, she had stopped worrying about how her mother must be worrying. Aside from her burned hands, the pain of which diminished day by day through the ministrations of the unicorns, the stay turned into a thing of almost pure delight.

When James suggested it was time to return home, Cynthia shed some tears over the thought of leaving her new world and new friends, despite a growing homesickness.

James shook his head and sighed. "You know we can come back, right? I said you might be able to see a pyr-genesis. You'd have to come back for that."

As Cynthia stepped through FireStorm's portal just behind James, she looked around at the muted browns and grey greens of late summer in the foothills of Montana. It seemed a bit drab after the rich colors of Trynoria. Still, it was the home she knew, and she was glad to be back to the familiar. Life among dragons and unicorns was not quite what she had would have thought. There were dangers that had to be navigated, some of which, she was certain, she still knew nothing. Yet, here she stood, safe beside the boy who had bravely faced down ember imps, thinking nothing of his own safety, to give her time to escape. She had little to fear with a friend like him.

Just then, Cynthia's mother called them to dinner. Cynthia wrapped her arms around James' chest.

"I've always wondered what it would be like to have a big brother."

James placed a protective hand on her back.

"You don't have to wonder anymore."

Shea'Mia Harrell learned to love reading and the English language from an early age. With many story elements chasing around in her mind, it was a natural progression to writing her own stories. Though her love is the novel, especially fantasy, and even more specifically the epic fantasy, her debut was a children's book "Boys Will Be Boys." Besides reading and writing, Shea'Mia enjoys the natural world of her Western Washington home, dancing, crafting, and playing with her inquisitive cat, Sherlock.

Learn more about Shea'Mia at:
Author Website | Good Reads | Pinterest | Instagram

H.T. Schwartz

After her mate was murdered and their egg broken, Skaltrath decided it was time to die. She laid down and gave in to madness.

The rain descended ceaselessly while they approached the village at the foot of the mountain. Blaza blinked through a mixture of tears and droplets and pulled her scarf to cover her mouth and nose. They were close enough now that the unmistakable smell of rotten flesh overpowered even the scents of mold and mildew in a land engulfed by storms. It had been raining for two years straight since the mountain's protector groveled before despair. And therefore, her despair had become the village folk's despair.

On the stone-paved road that led into the village, they passed a few carts pulled by thin beasts and whole families carrying ragged bundles. They all looked down not acknowledging Blaza and her mother.

"You are going the wrong way. There's nothing or no one there." A scrawny old man with a thinning gray mustache waved his equally weathered staff at them.

Mother gave him a polite nod and squeezed Blaza's hand reassuringly, indicating they would continue no matter what.

"The dragon, she's not blessing no more, no."

"I know." Mother replied and they pressed on as the rain grew heavier.

It was getting dark as they walked into the ghostly hamlet. Their wet clothes chilled their bones, and after days of walking, they were hungry and sore.

"Wait, sisters." Mother rolled her eyes as the old man called again. Despite the gloomy surroundings, Blaza giggled behind the thick woolen scarf. Mother was never the most forbearing with nosy people. Well, their art was not always welcome, so she understood why mother was defensive.

"Don't go up there at night. That's when she dreams. It's too dangerous, even for your kind."

Mother stopped her striding and squeezed Blaza's hand harder than usual. Blaza would complain, but she knew what that meant. Mother had a deep frown.

"We have a duty to see through, sir. Plus, I don't think there is anywhere we could stay."

"On the contrary, sister. You have a whole village for yourselves. We are the last ones to leave. Just pick a house." As he spoke, the old man used his staff to push a door open, seemingly at random.

"Kind sir, we appreciate the warning, but we don't mean to provide excuses for more persecution. That would be the perfect opportunity for any cunning fox to see two witches ransacking."

After a pause that seemed abnormally long due to the annoying tapping of the rain on their skin, the old man finally replied. "Then you are welcome to my home. Come. It is by the fountain. My daughter might have forgotten something we could eat."

Ugnath was soaring in the summer skies. His scales glistened gold when reflecting the radiating sun and Skaltrath was happy for a moment. That's how it always started, her dream.

Every night, when her fatigued body would finally surrender to sleep, Skaltrath saw her beloved Ugnath. Sometimes he was flying, sometimes drinking from the waterfall at the top of the mountain, which had been their lair for centuries. But that was just to aggravate the torture that existence had become. Soon those cherished memories would deform into nightmares.

She saw them coming to kill Ugnath. Again, she would see them raising their weapons against her beautiful egg. And she would relive that torment-filled episode over and over.

From the depths of her nightmares, Skaltrath screamed.

The rain suddenly turned into a furious thunderstorm. Blaza was relieved that her mother decided to stay the night instead of facing the weather.

"That poor soul." The man sighed and stared at his feet. "I don't know if you or anyone can do anything for her, sister. But we appreciate the intent."

"We will know when I take a look at her. If her heart still beats, there is still hope."

There would have been a moment of silence if it was not perturbed by the relentless sound of rain and thunder. Mother and the old man sat by the table on the only two existing chairs while Blaza chose to sit on the floor by the hearth. They had in fact found some stale barley for a meager soup that Blaza had trouble swallowing. The weird feeling in her stomach made her realize how terrified she was about the imminence of seeing a real dragon.

"We tried everything we could, everything we knew. We brought her our best sheep and honey. Everything is still rotting in there. We sang for her and even hired bards from the other villages because we know her love of music. Some of us would take turns keeping her company and even sleeping by her side. But we knew there is nothing we could do to cure heartsickness."

"I'm sure that she would appreciate your efforts, were she in her right mind."

"And dear Ugnath. What a terrible fate. There was nothing we countryfolk could do."

"What happened?" Blaza perked up.

"Oh, young one, I can try to tell you this tragic story, but I'm sure I will not do justice to all the majestic deeds of Skaltrath and Ugnath. But I don't suppose you like stories anymore for those are for little children." The man smiled for the first time and a web of little wrinkles formed around his eyes. Blaza knew he was just teasing her. She also thought he looked better when he smiled.

"I like stories. Mother says stories prevent us from repeating the same mistakes of the past."

Mother chuckled softly as she sat near the girl and undid her braids.

"Your mother is a wise woman. This story indeed tells of grave mistakes so listen closely and add those to the list of what not to repeat."

Skaltrath was born in the aqueous west, in a land no man has ever seen. During her first couple of centuries, she lived in a cave opened into an aeonian sea. And there she learned her kind's art. Skaltrath's lineage is one that can bend the sky's will and the water's temper.

A common thing to the hearts of any youth, no matter if man, fish, dragon, or horse is the longing for the unknown, for untrailed paths. So, when it was time, Skaltrath left her homeland to explore. She was young – for a dragon, at least – and naïve. And she flew to wealthy kingdoms and wastelands, jungles and deserts. She made acquaintances with humankind and beastkind. She observed their ways and grew wiser.

She watched as the beings in this realm waged terrible wars to feed their greed. But also, as she herself once told me, witnessed that fleeting and yet powerful moment when an artist births a masterpiece. Skaltrath recurrently found herself transfixed in wonderment thinking about how it is possible that beings from a same species, with the same faculties, could pursue such opposite passions.

She met other dragons, too. Some friendly and some belligerent. Among those serendipitous encounters, much to her surprise, she found out another dragon carried a piece of her heart she never knew was missing till then.

Ugnath came from the scorching east. Born of light and sand, his kindred tamed flames and heat with such easiness said to be envied by the Sun himself. Precisely like the threads of Fate weaved, these two dragons met and could never be apart.

They decided they wanted to aid this world they loved so much for it had given them the chance to meet. They shared their millenary knowledge with anyone who was willing to listen. They passed on to beast and human kings and queens alike the erudition to guide a nation; to farmers, they taught how to perfect their crops; to the healers, how to make miraculous remedies whose recipes were believed to have been lost forever. Skaltrath and Ugnath blessed every life they touched.

This very mountain used to be a place of fire and death. It blazed through its peak, burning everything around it. Ugnath appeased the flames and told them to go back to the womb of earth while Skaltrath washed the land's wounds. Together, they turned a barren soil into the plentiful steppe it was for a few centuries.

This village is but one of the settlements Skaltrath and Ugnath invited into their land. My ancestors arrived here escaping a great famine and, as my family remembers, none of us has ever suffered with hunger ever again. Until two years ago.

Some fatuous prince, blind with selfishness and excess that is typical to royalty, decided to tame a dragon. This preposterous and ignoble creature babbled about an ultimate weapon that would conquer and unify every piece of land and nation. Yet another war. He sent envoys to recruit Ugnath and Skaltrath and, while the first dozen or so returned with polite denials, the last two or three dozen were never seen again. But this deformed soul would not be detained. He insisted and he pleaded, and only after Skaltrath herself flew back to his father and not so gently threw this vile parasite in the middle of the court, he stopped his visits. Still, although it is rare - for our luck's sake - that putrid hearts like this escape purgatory, they will inevitably cause irreparable damage. In the depths of his scummy mind, this petty little prince concocted a plan that would harm not only our esteemed benefactors and our people, but a whole other tribe.

He initiated one of the bloodiest and cruelest hunts in the history of this realm. Using his father's soldiers without his knowledge, the prince secretly pursued, killed and kidnapped the witch kind. From a thriving tribe known to be endowed with marvelous powers, after seeing their relatives disappear and their name be smeared with lies, the witch clan has almost disappeared. This just so that an execrable man could harness their gift to subdue a dragon.

"But I believe you are familiar with this part of the story. Aren't you, child?"

Blaza nodded. She couldn't bear to face the man and kept her focus on the dying flames in the hearth. In her peripheral vision, she could see the dried trails of tears that had appeared on the old man's face at some point in the story. Mother had stopped untangling her hair. She hugged her knees and thought that dragons were not her biggest problem, after all.

Ugnath plummeted into the cave. One of his wings was impaled by a spear. He told her to hide the egg. She could hear them coming, a whole army marching, unanticipatedly close. Some of them, women and children in fetters and shackles. That fiend raised an odd scepter and all the people in chains squirmed and wailed until their eyes went blank. Skaltrath could not understand what was happening.

Suddenly, her whole body stopped responding. She felt like a humongous hand squished her entire being and even the ribcage movement of breathing became strenuous. She could see the same happened to Ugnath. They were pinned to the cave floor. Her eyes were fixed on the egg she had no time to tuck into the cavern's ridges. She watched as hundreds of armored soldiers swarmed around Ugnath and her egg. A pandemonium of limbs, weapons, and shouts. She tried to talk, to roar, to summon the waters, but, to her utmost dismay, she noted her vision started to blur and she passed out.

The next morning was gray like every day had been for two years. When they left the house, the rain had reverted to an annoying drizzle, tired like a child who is about to cry themselves to sleep.

Following the same main road they had used to enter the village, they left towards the mountain. The path was not paved anymore, and it was slippery and muddy, covered in footprints of dejected men and animals. It soon started to climb towards the once-idyllic top of the mountain.

They marched in silence, covering their mouths and noses. The higher they got, the fouler the smell. The old man who, as they found out, was named Jeno, insisted on coming along. He said his limp would be a hinderance to his family's exodus and that he never wanted to leave, so he would stay in the village until Skaltrath or himself drew their last breath. Still, Blaza was surprised at how well he kept up, but was too afraid to ask what happened to his leg and be scolded by Mother.

The climb to the entrance of the cave was half a day away, probably more considering everything would be muddy and slippery. To distract herself from the treacherous path Blaza leaned into her old habit of making lists. She thought of her family, and she thought of their gifts. Nana's was herbology; papa's was woodcarving; auntie Mina's was rhyming; older cousin Gliph's was weaving, and so on so forth. Blaza could remember the whole tribe's unique and quirky gifts by heart. She tried to visualize every single one of them well and alive as she proceeded with her list.

The track, however, did not seem to alleviate. Several times they passed unrecognizable animal carcasses and, other times, obvious human remains. Many of them wore the same black and purple armor.

At one point, about halfway, they stopped for a quick rest and to finish the cold barley soup. They could overlook the village and its neat collection of gable roofs. Blaza wondered how it looked under the sun.

The last stretch was the worst. The trail became narrow as a thread so Mother tied a rope around her waist and around Blaza's because they wouldn't be able to hold hands. They had to face the rock wall, with their backs to a fatal abyss. They continued climbing by slowly dragging their feet sideways, too afraid to lift them from the scanty floor. Once Blaza almost lost her balance but suddenly, she could feel something supporting her back. Old Jeno quickly used his staff to stabilize her back against the rock. Mother nodded at him.

By the time the sun was setting, the rain began to intensify meaning Skaltrath was falling asleep. At the summit, they found a clearing surrounded by dark rocky walls. On one side, a veil waterfall spit brown and murky water. On the other, piles of stones resembling two columns signaled the entrance to the dragons' lair.

And yet, she couldn't die.

Dragons only die when their hearts completely stop, and this only happens if they are pierced by something. In the beginning, Skaltrath thought about flying against stalactites, but she could never bring herself to do it. Now, after months without nourishment, she couldn't move. She thought the pain would pierce her heart and make it stop, but that moment of relief never came.

When she was awake, she sometimes thought about her native land and reckoned with regret that she would never see the ocean again. Nor Ugnath. Nor would she know the powers of her unborn child.

Her bleary eyes could still see the waterfall, one of her most cherished creations. It was now just a gush of filth.

But what was that? She couldn't focus her sight anymore, yet she thought she saw three humanoid figures. Terror seized her. Was it not enough to be humiliated and tormented? Was that demon back?

The stench of rotting flesh was unbearable. Blaza began dry heaving from the moment they reached the top and it took her long minutes to get used to the place's aura. There were uncountable bones on the clearing, some with the same purple armor.

They slowly descended into the cave.

"Skaltrath, oh, dear, dear friend! It's Jeno!" His voice cracked. His limp, hastier, came to a sudden stop.

Among the carcasses and urns of offerings, laid a great silvery drake, slumped on her side. Her scales barely glistened to their former majesty for moss and a profusion of fungi grew in nasty patches over her hide. Blaza was impressed by how thin she was, to the point of apparent ribs. A great pustule on her cheek facing up allowed to see some of her teeth. But what shocked Blaza the most was that the reek of decay did not come from the cattle and food the villagers tried to nurse her, but from Skaltrath's own body.

Her breathing was noisy and difficult. Blaza remembered many a horse nana healed with her teas. Sometimes they looked like they wouldn't come back at all, but nana could cure most of them and they would be up and hungry the next morning. She wondered if they would be able to do the same to that titan.

Blaza and Jeno froze as Mother walked ahead and unceremoniously climbed one of Skaltrath's legs. The dragon only snorted lightly but didn't move – much to Blaza's relief.

After poking and prodding, Mother stepped down and proceeded to kick a few rocks and bones in a circle in front of the large body.

"It's bad so we have to act quickly."

"Mom, I don't know what to do."

"Yes, yes, you do, Blaza. You have been taught and trained. I am counting on you."

"But Mom I- I…"

Tears started pouring freely and Mother stopped her frenetic cleaning to kneel in front of Blaza and gently hold both of her shoulders.

"We'll try. I know it's been difficult getting here and I know you are as tired as I am. I know you miss nana and papa and I miss them terribly too. We are doing this for them, Blaza. But we are also doing this because it is our calling. And if you are scared, just think of what this poor creature went through. She's missing her family, too. She is scared, too. And so am I. So we'll all be scared together and then maybe it won't be as scary anymore."

Blaza nodded. She suddenly missed nana and all her aunties and cousins more than anything.

"Is there anything I can do to help?" Jeno's voice seemed to break them both from a trance.

"I don't suppose you can play any music, can you, sir?"

She didn't recognize those people and she couldn't make out what they were saying amongst themselves. She realized she couldn't understand human languages anymore and that made her desperate. Her memory was draining with the water. As clouds invaded her thoughts, her memories were being diluted, dissolving, and falling to the ground with the persistent rain.

What she lamented the most was that, at this pace, she wouldn't be able to recognize Ugnath in the realm of the dead.

Why were they waiting so long to finish her off?

Mother sat in her customary position with her legs crossed. She produced her transverse flute - her favorite one, the one papa had carved for her - from the bundle tied to her back and started a cryptic melody, with long and low notes. Music, that was Mother's gift.

Mother kept blowing on her flute producing deep, mystic sounds like whales calling. She fixed her gaze on Blaza's in her motherly tender – and yet bone-chilling – way of saying "hurry up". Blaza, in turn, had never danced in front of someone who was not a witch. She kept her gaze down, hesitant, but Jeno seemed to understand it all. He closed his eyes, as he started stomping his feet and tapping the staff on the ground following Mother's song. With the weight of a vital duty on her shoulders, Blaza inhaled deeply and let her body speak through movement.

Every time Blaza danced, she told a story. This time, she needed to tell the dragon her own story, to make her remember. She started sitting on her knees and touching her forehead to the ground. She was an egg pulsating with the seed of life. She opened her arms and waved them; that's the ocean near where Skaltrath was born. Blaza had never seen the ocean, but that's how she thought an ocean felt.

Mother's song gradually sped up. Standing up, Blaza frolicked freely. She was young, still learning to control her wings. The girl's arms traced exaggerated circles in the air, and then they were gliding on high skies.

Mother's song was also telling the same story. The flute produced arcane and unimaginable sounds. They resembled distant lands; friends and foes; a life of adventures. Then the once erratic sounds assumed a single rhythm: sometimes mellow, sometimes torrential, but always fluid, adaptable. Water.

Skaltrath once could speak water. Yes, Skaltrath remembered. She could speak water, but she could also speak many languages. She remembered Ugnath's face. She started remembering faces from the nearby village.

Blaza spiraled around in the circle like a dragon's coiling her tail. She quickened her rhythm even more, clicking her heels. Jeno's tapping and Mother's flute followed. Hundreds of little clicks like raindrops falling incessantly.

Why was it raining for so long? It was then that Skaltrath remembered. The weapons, the chains, they took Ugnath and the egg. Alive. And cursed her, so she wouldn't move.

She now recognized the village's mayor with two witches trying to break the curse. Her heart was filled with such warmth she hadn't felt in years.

Skaltrath let the enthralling sounds and movements guide her consciousness. They led her to an inner place where she reached for her spirit. Upon touching it, she saw the red line of Fate that linked her to Ugnath. So, he was still alive after all. She saw the reflections of all her ancestors hovering over her soul. She clasped all the knowledge she had built through centuries. And she delved even deeper, plunging into the dark waters of her essence and there it was, right at the bottom. In an effort she thought would be her last, Skaltrath grabbed the curse and crushed it.

This was a moment Blaza would remember forever and tell her children and grandchildren about: the wondrous fleeting moment when a curse is broken. Blaza and the others could see when, for a fleeting instant, the droplets of sweat on their faces, the water in the cave, the rain outside, and the waterfall all ascended. The life-giving substance then floated, standing still in the air for less than a heartbeat. It felt like the world and time had stopped for the hold of a breath when unceremoniously, the water fell on its course again.

Blaza reeled, twisting her wrists over her head, and then plunged in a deep bow. The mountain protector was awake.

Skaltrath staggered until she was able to open her wings and shook her body violently. Moss, dust and mushrooms fell off profusely. Her joints ached, but they also craved movement.

She then scrutinized Blaza and her mother. They panted on the ground where they had sung Skaltrath back to life. They were exhausted after hours of playing and dancing. The dragon moved around delicately, sniffing until she found what she wanted. In one swift movement, she snatched a clay jar and broke it between her teeth drinking the delicious honey left for her. The pustule in her face started to fade.

Three perfect spheres of crystalline water appeared each one in front of Blaza, her mother, and Jeno. They seemed to shimmer. Blaza was so mesmerized by the one in front of her that she was slightly startled when Mother hastily drank hers. Tired as she was, she ventured a sip, and it was the freshest, purest water she ever tasted in her life.

"Skaltrath, mother of waters, bearer of knowledge, I am Vlasta from the witch tribe and this is my daughter Blaza. We know where your mate and egg are. They are alive and they are kept prisoners with our tribe."

"Words cannot thank you enough, honorable Vlasta and prodigious Blaza. And Jeno, dear friend, I apologize for destroying your home. I promise I will fix it, but for now let's heal and rest. I want to hear everything you know."

Skaltrath looked out the cave. The heavy clouds had given place to a clear sky studded with stars that had not been seen in two years. She anticipated the hunt that was about to begin. She began to brew a storm.

H. T. Schwartz is an English teacher with almost two decades of experience. She made speculative fiction her whole personality after her junior high librarian told her she should find something better than books about magic "and all that crazy stuff". As a scholar, she researches literary genre, science fiction, and anthologies. In your face, Ms. Librarian! She now lives in Canada, where she moved to for her PhD, and where a husband, a cat, a dog, and a baby joined her party. She has a couple of articles in scholarly journals, but the short story "Rain Reverie Dance" is her first ever creative text to be published.

Learn more about H.T. at: Instagram

<u>*The Art of the Dragon*</u>

Farzana Nasrin

A skin of bullets

weaves in an effortless dance

through the cotton bulbs.

His glass amber eyes,

lit by his soul's scorching core,

craves both life and death.

The dry air sizzles

before his great lungs exhale

a crimson ink spill.

Flames dye the canvas

as the low sun roams the sky

mixing their palette –

each breath a paint stroke.

My name is Farzana Nasrin and I am a graduate in BA English and currently study a MA in Creative Writing. I like to write poetry and personal essays (particularly about my pet budgie).

Learn more about Farzana at: Instagram | X

<u>*Worth Its Weight*</u>

Elisabeth Cherkas

A dragon's worth is determined by the size of his hoard. This is a fact of life, and it's how our world has always worked. The dragons of the East fight over their gold, the most powerful amongst them guarding caverns of riches so large it would take a man three days of travel to reach the other end. Those of the South gleam in the sun, covered snout to tail in glittering gemstones, the worthiest amongst them nearly more stone than flesh. In the West, dragons have taken to silver, covering the mountains in a reflection of their status. Across the world dragons can be found stashing away any scrap of wealth they find, fighting off both fellow dragons and the few brave humans who dare to claim dragon stones for themselves. It is a dangerous world with no friends to truly trust, nor family upon which to rely. It is a world that I left behind a long time ago.

I have been called weak, an imposter, and a fraud no longer worthy of the title Dragon. Yet when the others come to taunt me, to flaunt power achieved through terror and deceit, I remain. Not one has returned to try a second time. They assumed that because the halls of my cavern appear empty and void of any hoard that I am powerless. They are wrong.

My hoard has taken me a lifetime to gather. In that time, I have seen civilizations start from nothing more than a family with a dream grow to become fierce powerhouses of the world. Cities that were nothing more than a few huts surrounding a firepit, transform into feats of engineering that rival my height. These communities contribute to my hoard whether they are aware or not. I owe them my gratitude; I would not be nearly as strong without them.

When it comes time to expand my hoard, I have a world to choose from. Just down the mountain from my cavern is a small village. They don't have much in terms of gold, and even less in gemstones, yet they always have something to contribute to my collection. As I descend to their level, I am greeted with the sounds of life. Children dance through the street and let out shrieks of joy when they win a game that only they know the rules to. The parents look on, laughing in memorial of the days when they did just the same. The air is still full of the warm scent from the latest feast. Vibrant banners lace the buildings from their last festival, welcoming the fair weathers of spring. I can still feel the energy from that day, the joy passed around between the villagers. It was one of the biggest contributors to my hoard in recent memory. This festival is a day I look forward to each year. I walk along the outskirts of the village, with the softest footsteps I can muster, careful to avoid detection. While I have never considered bringing any harm to this village, or any other, the reputation of my brethren proceed me. Most humans aim to avoid other dragons, a decision I cannot fault them for. A young couple crosses my path, giggling in rebellion, embracing the nature of youth. I still, letting them continue on their way undisturbed, giving them my silent appreciation for their contribution to my hoard. When I can accept no more, I move on my way, drunk on the new additions to my wealth.

When I decide to add to my trove once again, I head to the south, where the sun warms my wings, its heat radiating through me. The dragons in these parts leave me to my own, knowing that I am not coming for their hoard, and they could not stop me even if I were. Here, I soar above the land, drinking in the golden rays of light. Below me sit rows upon rows of lush green plants, spotted with tanned humans, guiding the plants to maturity. Sweet sugar cane fills my nostrils as I descend, desperate to immerse myself in the oasis these people have created. A rainbow of florals surrounds me, laying on a bed of verdure, each bud reminiscent of the tender love of its nurser. I let the leaves of the trees caress my cerulean scales, savoring their soft touch contrasting the roughness of my back. When the sun loses its golden warmth, and the sky fades to twilight and rose, I leave behind the kaleidoscope of nature, and bring all that I can back to my abode.

The cities to the north cannot offer the same growing treasure, with their harsh winds and bitter cold. When I visit, I am greeted with the soft glow of candlelight, spilling from the inside of each home. There is no sun here to bask in, nor light to chase away the chill of the night. Yet the cold doesn't seep into my bones the way it often does when I'm left alone with my hoard. Shadows cast by firelight dance around me as I make my way through the town. The people here pay me no mind for they have all found refuge with their loved ones, creating their own fortress of community within their homes. I pass by each home, drawing in a sampling of the warmth for myself. The night is clear, and each star offers its own light to the town. My eyes trace the constellations, seeing how far they have shifted from when I was a hatchling. There is peace to be found here, peace that I can only wish my fellow dragons would be willing to share. When the firelight dies down and the people of the town cozy into slumber, I take to the skies. I fly amongst the stars, using them to guide my way home. I carry the warmth of the town with me, and my fire seems to burn just a little bit hotter tonight.

Before returning to my cave for a well-deserved rest, I fly to the end of the night sky and find a perch atop the tallest mountain. It's here that I welcome in the new day, absorbing each color that the sun creates as it brings life back to the world. Frost tickles my lungs as I draw in a breath, savoring the crisp mountain air. The sun rises, and with it comes the light, illuminating the valleys that hold my treasured humans and their villages. I watch as the darkness is nudged away by the sun and the life it brings. When the last of the stars have retreated from the sky, I stretch my wings and let the wind carry me home.

Back in my cave, I tread through the halls, noticeably empty of anything a respectable dragon might consider a hoard. Once upon a time, I too had collected gems that reflected rainbows along the walls of my cave with gold so shiny I could admire the reflection of each of my scales. I stopped that a long time ago. Now what I collect is so much more precious to me and something that no one can ever take away. I let the memories of the day play though my mind as I curl up, allowing them to lull me into a deep slumber. The hoard that I have collected over the years envelopes me, altogether worth so much more than its weight in gold.

Elisabeth is a university student completing her degree in Human Kinetics, but carries with her a childhood dream of becoming an author. As an avid reader and daydreamer, she is determined to share all about the worlds she has created in her mind. Elisabeth recently entered her first writing competition and was successful in making it to the top 60 writers in a field of over 3700 competitors. This success added fuel to her writing aspirations, and she is now pursuing her passion of filling the library shelves she used to empty each week.

Learn more about Elisabeth at: Author Website | Instagram

<u>*St. Osmund*</u>

Emma Space

When I sit in the attic of this barn, I know who I will always be. I sit in my father's old chair, in my grandfather's old house, and I feel as old as they once were and have become.

The floorboards creak underneath my feet as I sit at my desk. The fall air that is pressing through the worn siding is cold and crisp, and I can see through the open hay door that the sky is gray and carded with the heather cotton fiber of clouds. It turns to fall all at once here. Like God snaps his fingers and the Earth moves that much of a fractional inch.

Below me, I can hear it creaking in the wooden bower it has called home. I haven't had the chance to sex it, yet.

I googled how to sex it yesterday.

> *How to determine gender of dragon?*
> *How to find cloaca under tail of dragon?*
> *How to lift tail of dragon?*

The results were unhelpful.

I am worried that it will burn the house down. Mom thinks it will burn the house down -- she doesn't even live here anymore, she and Dad moved to a one-story an hour and a half south (Less weather, she says. More chance of someone finding us if we're croaked,), and she still worries about the structural integrity.

"It'll knock a support beam down, with all its prey thrashing," she said yesterday, before I thought to google anything.

"I don't think it's going to prey thrash," I said. I can't keep the eyeroll out of my voice when talking to my mother. I always sound a little disdainful, even when I don't mean to. "I mean, nights are getting colder, days are getting shorter -- I'm sure it's going into hibernation sometime soon."

"Well," she said. "God forbid it gets a rat in the meantime."

A rat? I don't think a dragon the size of this one would bother with a rat, but I didn't say anything. Then she would've been even more worried about the foundation. "God forbid," I said.

"You could always call the exterminators, Ozzy," she said. "You could call and ask for an estimate --"

"Ma--"

"It's not inhumane if it comes down to you or the creature --"

"Mom, it's so bloody, the way they just -- they don't use guns, you know that right? They do it the old-fashioned way." There's something grisly about that. Something grisly about tradition.

"Osmund," she said, and I can hear her holding my middle name on the tip of her tongue. "If it's life and death, it's not grisly. I know what I would choose -- I would choose you, every time."

"Thanks, Mom," I told her. I loved her and I hung up the phone and then I went to the computer and tried to figure out which gender dragon I would be killing if I called St. George's, as if that mattered.

I think I would feel guiltier if there was an egg involved. I would feel some sort of parental responsibility to a dragon egg. I don't think I'm ready to become a father.

I hear it thumping around from where I'm sitting. I can feel the vibrations through the floor of the barn, and I don't know if it's my mother's worry working on my overactive imagination or if the dragon is actually about to bring the barn down. I want to go down the stairs and take another peek, but I'm worried about that too, if too many footsteps will stir the beast awake.

The house is set up really nicely, an old millhouse built sometime in the first half of the 19th century. There's a fireplace in the living room that I sleep in front of when it gets too cold -- no need to cut the oil on for just one person. There are two and a half bathrooms and five bedrooms and more than enough room for me to store all of my stuff and all of my parents' stuff that they've kept safe for years and years.

The best part of this house is the barn. It's one of the reasons why I took it on after Mom and Dad decided to move -- it's like a whole second house attached to the first. Three stories tall. The top story was always my aerie, even when I was a kid. The wind would blow, the building would sway a little, and still, I was safe. I find some of my old army figures and matchbox cars shoved into nooks and crannies.

The barn's basement is made of dirt and a pile of coal. Absolutely flammable.

Shit, hadn't thought of that.

The barn doors open right out onto the bottom of the hill, and I figure that the dragon probably crawled in that way, but I don't know how, exactly. I don't have any doorbell cameras, and if I did, they wouldn't be set up to focus on those basement doors anyways. I can sort of see into the basement if I sit in the middle of the driveway and look down the slope towards the bottom of the hill; I can see through the door that has been thrust ajar.

From that vantage point exactly, and only if I hold my neck just so, can I see the scales of the dragon, can I see the curl of its neck. It's a sort of dun color, and it glints in the autumn light. I can't see its face or its wings or its tail, or any sort of other identifying features that would help me in my online searches.

"Doing alright there, Ozzy?" My neighbor, the retired Don Houston, asks me as he goes by on his daily walk. He's older than my parents, but not by too much. His hair is a downy white, and he walks now with a cane.

"All good, Mr. Houston," I told him, and I gave him a thumbs up. I didn't want to tell him there was a dragon in the neighborhood -- he'd call the exterminators for sure, or his wife would. "Thanks for looking out."

He waved me off and kept on down the street.

I watched him go, then went back to craning my neck at an angle to see through the open door. I wish I was brave enough to go down there, to lift up the dragon's tail, to determine its gender and to see what was really living underneath my house, but I don't think I am. Instead, I sit as quietly as I can in the attic, trying not to scrap my feet over the floorboards for fear that the echoes of my movement could be heard all the way in the basement.

My mom sent me the number of our local chapter of St. George's, so I called, just to get an estimate. Just in case. The beast has been twisting and turning in its sleep, and when I came down for breakfast this morning, I could hear a *whumping* throughout the whole first floor of the house. It sounded a bit like the house had a heartbeat.

So I called for the estimate.

One of the Georges came out this afternoon -- he was a burly guy, for some reason bigger than I was expecting. He was wearing a jumpsuit similar to a firefighter's protective gear, and he had a sword strapped to his back. He was clean shaven, and his hair was cropped very short. His chin was blunt and square, as though someone had hit him in the jaw with a brick. He nodded at me gruffly when I opened the door.

"Where's the beast?" he asked, without preamble.

I, in my pajamas and my ratty shirt that was too thin to hold out the wind, walked across the driveway to point down the hill. "Down there. She's mostly peaceful," I said. I have been subconsciously referring to the beast as a she, for better or worse.

The man sucked his teeth. I noticed he had a medallion on his chest, an Order of St. George. "Probably because it's hibernating. Wouldn't want to be around one like that when it starts to thaw. I'm going to take a closer look," he said, and he went down the hill. I watched with bated breath.

The George approached the door and pushed it open, so more of the dragon in my basement was visible. I could see the curl of the dragon's back, could see how the scales glimmered in the light. She was beautiful -- for a beast. Small rainbows scattered off the back in the light from the basement window, and I could see its side gently rise and fall. The exterminator tried to open the door a couple more times, but the bulk of the dragon must've been pushed against it, because he couldn't move it open any farther.

"Four thousand," he said, coming back up the hill. "You got a big 'un."

"I don't have four thousand dollars --"

"There's financial aid you can apply for. Go on the website, it's a government program." The George didn't seem too keen on sticking around and talking. He wiped his forehead with the cuff of his fire-proof coverall. "We'll be here when you need us," he said, and he got back in his truck and left.

I called my mom and told her what happened. "I don't have four thousand dollars," I told her, and she said she would lend me something, to think of it as an investment in my health and in the continued well-being of the house.

"I just don't know how this happened," she said over the phone, and I could see the downturn of her lips. "All the time your father and I lived there, we never had a dragon in the basement. We never even had so much as a mouse!"

How could I forget.

I bit back an apology. I didn't need to apologize. I hadn't kept raw meat on the basement floor. She promised to send me a check for three quarters the amount, and we said our goodbyes.

I crept down to the basement last night. I just shimmied up to the doors, sort of scootched on my butt. I sat at the door, with my feet pressed against the wood, so I could see inside. The beast was sleeping, and I could see horns highlighted in a glimmer of light.

I've been seeing this beast in bits and pieces -- a scrap of claw through the open door, then its spine highlighted in the setting afternoon sun. Sitting right at the threshold, my view was greater, but perhaps no clearer. I could see the side of the dragon's face, could see the way her forearms were curled up underneath her, sort of tucked against her chin. I couldn't see any back legs, but the way that the dragon is curled, her tail is pressed directly up against the door, holding it closed. I thought I would be frightened, to be so close to a dragon, but I felt a warmth I haven't felt all fall.

"Listen," I told her. "It's going to take so much money to get you out of here. And honestly, I'd rather not -- the whole thing is pretty inhumane, if you ask me. Not that I think you're human --I just would appreciate it if you got out of here on your own. Would solve a lot of problems." I kicked my foot forward a little bit, to press the toe of my boot against the dragon's hide, just across the threshold.

The dragon made a noise in its sleep, a bit of a grumble. She didn't wake up though, didn't spit fire. I think I've been going about this all wrong.

My mother called the Georges without telling me. They showed up yesterday at the foot of my lawn in a pick-up truck with lances in the trunk. I ran out down the driveway to meet them, still in my pajamas, my robe flapping out around my heels.

"What the fuck!?" I shouted, which was unprofessional.

The big man who had come to my house three days ago, greeted me by crossing his arms over his chest. "The owner of the house called, asked that we --"

"The owner of the house? The *Owner* of the house?" I was spitting. I could feel the wildness in my eyes. "I bought this house free and clear three years ago, the mortgage is all my own --"

"I'm sorry, sir, but we have been told that the dragon underneath your house is damaging the structural integrity, and in such cases we have state jurisdiction to ensure the safety of its residents. So --"

"She hasn't even seen it!"

The Georges were no longer listening to me. They were all wearing identical fire-proofed suits, and all of them were wearing masks that they pulled down over their faces, so they became obscured. They armed themselves and took off down the hill without me, their lances at the ready. I came behind them, huffing and puffing the whole way. One of them told me to shut up, and I did, feeling like an untrustworthy and petulant child the whole time. Who did my mother think she was? It was *my* house.

There were six Georges total, and they lined up outside of the door in two columns of three. One man ran into the door and burst it open in an explosion of splinters, and he tumbled on over the dragon, who woke up with an explosive roar. The sound shattered my ears, rumbled through my rib cage, shook through my shoulders and through my arms. Her roar was so loud it was physically painful, and I momentarily doubled up on myself.

I scrambled back up the hill, still curled over with my knees pressed close to my chest, my slippers sliding on the frost. The men threw themselves into action, metal swinging as they rushed the dragon. They scrambled, lances flashing, spurts of red in the morning light. The dragon was trapped, stuck in the basement that had only one way out.

I called out to her, but my voice was lost in the hubbub, lost in the other masculine shouts, the crash and glint of metal.

One way out.

I stood up and ran back down the driveway, back to the George's van, which was still bristling full of weapons. I grabbed a shield, a lance, kicked off my slippers so that I could run on the ground on the dew. I ran back, tripping over my knees and the shield as I ran back to the Georges, who had moved inside the barn and were surrounding the dragon, their lances pinning her into the dirt floor of the basement.

She was still making noise, the low rumble shaking the ground.

I banged the lance on the shield, loud and clear as a bell in the crisp fall morning. Some of the Georges turned to look at me.

I rushed them. Without thinking, I ran forward, towards the group of men who were standing in *my* basement, stabbing *my* dragon, without *my* permission. I rushed them with the shield up in front of my face. Instinctually, all of the Georges pulled their lances up from the ground, angling them at me --

And that was all she needed. She twisted, perfectly, knocking all of the men off of her and knocking me to the ground. She plowed half of the Georges down and ran through them, ran through me, her underbelly raking across the top of my head as I tumbled to the dirt. For a brief second, I thought I was suffocating, that her bulk was going to press me down into the ground, grind me down into nothing.

The feeling only lasts for a second. The moment the pressure is removed, I turn on my stomach and turn my face skyward, in time to see her limping over the rooftop of the house across the street, her wings thrown wide, her tail whipping back and forth, propelling her forward. Even from this distance, I can see that she has left drops of blood on the asphalt of the street.

"That was damned stupid," the George who came to my house first said, clamoring to his feet and standing over me. He pushes his mask back so I can see his face and his square, unhappy jaw. "You could've gotten us killed."

I find it difficult to be repentant, lying on my stomach in the basement. "Yeah," I say. "Well. *I'm* the homeowner."

Emma Space is a recent graduate student of the UNC Charlotte's Creative Writing Master's program. She grew up in New England and developed her love of the outdoors underneath the changing colors of the leaves. Currently she enjoys working on farms and writing science fiction and fantasy.

Learn more about Emma at: Author Website | Instagram

Cassandra R. D'Alessandro

"The legends say, dragons first came to Iaxanara, from the moon." Galdor, the head elder of Gwendolyn's mountain village, began to tell the history of their tribe.

Everyone had gathered around the giant bonfire after the ceremonial feast and were listening to the five elders tell the Sacred Tales that made up their history.

Gwendolyn sat on the ground next to her aunt and two younger cousins. She felt the cool grass on the soles of her feet. Her long, wavy copper hair was braided in the traditional warrior's braid of her people, and she wore her fanciest fighting leathers, just like every other member of her tribe.

"The moon rose every night and watched all the creatures. She loved all the beings of Iaxanara, but there was one group of beings that she loved the most, mortals." Galdor continued the story and even though Gwendolyn had heard the story every year on the spring equinox, she still sat with her silver eyes wide, savoring every word that came out of Elder Galdor's mouth.

"The moon found mortals to be very curious creatures. The way they felt so many emotions intrigued her. She watched them build and destroy and she fell in love with their wild hearts. One day, the moon decided she wanted to give her beloved mortals a part of her. From her luminous light, she birthed the first dragons." Galdor paused as the children in the crowd gasped in wonder at the mention of the fire breathing beasts.

Gwendolyn remembered when she was a child and had first heard the legends of the birth of dragons. She had been so consumed with the idea of one day being a dragon rider that she convinced the five elders to let her start her warrior training when she was only ten. Over the past seventeen years, she trained in countless forms of combat and was now one of the tribe's deadliest warriors.

"The moon had intended for the dragons to inspire the mortals. She hoped that the mortals would cherish this beautiful part of her soul as much as she cherished them. But not all the mortals saw the dragons as beautiful treasures. Some saw their giant bodies and mouths full of teeth and decided the dragons were a threat to them and their families. Others saw the dragons as a way to harness more power, and they desired to control them. And so the wicked mortals started to hunt down the dragons, using them, torturing them, and killing them." Galdor told the story with so much passion anyone would've thought he was there 500 years ago and witnessed the events he spoke about with his own eyes.

"The moon's heart was broken, and it is said that she was in so much sorrow that she turned red for a fortnight."

A few gasps came from the children again, and Gwendolyn heard a child close to her whisper sweetly, "Mama, did the moon really turn red?"

"But the moon found one mortal man, Zave, who was not afraid of the dragons, nor was he eager to kill them or use them for power. He was an honorable male, and the moon could see his gentle spirit and curiosity toward the dragons. The moon blessed him with magic and gave him the title Dragon Keeper."

Some warriors in the crowd whispered the title, "Dragon Keeper" as they placed their fist over their hearts and gave a quick bow of their head.

"Zave and his sons and daughters took oaths to stand with the dragons. They trained to become fierce warriors, and they fought to protect them against other mortals and beasts. They became friends with the dragons, and they coexisted in harmony. Some of them bonded with the dragons and rode on their backs flying so high they could almost touch the stars."

Gwendolyn grabbed the dragon eye pendant that she wore around her neck, the pendant that all Dragon Keeper warriors wore, and she held it to her palm.

"From Zave's line, our tribe was created here in Iaxanara. Our ancestors kept their oaths and continued to aid the dragons throughout the years, until one spring equinox when the dragons disappeared. The legends say they were called home to the moon. Even though we have not seen a dragon, and there has not been a dragon rider in hundreds of years, our people are ready to protect them and fight with them when the time comes. For when the dragons are ready to return, they will come back here to Iaxanara."

"But Elder Galdor," a young girl with brown curly hair who was sitting right in front of Galdor interrupted, "how do you know the dragons will return?"

Galdor smiled widely, the corners of his mouth touching his eyes. "Because my dear Kisya," he started as he patted her head, ruffling her ringlets, "they left us this." Galdor opened the golden encrusted wooden chest that sat on the tree stump beside him.

Every member of the tribe, including Gwendolyn, went silent as Elder Galdor reached his hands into the chest and pulled out a black dragon egg. Everyone watched as Elder Galdor stood up, stretched out his arms and held the egg above his head for all to see. Flecks of gold shimmered on the egg's black scales as the egg caught the light of the massive bonfire.

"The dragons left us the last dragon egg that was birthed. This is a sign that they will return one day. And when they do, our Dragon Keepers will be ready to fight alongside them. And we will see the days of the dragon riders return."

Gwendolyn couldn't help but feel excited and hopeful at Galdor's words. She had dedicated her whole life to dragons without even seeing them. She looked up to the sky, found the bright crescent moon, and let out a prayer asking the moon to allow the dragons to return in her lifetime.

Galdor put the dragon egg back in the chest as Elder Craith started on the next story of the Sacred Tales. Gwendolyn sat and listened with the other tribe members as each elder told legend after legend.

Suddenly, a whispering whoosh rang through the air. The Dragon Keepers looked out into the dark forest that surrounded their camp, searching for the source of the sound.

A sudden pain erupted in Gwendolyn's shoulder. She looked down and to her surprise, there was an arrow sticking out of her. She made eye contact with her aunt, and then Elder Galdor. Both of them paled as they looked in shock at the arrow.

The next few moments were in slow motion for Gwendolyn. One moment she was looking down at her shoulder, the next, she watched as arrow after arrow came flying out of the forest and member after member of her tribe fell to the ground.

This can't really be happening, Gwendolyn thought to herself. She shook her head, trying to wake up from this nightmare, willing this devastating scene to disappear, but it didn't. It only got worse. Soldiers wearing some sort of metal outfit came running into their camp. With weapons in their hands, they came charging out of the darkness.

The other Dragon Keepers and men grabbed any weapon they could find and fought against the intruders. Gwendolyn watched in horror as the soldiers in the metal outfits so easily took down her people.

Within seconds of the foreign soldier's arrival, a fire started, and instantly burned its way through their tents. Fear, pure fear, started to rise up inside of Gwendolyn, as the flames grew brighter.

The loud screams of women and children created a terrifying melody as the clanging of steel hitting steel rang out into the night. Gwendolyn's silver eyes were wide as she looked around at the damage to her home. Everything around her was burning. Her people lay dead on the grass, their crimson blood soaking into the earth.

The fear that was festering inside of her turned into rage. She looked down at the arrow that was sticking out of her shoulder. She grabbed the end of it and pulled it out in one swift movement. She barely felt the pain of removing the arrow from the shock and adrenaline that was pumping through her veins.

A male scream sounded beside her, and Gwendolyn turned to see an arrow sticking out of Elder Galdor's chest. The old man stumbled backward. Gwendolyn reached out to grab him, but he fell to the ground before she could reach him.

"Elder Galdor!" She screamed as she ran to his side.

Elder Galdor looked directly into her eyes. Mustering all of his strength, he said, "Protect the egg." His voice was barely more than a whisper, and Gwendolyn knew he was dying. "Take the egg. Make sure it is always safe. You must do this. Go now."

All Gwendolyn could do was nod as she watched one of her elders pass on to the afterlife. She got up and ran to the wooden chest. Quickly, she grabbed the egg and held it close.

Chaos was still erupting all around her. She looked around, searching for her aunt and cousins, but she didn't see them amongst the death and flames that surrounded her. She prayed to the seven stars that the three of them had escaped or at least found a good place to hide from these deadly intruders.

Gwendolyn didn't waste any more time. She held on tightly to the egg and ran towards the trees. She dodged her fellow Dragon Keepers as they fought against the intruders, unknowingly giving her the distraction she needed to escape.

Out of the corner of her eye, she watched as another Dragon Keeper fell to the ground. Her heart broke, and she longed to stop and defend them. But she knew the importance of her task, knew what the egg meant to her people. So instead of joining in the fighting, she held onto her people's most valued treasure, and continued to run towards the trees.

The fire had completely surrounded the camp. Flames blocked her path to the forest. She stopped and looked around. The unknown soldiers seemed to be multiplying. Everywhere she looked, there were people running, fighting, and dying.

The chaos and death behind her were a thicker barrier to the forest than the flames before her. Gwendolyn had no choice but to go forward.

She whispered part of the oath of the Dragon Keepers to herself, "Born from ashes, with fire in our blood. We are the flames that walk the earth."

She ran toward the flames, tucking the dragon egg close to her chest. Using all of her strength, she flung her body over the flames. Gwendolyn hit the ground on her side and rolled a few times until she was lying on her back, looking up at the tree branches. The dragon egg was still in her hands. Gwendolyn checked to make sure no damage had come to it. She breathed a sigh of relief and said a quick prayer of gratitude to the moon when she saw that it was perfectly intact.

She listened for a moment and heard the screams of her people mixed with the sound of fire crackling and the clanging of weapons. Gwendolyn got herself up and disappeared into the dark forest, searching for a place to hide.

Gwendolyn had wandered as far into the forest as she could in the dark. Her eyes stung from the smoke, and no matter how far she walked, she couldn't get the sound of her people screaming out of her head.

She had no idea what to do with the sacred dragon egg, or where she could go to hide. She prayed to the stars and the moon and asked for guidance. They led her to a giant, fallen, hollowed tree, and she crawled into it. Gwendolyn waited there, trying to come up with a plan to get the egg to safety.

A little after the sun rose, the sound of voices and the crunching of boots trampling over leaves and twigs on the forest floor pulled her out of her thoughts. Gwendolyn crawled out of the tree, bringing the egg with her, as she would sooner die than part from it.

Hiding in the thick bushes, she watched as the invading soldiers walked her way.

"Are you sure she ran this way?" one soldier questioned.

"Yes, I am positive. A red-headed bitch grabbed the egg and ran into these woods."

Shit. She thought. *They saw me.* Panic started to rise in her, but she used her years of training to still her mind. *Fear leads to a sloppy warrior.* She could hear Elder Galdor's voice in her head.

"I can't believe the legends of the last dragon egg are real." Gwendolyn heard someone call out.

"Aye!" another man said. "All this time a small part of me thought the King was going mad listening to that oracle witch."

A few of the other soldiers grunted their agreement.

"I wonder what dragon meat tastes like?" Another man said.

Gwendolyn felt sick at the thought of these wicked men eating a dragon. Their disrespect was shocking.

"That's just like you, Joff, to be thinking about your stomach." A soldier answered, and some others laughed.

"It is a pity we killed so many of them Dragon Keepers last night. They would've made good slaves."

"Don't be ridiculous. These people are wild savages. It would be impossible to train them to behave respectably."

"Come now, anyone can be trained to behave, if you break them in right."

Gwendolyn prayed to the sun, asking him to burn these despicable men to ashes.

"Once we find the dragon egg, we can go back to the village and take a few savages home with us."

"No," the man they called Joff said. "The commander already moved the army out of the village back to the coast. He said the King's orders were very clear. Bring him the egg first. Then, on the next trip, we will conquer the people."

Conquer the people. Gwendolyn repeated in her head. These foreigners had already murdered members of her tribe and now they wanted to steal their dragon egg and then come back and turn her people into slaves.

A pure rage started to consume her. She would not let that happen. Gwendolyn didn't know how, but she vowed to the moon that she would not allow these wicked men to succeed in their sinfulness.

She looked down and picked up a rock that took up the circumference of her palm and, without thinking, she threw it hard at the back of one of the soldiers' heads. The soldier stumbled forward as he let out a cry of pain. All the soldiers turned to their hurt comrade before each of them stared at Gwendolyn.

"You stupid bitch!" Joff cried out as he looked at the egg in her arms. "She has the egg, get her!" He barked out the order.

"Shit." Gwendolyn said to herself. She immediately regretted her decision. She spun around and like a deer running from a pack of wolves, she sprinted deeper into the forest. She could hear the group of men getting closer, but she dared not look back. That would only slow her down. She could not be caught, not when she now knew for certain that they came for the egg.

This is what I was born to protect. I will not fail. Gwendolyn repeated in her head, as pushed herself to run.

She looked up to the sun and cried out with all her heart, "HELP!"

Faster and faster she ran until her barefoot caught on a root and she tumbled to the ground, the egg slipping from her hands as her body landed on the cold floor of the forest.

"No!" Gwendolyn screamed in frustration as she watched the sacred dragon egg roll away from her.

A big black boot placed a foot on the egg, stopping it from rolling any further. Gwendolyn looked up to see one of the soldiers giving her a wicked smile.

"Hello *Dragon Keeper*," he said mockingly. He shouted to the men behind her, "Pick her up, we will bring her to the commander for questioning."

Gwendolyn felt two sets of hands pull her to her feet as she watched in horror as the soldier in front of her picked up the dragon egg and placed it in a sack. The men wrapped a rope around her wrists and pulled her along as they trekked down the mountain. She did not speak to any of the soldiers, she only listened to their monstrous talk of conquering and killing.

The further they travelled, the more Gwendolyn's heart sank in her chest. Her enemy had the sacred dragon egg. She failed her tribe. She failed her ancestors. She failed the dragons.

It took them a while to reach the invaders' camp along the coast. When they did, Gwendolyn saw their hundreds of black tents and giant wooden ships with black sails, all along the beach.

This was the largest army Gwendolyn had ever seen. *How could their tribe be so large?* She wondered to herself.

The flag they bore was one Gwendolyn had never seen before. It did not belong to any tribe of Iaxanara. These soldiers must have come from somewhere across the great ocean.

She remembered the words the soldier had spoken in the forest, *"... the King's orders were very clear, bring him the egg first. Then, on the next trip, we will conquer the people."* If this was the amount of soldiers this king sent for the egg, how many would he send to conquer all the people of Iaxanara? Gwendolyn didn't want to find out.

The men who had captured Gwendolyn brought her straight to their commander. A tall, older man with short brown and grey hair was sitting at a desk inside one of the larger black tents. The soldiers handed the man the sack with the egg in it and removed the ropes from around her wrists.

The commander pulled out the dragon egg and smiled. He praised his men and then rose from his desk and turned his attention towards Gwendolyn. 'Tell me Dragon Keeper, where are the dragons?"

Gwendolyn glared at him.

"The oracle said once we have the egg, the dragons will come. Now, where are they?" He paused for a moment, waiting for an answer. "Are you too much of a savage to speak?"

Gwendolyn decided she hated this man.

"I don't have to answer the questions of evil men who spill the blood of my people." Gwendolyn spoke the words, and when she was finished, she spat at the man. Her spit landed on the crest on his black jacket.

"You truly are a savage." The commander mumbled as he grabbed a cloth that was on his desk and wiped the spit off. Without warning, he struck Gwendolyn's face with the back of his hand. Pain erupted on her cheek, and when she turned back to look at the commander, she laughed at him.

"You pathetic worm," she taunted him, "no one has seen a dragon in hundreds of years." She laughed again.

The tent had gone silent, and for the next few moments, the sound of waves crashing on the shore and the distant sound of thunder were the only sounds to be heard.

The thunder kept rumbling, getting louder and louder as if the storm was moving closer to the camp. Suddenly, a mighty, loud roar pierced the air, and a few of the soldiers covered their ears with their hands. Screams from the men outside of the tent rang out as another shirking roar boomed.

The sound sparked something in Gwendolyn. Something ancient had come alive in her, she could feel it vibrating in her chest. Even though she had never seen it before, she knew what creature made that powerful roar.

Gwendolyn's silver eyes widened in disbelief. The commander looked at her shocked expression, and a wicked smile spread across his face.

"You liar," was all he said to her as he strode out of the tent, the dragon egg in his hands. "Bring her," he shouted to his soldiers.

Two men pushed Gwendolyn to her feet and out of the tent. Gwendolyn stopped dead in her tracks as she looked up at the sky. Her jaw dropped open in amazement.

She had been waiting her whole life to see a dragon, and now the wait was over. Circling the camp, getting closer and closer to the ground, was a giant red dragon.

Sister. The magical ancient spark that had awoken inside of her whispered the word in her heart as she watched the magnificent beast land on the ground. All four of its claws touched down on the sandy beach, and the ground shook. The red dragon looked at the soldiers and let out a loud, furious roar from its sharp tooth mouth.

Screams came from all around her, but Gwendolyn blocked them out and focused on the dragon in front of her. Tears started to form in her eyes, not from fear but from pure joy and adoration of the beautiful dragon.

It was the largest thing Gwendolyn had ever seen. It was at least fifteen times bigger than any horse, and its wingspan was even longer than its length. The dragon was covered from nose to tail in burnt red scales with giant, red leathery wings to match. Claws stuck out on the top of its wings. It had a long snout, a mouth full of razor-sharp teeth, and two large horns on its head. The dragon smelt like smoke and ashes; Gwendolyn breathed in the glorious smell.

The dragon's eyes stood out to Gwendolyn the most, bright silver, just like hers. Beside the shape and vertical slit pupil, they were identical to Gwendolyn's.

The smell of urine filled Gwendolyn's nose. She turned and realized all but one soldier had fled. The one left behind her stood there with his mouth open and urine-soaked pants.

Cowards. Gwendolyn thought, and she could've sworn the dragon huffed in agreement.

"Is this what you want?" the commander carelessly waved the dragon egg in the air in front of the dragon.

The red dragon looked directly at the commander and roared again. This time Gwendolyn could see fire start to rise in the dragon's throat.

"Yes, it is," the commander continued. "I have your egg. You will listen to me or I will destroy this egg and kill you." The arrogance radiated off of the man. "Together, you and I will conquer kingdoms until the world is mine."

Gwendolyn had enough of this awful man's disrespect. The dragon snapped its jaws at him, as its tail snapped to one side like a whip. Taking advantage of the dragon's distraction, she grabbed the stunned soldier's sword from his hip, and in one fluid motion, she cut off his head. She didn't wait to watch his head roll away, instead she ran towards the commander and drove the blooded sword into his back, barely missing his heart.

The commander was so distracted by the dragon that he didn't hear her coming. He screamed as he fell to the sand, his blood poured from his wound.

Gwendolyn took the egg from his hands. The moment her skin touched the black scales of the dragon egg, the red dragon lifted its head to the sky and let out three quick cries.

Instantly Gwendolyn heard the thunderous sound of dragon wings. She looked up and saw six more dragons heading straight for them. Slowly she got on her knees, bowed her head and lifted the egg up in offering to the magnificent beast.

The red dragon brought its face down to Gwendolyn's head, sniffing her. Gwendolyn willed her body not to tremble as a soft growl came from the dragon. It pulled back its head, and slowly Gwendolyn looked up at it.

She felt the ancient spark again whisper, *sister*.

She looked into the dragon's silver eyes, and a sudden shock rippled throughout her body. A bond had formed with this dragon and it had attached itself to her very soul.

It wasn't a physical bond, but an emotional one. Gwendolyn could communicate with the dragon, not with words, but with an intuition of sorts. She could feel the creature's emotions and thoughts. She was completely aware of its needs and wants. Gwendolyn couldn't truly explain this connection, even in her own mind. But without a doubt, she knew the red dragon before her was named Kaida and they were now bonded for life.

"Sisters," Gwendolyn said, and she reached out her hand and touched Kaida's scaled nose.

A loud roar and a wave of screaming interrupted their moment.

Gwendolyn watched as the six other dragons circled the camp, raining fire on all the men, their tents and their ships. Within moments, the entire camp was ashes, except for the commander's tent and the slow dying commander who still lay on the beach next to them.

Gwendolyn stood beside her bonded dragon watching a black dragon that was somehow larger than Kaida, lead the others back towards the mountains.

"You think this is over?" the commander laughed, blood spewed from his mouth, as he lay on the ground waiting to die. "More of us will come. The King wants these lands and your dragons. He will see that the legend of dragon riders is true, and he will send more men to conquer these lands. He will come."

Gwendolyn looked at the dying commander. She kneeled down beside him. She felt his spilled blood soak into her pants.

She brought her mouth close to the commander's ear and said, "Let him come." There was no warmth in her tone. Her voice was as cold as a winter storm as she spoke to her enemy. "We will welcome him with flames of death." She spoke every word with a terrifying confidence.

Behind her, Kaida let out a mighty roar in agreement.

Gwendolyn looked at the commander's face. His eyes were wide with fear. She flashed him a murderous smile.

Gwendolyn ran into the tent and grabbed the sack the egg had been in. She placed it back inside and tied the sack securely around her body.

Kaida lowered her wing and Gwendolyn excitedly climbed up it. Feeling the hard leather and thick scales under her hands and bare feet, she made her way to Kaida's neck, and wrapped her legs around it.

Kaida let out a growl, and Gwendolyn knew what she wanted.

"Eat Kaida," was all Gwendolyn said, and Kaida stepped toward the injured commander. The commander screamed as best he could with his injuries, but soon his voice was replaced by the crunching of bones. A moment later, he was nothing more than a memory.

Her first dragon ride was even better than Gwendolyn had imagined it would be. It felt like pure freedom.

Kaida took her high up into the clouds and then dove down back towards the earth. Gwendolyn giggled like a little girl, as she admired the beauty of Iaxanara. It was the most exhilarating experience she had ever had.

I am a dragon rider, was the only thought to go through her head as they soared in the sunshine making their way back to Gwendolyn's mountain village.

Nothing in her life had ever felt so right.

Kaida landed, and the earth shook.

Many of Gwendolyn's people had survived the attack, and they had already started repairing the village, attending to the injured and gathering the dead.

All of them now crowded around, staring at Kaida.

Gwendolyn dismounted her dragon, as Elder Craith came pushing through the crowd.

"Is the egg safe?!" He shouted in a panic.

Untying the sack from her body, she smiled at him. She lifted the black dragon egg out, and he sighed in relief. The rest of her tribe cheered.

"Gwendolyn!" someone yelled from beside her, and she turned to see her cousins and aunt running towards her. They wrapped their arms around her and squeezed her tightly.

Kaida growled, and Gwendolyn turned around and introduced her to her tribe members. They all looked in wonder at the beautiful red dragon. All the Dragon Keepers bowed in respect.

Gwendolyn took the egg and placed it on the ground in front of Kaida. Clutching the egg in one of her claws, the dragon let out a soft growl and flapped her wings once, then twice. The crowd parted for her as she took a few steps and then leaped into the air. Gwendolyn felt Kaida's gratitude and warm goodbye.

"The days of the dragon riders are just beginning." Elder Craith said, a large smile spread across his face, but Gwendolyn swore she heard a hint of worry in his voice.

The surviving Dragon Keepers gathered around Gwendolyn, and in unison they spoke the Dragon Keeper Oath as they watched Kaida fly away.

Cassandra R. D'Alessandro is a writer from a small town in Ontario. She writes short stories, poems, and novels across various genres such as fantasy, romantasy, thriller, and mystery. Her favourite subjects to write about include vampires, daring quests, werewolves, epic love stories, witches, magic, fae, and dragons. Outside of writing, Cassandra enjoys traveling, spending time outdoors, trying out new wellness trends, socializing, and reading.

Learn more about Cassandra at:
Author Website | Instagram | Wattpad

Kyle Derek McDonald

CANTO XVIII: Ascension

I

"Two months!" thought Magnus as he Fanthar rode,
    The dragon whisking them unto the East;
"Did hunger not my welfare discommode?
    Did not my throat crave barley, hops, and yeast?"
 The answer to his query came as it was posed:
"He gave me that refreshing liquor whilst I dozed…"

II

With his accoutrements a skin he'd found;
    Believing it to be with water filled,
He then unto his girdle saw it bound,
    That later, hot with strife, it might be swilled.
He grabbed the brimming bombard[1] and the cork removed:
That it with healthful liquor teemed, his nose approved.

III

"This must some Godly nectar be," thought he;
    "What rarer secrets doth their hold possess?"
Thinking again upon his destiny,
    He looked about, their progress to assess:
Below them he beheld with awe but boundless sky:
No archipelago or sea could he espy.

IV

"Here is the canvas by the Gods neglected,
    Across which void this dragon doth parade.Too
What would occur were I to be ejected?
    Would I for an eternity cascade?"
He pondered over this and all his other cares
Until, at last, the wyrm approached the hallowed stairs:

---

[1] leather jug

V

> "It is a mountain, then," remarked the Knight
>> As he observed a floating mass of rock
> Whose peak by cloud was hidden from his sight;
>> Upon the base he saw a likely dock:
> "There shall the Godly challenges begin, I think."
> Fanthar deposited the Hulk upon that brink.

VI

> Magnus dismounted then the drake addressed:
>> "Gramercy for thy succour from the fray;
> How thou did'st know…such means cannot be guessed,
>> But certainly, thou kept'st dark Death at bay;
> And for thy friend's demise, apology is due,
> For, I know what it is to lose companions too.

VII

> "And, if thou wilt accept, here is my pledge:
>> In me thou dost behold a friend eterne,
> And I will swear't upon keen *Scalpel's* edge;
>> And fear thee not: thy trust I'll strive to earn."
> "Who is this lurden,"[2] came a voice, as though from air,
> "Who speaketh unto dragons on the holy Stair?"

VIII

> The voice was lewd and wry, its wont to taunt,
>> A scornful insolence behind a smirk;
> "Here is a place for Gods, not beasts: avaunt!"
>> Virilus spoke: "who 'midst the mount doth lurk,
> And jeereth like a coward from the craggy shade?
> Come nearer, knave, and see of what a God is made."

IX

> Fanthar at once departed from the wharf,
>> And darted off into the stretching sky,
> Whereat before Virilus leapt a *Dwarf*,
>> Who did not even reach his burly thigh.
> "Thy wingèd paramour hath fled, alack for thee!"
> A chafing laugh accompanied this ribaldry.

---

[2] dullard

X

Virilus with bemusement scanned this mote[3]
  Who stood akimbo in a jester's weeds.
"How now, tall tewel![4] Silent? Dost thou dote?"
  "'Tis not my habit to discourse with reeds."
The Dwarf then cachinnated, rolling on the ground,
Which served to further the Elect of War confound.

XI

This mite appeared to be a score in years,
  His countenance like to a babe's, all bare;
His mouth was broad, and ruddy were his lears;[5]
  His eyes were hazel; azure was his hair;
All this discorded horribly with his array,
Which nearly every worldly colour did portray.

XII

"Long hath it been since laughter pinched my cheek!
  Scurrin, I'm clept," the Pygmy then announced.
"I am Virilus; Ichora I seek."
  "Then, Pilgrim, ready thee to be betrounced!
Although…another through the contests swiftly sped…
But, he had sacrificial mutton that he bled!"

XIII

"When did he pass this way?" enquired the Knight,
  Certain that Scurrin of the Warlock prated.
"Within this twelve hour he achieved the height,
  Though by the end with mutton was unfreighted."
"Alack! If only yesterday I had awoken!–
But once again of lambs and slaughter thou hast spoken…"

---

[3] mite, small thing

[4] anus

[5] cheeks

XIV

  "Yea! But not lambs of flesh and blood, I say–
    But hold– of blood and flesh, but not of lamb,
  For tropically[6] this tiding I relay!"
    "I am aware, confound thy dithyramb![7]
  Who were these hapless lambs that with the wretch traversed?"
  Asked he, afeared it was the Blessèd who were cursed.

XV

  "A servile flock, with loyalty replete,
    E'en though they were being led unto the block!"
  Magnus now in his spleen felt fury's heat,
    And thought to cast the Pygmy from the rock,
  But then he paused: why had not Xolis done the same?
  Perhaps this was a challenge he was meant to tame.

XVI

  He trampled down his choler, then he said:
    "Peace dwell with thee, but I must forward yede,
   For I must hurry to the castle's stead."
    "Together, then, O oaf, shall we proceed!"
  Exclaimed the Dwarf while clambering up the mazèd Knight,
  Ere he his little frame upon his shoulder pight.

XVII

  "Ho ra, ho ra! Now gallop, cumbrous[8] steed!
    Betake thee, lest my spur should gall thy side!"
  "So be it, Dwarf," quoth he, "behold my speed."
    He dashed and offered up a bucking ride
  As his unwelcome and imposing little guest
  Clutched with surprise and fear his coriaceous[9] vest.

---

[6] as a metaphor

[7] wild speech

[8] burdensome, unwieldy

[9] leather

XVIII

    Up the acclivity Virilus sped
        While Scurrin screeched like a delirious child;
    They soon approached a slab, which to be read,
        Required the Hulk to make his pace more mild.
    He saw an ebon door above the tablet stretched:
    "Here is a tablet with the Flame God's sigil etched…"

XIX

    He scanned the portal: it was firmly shut;
        Its frame he dared not vault nor obviate,
    Lest he the rightful ritual did rebut;
        But ere he further could investigate,
    He heard a murmur from the rubble to his right;
    As he looked closer he beheld a buried wight!

XX

    He swiftly pulled away the larger stones,
        And saw beneath the Fire God's elect
    With lacerated flesh and broken bones:
        "Cratus! How comes this sanglantine[10] effect?"
    "My strength…" moaned Fervides, "the dastard filched it all…
    Forgive me, Thunderwold…I was Ambition's thrall!

XXI

    "The others served, they by his arts compelled,
        Whilst I aligned with him to Godhood claim…
    Here is my guerdon, Fervides is felled,
        Dishonoured now in body as in name…"
    He sputtered, casting blood from mouth to concave breast;
    "The wicked Warlock drains the powers of the Blest…

XXII

    "This is the means by which he opes the doors…"
        "How doth he this? By craft, or by device?"
    "…Avenge us…I depart for deeper shores…
        Though unto Abaddon, or Paradise…?"
    His expiration interrupted his lament,
    And his expectorated shade began descent.

---

[10] bloody

XXIII

      "Had but more wisdom in his mind resided,
         What honourable friends we could have made."
      "Instead, with darkness' impulse he confided,
         And perished as a bloody marinade!"
      "Here is no time to jest." "'Tis always time to jest!"
      "Didest thou know the Warlock could denude the Blest?"

XXIV

      A shrug and titter was the Dwarf's reply.
         "Stokastor bade me use the maul and chance,"
      Muttered the Hulk, "I comprehend now why.
         But come, beyond this gate we must advance."
      He strode unto the portal, then the panels pressed:
      Before his trembling might, the ebon slats recessed.

XXV

      "So many sinews," quoth the Dwarf; "no brain!"
         Thunderwold grumbled, passing through the door,
      While Scurrin loudly sang a merry strain
         Which was with melody and key at war.
      The cobbled slope the pair continued to ascend,
      Where at another gate their path came to an end.

XXVI

      "Here is the Wind God's gate," declared the Knight
         Who saw the sign of Ventus on the stone.
      "Ah, Wisdom!" mocked the Dwarf, "thou'rt quoited quite!"
         "Quoth he whose wits are brittle as a bone…"
      But then, amongst some rocks, Virilus spied a heap:
      The rumpled body of a man in mortal sleep.

XXVII

      The face he could not see; the robes he wist:
         Venerable Geros was the sorry slain,
      Once whole of stalk, but now reduced to grist;
         "And yet, no carnage doth his flesh profane…
      His death is not like that of Fervides, methinks…
      'Tis from his frailty rather than assault he sinks."

XXVIII

  "Too wise to live," the flippant Dwarf averred,
    Who now with a courtly weariness protested:
  "For what is life but pain and joy deferred?
    We sweat and die to be by worms ingested."
  Now Magnus: "is thy cunning parcelled like thy height?
  I see short wit retiring into Castle Trite."

XXIX

  "O ho! Beware the large one's furious sting!
    To rouse he's slow, but once aroused, he's savage!
  And of this repartee I'll freely sing,
    And all the ears of all the lede[11] I'll ravage!"
  Another maddened madrigal the Dwarf commenced,
  Which even further Music's dignity offenced.

XXX

  His caterwauling Thunderwold ignored,
    And turned again unto the puzzle's slate,
  Over which he for but a moment pored
    Before he pushed upon the portal's plate:
  The ebon doors receded without more ado,
  And thus, he had completed trial number two.

XXXI

  Scurrin, with grudgeful admiration, spoke:
    "The other squandered *hours* upon that door;
  How is't so swiftly thou this riddle broke?"
    "A simple precept," quoth th'Elect of War;
  "One must attempt the path ere he declares it blocked:
  Not every pass is barred; not every door is locked."

XXXII

  Unto the tertiary gate they strode,
    Where Magnus saw a sight that grieved his eyes:
  Defoiled before the slab, the Master's Mode,
    And, in it, one he feared would never rise!
  "Sagir!" he cried as to inspect his friend he rushed;
  "What hath befallen him? Hath he been pierced, or crushed?"

---

[11] people

XXXIII

> The Wizard's back unto the Hulk was turned;
>> Virilus, careful, rolled him on his side,
> And, happily, no injuries discerned,
>> And more, that he was living verified:
> "He breathes!" Now gently on his back Sagir he lays,
> And with his probing eye his health seeks to appraise.

XXXIV

> The Sorcerer awakes and groans in pain,
>> Then over him the friendly Magnus sees:
> "Virilus? Are we in the shades' domain?
>> Have we succumbed unto our enemies?–
> But soft…about thee I behold some lofty change…
> Thou'rt grander, teeming with refulgence; it is strange…"

XXXV

> "That is a story for another day,
>> But say at once: art hurt? How dost thou fare?"
> "My magic, Magnus, hath been filched away!
>> My intellect, as well, hath been laid bare!
> What erst was uberous,[12] now plain and fallow lies:
> Without the gift of genius, all invention dies!"

LVIII

> Virilus pondered over what he'd heard,
>> Then to the looming portal turned his gaze.
> "The passage by a puzzle is obscured:
>> Thou must needs solve an ever changing maze.
> If I were with my Blessing pursed, I would abet,
> But I here sit an indigent[13] o'erwhelmed with debt."

LIX

> Magnus said nought, then touched the towering door:
>> A sprawling labyrinth raced across its face,
> Its ivory contours spreading top to floor,
>> Entwining the whole door in its embrace.
> To see the maze in full, he had to step away;
> How intricate and difficult was this display!

---

[12] bountiful, productive
[13] beggar

LX

    He saw the narrow entrance at the top,
        And the one hundred chambers at the bottom;
    "But one of these is the ordainèd stop…"
        "But do not dare upon the door to plot 'em!"
    Added Sagir, "for if thou touch not what is apt,
    Thou'lt banish it, then face another, but remapped,

LXI

    "And twixt this change an hour thou must abide!
        I watched for hours as Xolis gleaned this clue."
    "Thy counsel shall be dutifully applied–"
        Abruptly Scurrin from his back withdrew,
    And, brandishing his finger, capered towards the gate:
    "And how if I this labyrinth should digitate![14]

LXII

    "And wherefore would'st thou seek to cross my quest?"
        "For I am bumptious! Dost thou not recall?"
    "Meddlesome too, a veritable pest!"
        "To heap on further hate thou hast the gall!"
    The Dwarf approached the gate and menaced with his hand.
    "Thy minute digits on that door shall never land."

LXIII

    "For that thou wilt eject me with thy thew?"
        "I have no need to pitch thee from this rock:
    Who was't that round thy mouth a towel drew?
        I may rebuff thee, but I let thee talk.
    Should'st thou protract my journey, *him* thou dost condone."
    Bested again, he said, "I'll let the door alone…"

LXIV

    Grumbling in umbrage Scurrin moved away,
        Whereat Virilus towards the gate advanced;
    "'Tis two-and forty," mused the Chevalier.
        "Be warned! A rapid guess cannot be chanced!"
    Aquinus to the Imperator spoke with haste.
    He pressed the chamber, and…the puzzle was erased.

---

[14] touch with the finger

LXV

 "Virilus, ah! Thy valour I commend,
  But here's a task for the Immortal Gods!
 If I had wits, my wits to thee I'd lend,
  But, to prevail in this…low are the odds–"
 "Two thousand unto one success attends," spoke he.
 The Archon bit his fingers in dubiety.

LXVI

 But then the plated portal open swings,
  Before Virilus' acumen receding;
 "By Aquin's briny wave!" the Wizard sings,
  "The barrier before us is retreating!
 How is it thou the hidden path so deftly lined?"
 "The many passages I plotted in my mind."

LXVII

 "All whilst debating this unruly imp?
  Such was the sapience I once possessed!
 But now my mind is sluggish, dull, and limp!"
  The Pygmy: "fie, puler![15] Art much obsessed?"
 "Enough," commanded Thunderwold, "he is aggrieved:
 Of his most potent pleasure he hath been bereaved.

LXVIII

 "If means exist to remedy this curse,
  Know, Archon, I will put it in thy hent,
 But we must succour Thalia and the Nurse;
  Already in debate much time we've spent."
 "Wisdom adorneth thee," Sagir replied, "let's go,
 And I, like to a man of worth, shall bear my woe."

LXIX

 "Commendable! Now take a sip of this,"
  Said Magnus, offering the drinking gourd;
 Sagir imbibed then said, "why, here is bliss
  That to my weary limbs doth strength afford!"
 Therewith, they passed the gate and climbed the dreary Stair.
 Anon they came unto another frankered[16] pair.

---

[15] whiner

[16] closed

LXX

    "What challenge here awaits?" inquired the Knight,
        As he his scouting eyes cast to the ground,
    His fair inamorata[17] yare to sight;
        But, Thalia was nowhere to be found.
    "'Tis Thona's gate," averred Sagir, "here is her rune."
    "Then something beautiful…perhaps a dulcet tune."

LXXI

    Then Scurrin: "Thou a door wilt serenade?
        Perhaps thou can'st some pretty flowers pluck,
    Or put thy locks into a dazzling braid,
        Or better: balter[18] to improve thy luck!"
    The Imperator once again ignored the knave,
    And sang the lay he wrought before his sister's grave.

LXXII

    "Was thine innocence so great
    That Elysium could not wait
    To adorn thee with her pall,
    And to house thee in her hall?
    Was thine innocence so great
    That Elysium could not wait?

LXXIII

    Now how merry death shall be,
    For that I will be with thee;
    Naught remains for me above,
    For in Death dwells all my Love.
    Naught remains for me above,
    For in Death dwells all my Love.

LXXIV

    The song concluded and the doors withdrew.
        "When I composed that, I was ten and five;
    It wants sophistication, but 'tis true."
        "Truth in simplicity doth often thrive,"
    The Mage, "the Gods' delight thy chanson[19] doth arrest:
    Thy canorous rehearsal hath appeased their test."

---

[17] lover

[18] dance poorly, but with passion

[19] song

LXXV

    Scurrin, yet silent, masked his running tears
        By sauntering before the mournful pair,
    The haunting lay still ringing in his ears;
        And so, all three continued up the Stair.
    They came unto a large plateau beneath the cloud,
    And were astonished to behold an ambling crowd:

LXXVI

    Despite his Godhood, Magnus swiftly hid,
        And pulled his two companions from the road;
    He covered Scurrin's rictus lest he chid,
        And glanced at those who on the plateau strode.
    "The Ephors!" hissed Sagir, heart wrung with wrath and dole.
    "And not alone…Stugnetos too is on patrol."

LXXVII

    The Mad One stalked amongst the cassocked cluster,
        His lecher's smirk unusually grand;
    Then Magnus spied the reasons for his fluster:
        He saw a length of chain within his hand,
    Which, as he tugged it, pulled two women to his side:
    These were the comely Mistress and Salubria's pride!

LXXVIII

    Pinioned like beasts, and of all clothing stripped,
        These vainly strove their nudity to veil,
    But were too often pulled and pushed and tripped,
        Their guardless flesh contused by the rough trail;
    Still greater their humiliation: set in branks,[20]
    They could not even rail at his remorseless pranks.

LXXIX

    "By Heaven…" said the Archon in abhorrence,
        "What felon keepeth Damosels in chains?"
    These words the Hulk scarce marked for vengeful torrents,
        Which surged and pounded through his swelling veins.
    But, twice five Ephors! – all in magic's usage apt!
    Would he not be all frozen, burned, and thunder clapped?

------

[20] headset used to prevent speaking

LXXXI

He moved to rise, but felt the Archon's hand:
    "I cannot aid thee," uttered he in tray.
"I know," replied the Knight, "but I must stand;
    But, tell me quickly of the Wizard's way:
How doth a Wizard conjure? Is it words, or sense?
It is not tinctures, for with those thou did'st dispense."

LXXXII

"How strange a question for this pressing hour!"
    "I prithee, answer me with all thy haste!"
"Soft now…it is…a feeling, or, a power…
    Though some are smells, whilst others are a taste…"
Lost on this novel sea, Virilus grimaced sore:
What he would give to spy an inkling of the shore!

LXXXIII

Aquinus, seeing his distress, exclaimed:
    "'Twill come if one can see it in his mind!"
This offering his apprehension tamed:
    "Stay couched: unto this rock ye are consigned."
Out comes the hungry Scalpel, long deprived of meat:
At last, of her opponent's flesh she'll duly eat.

LXXXIV

Stugnetos, meanwhile, at the Ephors grumbled:
    "Deploy the portal! My sweet Brides await!"
 All Thalia's defiant cries were humbled,
    While limp Iréna could but lachrymate,
Her suffering redoubled by her rough-shorn strands,
Whose glossy skeins now dangled from Stugnetos' hands.

LXXXV

Like all of those whose minds are fraught with rot
    Who in all things see implements of scorn,
Into a scourge he turned this braided knot,
    And whipped the maid from whom the lash was torn.
The branks annihilate her retching, plaintive sounds,
Which, lief to hear, Stugnetos ever harder pounds.

LXXXVI

Amidst this wrack, the portal is deployed,
    But, ere the Ephors can its window thread,
The foremost traitor Wizard is destroyed,
    And, with her entrails, all is painted red!
What erst she was, was nothing now but pulp and spatter:
Hers was the gruesome image of how bodies shatter.

LXXXVII

Stout Scalpel quivered in the stone behind,
    Embedded halfway down the dripping blade;
All turned to see, as if of single mind,
    From whither came this fatal ambuscade:
Here they beheld Virilus with a mien of wrath.
"How *is* it, that I find thee stalking on this path?"

LXXXVIII

Stugnetos asked with choler of his own;
    "He follows me unto the world's end!
Enamored, art thou? I shall make thee groan,
    And *then* unto thy harlot I'll attend…"
He pulled the chain, and Thalia fell unto her knees;
Though she could not be heard, here eyes were filled with pleas.

LXXXIX

"Coward!" Virilus roars, and shakes the rock,
    His thunderous voice itself a raging wave;
"Know, from thy neck thy head I will undock,
    And, not with sword shall I that pustule shave,
But with these hands a slow divorce I shall enact."
Stugnetos pales before the promise of this pact;

XC

"Obliterate this wretch!" he bawls in fear.
    The Ephors of their tinctured stores avail,
And hurtle at the hulking Cavalier
    A hurricane of fire, bolt, and hail!
In his legerity, around these blasts he leapt,
But could not long avert, no matter how adept.

XCI

    First, by a wall of ice he was confronted;
        Then, ere he could demolish that frore mew,
    He by a bomb of rasping fire was shunted;
        Then was he shocked by heaven's forking spew;
    Aflame and rife with current, doused with melting ice,
    The Ephors froze the lot again by shrewd advice.

XCII

    Virilus found himself in ice encased,
        Yet, for the Mages, this would not suffice:
    They, with a flashing bolt (by thunder chased),
        Cast down a titan boulder on the ice:
    A peak above the Stair cascaded on the Knight:
    The sky fell dim again, bereaved of magic's light.

XCIII

    Stugnetos with incontinence exulted:
        "Ha ha, well executed! What a sight!"
    He with the captive Damsels next consulted:
        "What say ye, sluts? Is't not a sweet delight?"
    He wrenched the links, but a disturbance drew his eyes:
    The sundered peak above the ground began to rise.

XCIV

    The Ephors, too, in consternation gazed:
        Still hot from the encounter, Magnus smoked,
    As he above his head the weighty boulder raised:
        Stugnetos on his terror nearly choked.
    Virilus' eyes, again, were like great stars illumed,
    As round his steaming body numen's bounty plumed.

XCV

    He heaved the boulder off the mountain's brink,
        Then slowly raised an arm with open palm;
    He closed his eyes and seemed to inly think,
        His visage smoothed by an uncanny calm.
    Within his hand a blue and sparking bolus formed,
    Even as furcate[21] tendrils up his forearms stormed.

---

[21] forked

XCVI

    Nor he nor they could credit that which followed,
        For, from his hand a crackling spike emerged,
    Whose fry the bosom of a Wizard swallowed,
        And whose vitality was quickly purged.
    A smoking husk, the Ephor fell unto the ground
    While Magnus sought another salvo to expound.

XCVII

    "Assail, assail, ye damnèd dumbstruck curs!"
        Stugnetos with resurgent terror cried;
    "The Mode to him that this curst Knight deters!"
        Before they could engage, another died,
    Her face excoriated[22] by a sparking bolt,
    While her unruddered body shuddered in revolt.

XCVIII

    The seven Sorcerers who yet remained
        Assaulted Thunderwold with all their means,
    And, though his was a craft by recence strained,
        The Wizards felt as though they battled fiends,
    Setting upon them from all corners of the fray,
    And not just one indomitable Chevalier;

C

    The contest, like a maelstrom in the seas,
        Rotated, and expanded and contracted;
    The tireless Imperator, by degrees,
        From desperation, dominance extracted,
    And, by good accident, reduced his foes by two,
    A pair exterminated by a single coup.

CI

    His magic, from his essence culled, was fresh,
        And never did he wane, or tire, or dodder;
    The Wizards, though, were made of mortal flesh,
        And found their tincture pouches scant of fodder;
    Virilus pressed, their backs now facing either ledge:
    In little time, he'd drive them from the mountain's edge!

---

[22] peeled off, flayed

CII

Stugnetos, prescient of his demise
    Should all the Sorcerers default,
Then undertook an ugly enterprise
    That would the Imperator's triumph halt…
Amidst the clamour, Magnus heard another bruit:
A woman's cry from pain, both sudden and acute.

CIII

He paused to look for Thona's acolyte,
    And what he saw induced his hands to drop:
Thalia, her supple waist with carnage bright,
    With her free hand a river strove to sop,
Whose estuary was a wound upon her side,
Which by Stugnetos' darkened dagger was applied.

…

CV

"Forbear!" Stugnetos shouted, "or she dies!"
    "What would'st thou have of me, thou reprobate?"
"I like the predator the best that flies:
    From off this ledge thou must precipitate."
Virilus growled, "impossible." "Then she will bleed."
"Ignore him, love," said Thalia, "do not recede!"

CVI

The Mad One snickered: "Love? How light thy heart!
    How finical![23] She served my sire, her Lord,
And after but one evening of thine art,
    My father is forsworn, whilst thou'rt adored!
But then, she's captured, and returned unto the fold,
Whereat to Xolis she converts thy Thunderwold!

---

[23] finicky, flaky

CVII

    "And now this strumpet calls on thee once more?
        O, how these hoydens[24] change their hue at will!
    Much like that busy, buzzing, Sylphid whore,
        Whose oscillations have since grown quite still…
    Would'st care to see another of thy callets[25] perish?
    How much dost thou this light and wayward hussy cherish?"

CVIII

    The Mistress for the want of blood grew pale,
        And only by Stugnetos' arm could stand.
    "O, champion, her staving makes her frail!"
        The Madman gleeked; "obey, then, my command."
    "She will become a lecher's thrall if I comply…"
    "Destroy them all!" cried she, "for I would rather die!"

CIX

    He looked upon his lover, then the Maid;
        He then upon the puffing Ephors glared;
    Then long his eyes upon the Mad One stayed.
        "The time is now!" the Warlock's son declared.
    "I will…obey," the Imperator acquiesced,
    Which garnered sobs and whimpers from the whilom Blest.

CX

    "But I shall not descend alone!" says he,
        As from his hands he sends a sudden gust,
    Which hated rivals and the Blessèd three
        From the plateau immediately thrust,
    Committing all unto the vasty, floorless waste!
    Virilus leaps and plummets after them with haste!

CXI

    A hawk amidst disordered prey, he dives;
        The Ephors struggle in their flapping raiment,
    While Xolis' bastard his revenge contrives,
        Preoccupied alone with swift repayment:
    Whatever fate awaited him, he little cared,
    So long as by his means the women's lives were pared.

---

[24] carefree girls

[25] callgirls

CXII

    Despite the puissance of the sudden storm,
        He did not drop the dagger, nor the chain,
    And, though he did relinquish Thalia's form,
        He need but pull to reassert his reign.
    He saw the damsels tangled in these links below:
    They'd sped beyond him with no garb their chute to slow.

CXIII

    The chain to collars round their necks was gird,
        And they could never hope the link to rend;
    Stugnetos looked behind and saw the bird
        Who to the wobbling Wizards put an end:
    They could not reach their tinctures, so they could not cast:
    They were expunged, one at a time, by fiery blast.

CXIV

    One managed, ere in hungry fire he died,
        A magic door's circumference to call;
    His body, by Virilus' fury fried,
        Into that portal did directly fall:
    Whichever region that received that purple rift
    Was forthwith furnished with a most unwelcome gift.

CXV

    The Dark One, of his retinue bereft,
        Pulled himself down along the clinking cord,
    Even as Magnus through the aether cleft,
        His body rigid as he deftly soared.
    Stugnetos closer to the pallid Mistress drew
    Who languished in a swoon for loss of vital dew.

CXVI

    Below, Iréna saw him with her close,
        Then spied the glinting dagger in his grasp;
    His progress she desired to oppose,
        And so she seized upon her collar's hasp,
    Then with her other hand, she pulled upon the line:
    Her might was slight, but in the flight, 'twas leonine.

CXVII

 The chain grew taut, and Thalia therewith sank;
  Stugnetos growled and pulled with greater might,
 And, once again, the distance twixt them shrank,
  Though, near behind approached the racing Knight,
 Who sought to take in hand Stugnetos' kicking heel
 Just as the Dark One moved the Mistress' fate to seal.

CXVIII

 Within in his teeth he had enclosed the blade
  To liberate both hands to catch his cony;
 Contiguous at last with the pale maid,
  He clasps the knife, and, without ceremony,
 Embeds the point into her heart through her soft breast:
 A stroke that sends the Mistress into mortal rest.

CXIX

 Her blood ascended past the wicked pest,
  And splashed, still warm, on the Elect of War,
 Coating his countenance and brawny chest
  With his inamorata's littered gore.
 From his extended limbs he felt the fight depart,
 Much like the child who withers from a sudden smart.

CXX

 His hand, so close to vile Stugnetos' heels,
  Collapses and falls flaccid in despair,
 While all his coursing blood in grief congeals.
  His bulk, unfettered, slowed him in the air;
 Stugnetos saw, with much delight, the Hulk recede,
 And then endeavoured to complete his final deed…

CXXI

 He bit the Mistress' unmolested pap
  Ere he commenced descent unto the Nurse;
 His true desire was to defile her lap,
  But time and circumstance were too adverse.
 Iréna thrashed and wept, and pulled the links in vain:
 She could escape and die elsewhere, but for the chain!

CXXII

Virilus, meanwhile, took his love in arm,
    And sought her ruptured breast to seal again,
But no amount of care relieved the harm;
    All that remained was to avenge the slain.
He clasped her close, and softly moved her to his back,
Then round them coiled the cable, like a winch-drawn rack.

CXXIII

Stugnetos and Iréna up were drawn,
    As Magnus ineluctably descended;
The Dark One pressed to reach his dangling pawn
    Ere he by Thunderwold was apprehended;
He caught Iréna's slender arm and pulled her near:
He raised the knife to strike, and glowered with a sneer.

CXXIV

But ere he struck, his arm in chain was trapped:
    Virilus, with his sure and supple wrist,
Saw to it that Stugnetos' hand was wrapped,
    And that he could not free his daggered fist.
"I am the Lord of turmoil!" Xolis' son exclaimed:
"If not by blade, then by my hand she will be maimed!"

CXXV

To face the void he turned helpless Maid,
    Then on her collar pulled with wonton hate,
Which unto breath erected a blockade:
    She would not bleed, but she would suffocate.
Or so she would have, had not Magnus firmly caught
Stugnetos' flailing unctuous and braided knot.

CXXVI

With a swift wrench the Madman's neck he broke!
    The bastard son of Xolis roared in pain
As he released the Damsel from the choke;
    Though nullified, he was yet far from slain;
Virilus coiled a burly arm about his head,
And placed his other hand upon his shoulder's stead:

CXXVII

He then one from the other 'gan to pull;
	In agony Stugnetos screeched and cawed,
And, like a hatchling set on by a bull,
	Was quickly overmatched and overawed;
Virilus tweaks his brawn; it's over in a breath,
As head from trunk is torn, his soul bequeathed to death!

CXXVIII

That final sound would ever haunt the Maid:
	A gnashing snap commingled with a howl;
Virilus clutched the cranion[26] by the braid,
	Then flung the corpse aside like meatless fowl;
The headless corpse by the abyss would be consumed,
The monster, rightly, in oblivion entombed.

CXXIX

He reached the Maid, then broke and doffed the branks;
	Into his bulk she pressed her frightened face,
While sobbing and resounding with her thanks;
	He wound the lady in the chain's embrace,
That neither she nor Thalia could drift away;
"In life, or death," thought she, "together we shall stay."

CXXXI

Then, something in the wind disturbed her ear,
	Just as her tender skin felt less abraded;
By sound and breeze, she felt some mass was near,
	But what, besides the three of them, cascaded?
She dared a look, and then misdoubted what she saw,
For there appeared a dragon diving like a daw!

CXXXII

"A dragon!" she unto her host asserted,
	His eyes ashimmer with a golden glow.
"Fanthar," replied the Knight; "we're not deserted."
	The dragon, with precision, dipped below,
And, carefully, beneath the dropping triad rose,
That, without danger, on his back they might repose.

---

[26] head

Kyle is an award-winning poet and voice-over artist, a Toronto based actor, operatic bass, writer, digital composer, director, and producer. He's also the co-founder of Indie Opera Hub, and the Managing Director for North American Operations at Octant Aerospace Consulting. His current claims to fame are voicing Drago on the animated series Bakugan, and Batman on the fan-made series, Batman: Just A Mortal.

As a writer, he's been produced as a playwright (Macbeth's Head, Don Juan: An Episode), and screenwriter (Street Smarts, This is Bill, Revenge for the Duchess of Malfi, Movies Matter, Actorapists, The Car, Gamers Anonymous), and has written libretti for three original operas, The Lion Heart, The Bat and the Bells, and Possession, and created the book and score for two new operas in pasticcio, James Bond: A Convenient Lie, and Conan and the Stone of Kelior. He was awarded the Winning Writer's War Poetry award for The Rose Of Ilium (now called Achilles and the Queen), a poem composed in heroic couplets that tells of the doomed love between Achilles and Penthesilea, and, after a long break, he's returned to poetry recently having completed the writing and recording of his novel length epic poem, The Blessed, a selection of which is featured in Dragon Dreams, and which is pending release. He's currently assembling a chapbook of his love poetry called Ravenous.

Learn more about Kyle at:
Author Website | YouTube | Instagram | Amazon

Kathryn Malcolm

Chalky smoke billowed over the water. A grimy film settled on the surface before fracturing and washing away with the tide. Lilja pulled her cloak over her mouth and nose, though she'd already breathed in much of the stuff. It caked her nostrils and clung to the back of her throat, earthy and metallic. Beneath her, Ylvastrya, her dragon huffed out a purifying breath, rippling the sea with her stomach muscles. Lilja's half-submerged feet stirred with the movement, and she raised her pale eyes to the inferno that was the burning shore.

This was not what her mother had wanted of her. The colour would leach from her face at the knowledge of what she'd done. What she'd taken part in. What she'd *allowed* to happen. Lilja shuddered. Her cloak couldn't quite rid her of the acrid taste at the back of her tongue. The scent of burning flesh.

In the burning ruins of the harbour town, a few dragons roved without their riders, basking in the heat of the flames. The mortals didn't stand a chance. The inhabitants of these distant shores thought the likes of dragons and their fae riders no more than a myth until recent days. A story to delight and frighten children in equal measure.

"There is nothing you could have done to stop this," the voice of her dragon purled into her mind. "They would have continued the attack regardless of your opinion."

Lilja lowered her head. Ylvastrya was right. Besides, she was The Seasprite, a warrior famed for her bravery in the battles against other northern clans. It was she who had led them to victory and brought peace amongst the fae of the sea and mountains. If she were to refuse, if she'd spoken out against the other warriors, her leaders, *men*, then her reputation would shatter as quickly as it had formed.

"Maybe so. But now I am no better than my former enemies."

She adjusted the sturdy leather straps that crossed over her chest, holding her sword and shield in place. Instantly, she regretted doing so as her gaze caught on the body of a young girl floating in the water. Her arms sprawled as if in welcome, dead eyes gauzy with grit. She wasn't sure if her tangled hair was red with blood or if that was the true colour. Lilja swallowed bile.

Other riders and their dragons circled overhead, gradually spiraling in their descent before settling in the water. The wavelets nearly reached Lilja's waist. Like her, the other warriors all wore the same thick oilskins, skin-tight under their leather armour. Dragon-scale spaulders and mail adorned the most honoured of their warriors, including her. Lilja was flush with them. Even her ice-blonde hair, drawn back in tight braids, was flecked with the tiny sapphire-blue scales of an enemy clan.

From their distant shouts, she gleaned their next move. It was over. Back to the Viperlord, their victorious leader.

No sooner had she thought of it than did Ylvastrya ripple with pleasure. The Viperlord's dragon, Vardhr, was her mate.

Lilja gripped the reins and directed Ylvastrya to the west. She raised her silvery head from the water. Pearls of moisture cascaded off her iridescent scales, flashing orange and blue in the firelight. She glided slick as a sea snake before beating her powerful wings. Sea spray tinged with red scattered across Lilja's nose like liquid freckles. Along the coast, the clean air beckoned. As did their next conquest.

The Viperlord held his court upon perilous rocks in a maelstrom of sea, protected by his gargantuan dragon as he

Like his rider, Vardhr was much darker in hue than most. Iron-grey scales reflected the stormy waters, and he reared his great head up as Ylvastrya approached. He dwarfed most of the common dragons flocking to the rock. Burning eyes bore down at her. Lilja couldn't glean any sort of tenderness in them, but evidently, something about his attentions pleased Ylvastrya.

Lilja dismounted, marching towards The Viperlord and sheets of rain pelted her face. He was reclining on the tail of his dragon, as relaxed as if he lay in a sunny cove.

"Ah, The Seasprite!" He greeted her. "I was beginning to think you'd never visit."

Lilja offered a perfunctory bow of her head, then raised her voice over the storm. "A moment of your time?"

"Anything for my men's favourite warrior." He cocked his head obnoxiously, inviting her closer.

Lilja glanced at Ylvastrya, who was busy with her mate. It was the only time she paid little heed to her rider. Though she knew she shouldn't, Lilja resented sharing her attention.

"Our homeland," she began. "Remind me why we cannot take it back from the mortals who stole it? Is it the mists?"

The Viperlord jumped down. His heavy boots crunched on grit, scattering shards across the barren rock. "If we could take it back, we would," he said, his expression stony. "If only it were that simple. The mortals have damaged the mists of the Faery realm beyond repair."

"There are no Faery mists here. No dragons. Why take these lands when there is no mist to sustain our magic, our dragon's lifeforce?"

Ylvastrya and Vardhr were paying attention now. The mists which coated the sea and the mountains in the north were not only the singular environment in which Faery magic flourished, but it was the only one in which they and the dragons could be born in. Without it, where Faeries had relied on the dragons as their source of power when travelling out of the Faery realm, they now relied on them always.

The Viperlord clenched his jaw. It was an impossible question to answer.

Lilja squared her shoulders and held her ground. There was no reason to attack these southern mortals, and he knew it. Even if it were for revenge, these country folk were not the ones responsible for the destruction of their realm.

"You're wrong," he said eventually, arching a brow. "There are Faery mists here. Our scouts have reported it farther inland."

"Inland?" She repeated, voice straining over the crashing waves. It was certainly unusual for the mists to be so far away from the coast. "Is there a mountain?"

He shook his head, dark braids heavy with water lazily brushed his shoulders. "It is a forest."

Lilja gaped. "And is this the land you truly intend to take?"

His usual countenance of bored amusement soured. "We do not know if there are Fae within, or if they have dragons. If we are to take them, we must first know how powerful they are."

It was all she could do to keep a straight face. It was understandable for Fae and dragons to torment mortals, even before their homeland was taken. It had always been the way. Poor wandering mortals who ventured into the mists accidentally were to be the playthings of the Fae. Young girls and boys were sent in to appease the appetites of the dragons. But for the Viperlord to intentionally wish to do battle with their own kind chilled Lilja to the core.

"Let me be the one to go," she offered. "Let me find out what kind of Fae they are, what they're capable of."

The Viperlord scratched his chin, the tiny beads ornamenting

"Please. I can be there and back in a day."

He tilted his head. A casual consent.

Lilja was walking backwards to Ylvastrya as she nodded her thanks. "Let's go," she said in a voice only her dragon would hear. She was in no mood to wait for her and her mate to pry apart from one another. With some reluctance, Ylvastrya turned for Lilja to mount.

Ylvastrya was in a mood the whole time they flew over the land. Lilja ignored her. She'd come round as soon as she saw Vardhr again, and she'd already promised over and over to let them spend longer together.

The weather grew fair as they flew over the emerald land below, skimming the tips of evergreen forests. Pure, undiluted winter sunlight warmed Lilja's face for the first time in months. She closed her eyes and tilted her face into the sun.

In a rush, Ylvastrya's body relaxed. "I am carrying an egg."

"What?" Lilja said with a jerk. "How?"

"I have been carrying it for a long time. I had thought that I might never lay, that it would either fester in my womb or become as a stone without. I could hatch it in these mists if they exist, once they are ours."

Lilja's stomach plummeted. "Would you not rather lay on your home mountain?"

"Of course, I would," Ylvastrya hissed. "But that is not possible."

"What if it were?"

Ylvastrya tensed. "Speak plainly."

"I cannot continue to partake in mortal massacres in the name of a realm we lost which they have no notion of. I must do something," she breathed. "I don't understand the need for conquest. We need more land, yes, but why burn the homes of the innocent like this? And why so many? We could settle here easily enough, but the Viperlord will soon have his sights on other towns. And for what?"

Ylvastrya huffed a breath, which was as close as Lilja was going to get to an agreement where the Viperlord, or more specifically Vardhr, was concerned.

"What are you planning?"

"To make peace with the Fae or dragons of these mists, perhaps they can help us."

"And what if there are none here?"

Lilja shrugged. "Then the land belongs to no one. I will live here peacefully; you can hatch your child and I will never raise my sword in anger again."

"I hope that is the case," Ylvastrya said in a faint, forlorn voice.

The mist of the mysterious Faery realm appeared distant at first, a dense fog hovering above the forest. An unusual greenish hue within glinted now and then, though it seemed independent of the trees. All at once the mist rushed upon them, thick and cloying, stinging Lilja's eyes like smoke. Ylvastrya veered and groaned in displeasure.

Despite the visual hindrance, Lilja's blood sang in her veins as the mist's magic swelled in her. She allowed her heartbeat to attune to this new melody, similar in some ways and vastly different in others to the dispatched mist of her homeland. Eventually, though still ever-present, their eyes adjusted.

A river slashed through the forest, granting relief from the canopy which webbed and intertwined across the landscape. Perhaps it was Ylvastrya's affinity to water which drew them to it; they had passed several small clearings already.

Lilja had seen forests before in the mountains of her people and at the edges of her seascape homeland, but none such as this. The colours were vibrant despite the season, vivid with evergreens and frosted berries like rubies amongst the pines. The very ground beneath her feet had an uncanny warmth to it, soft with moss and life-giving detrition. The scent of the place, damp soil and dew, was inescapable.

Ylvastrya emerged from the frigid river, incongruously pale amongst the backdrop of the forest. She raised her head, her slit nostrils dilating as she tested the air. "The mist is not the same as ours, but it is just as strong."

"Let us proceed cautiously," Lilja said, checking her weaponry was all easily accessible, "I think there is a path up ahead."

Gentle wisps of snow drifted miraculously through the canopy. As Lilja pushed aside the bracken, her Fae eyes noted every detail of the flakes, every minute ice crystal. When one landed on her lashes, it did not melt. She was of the Northern Fae after all.

Lilja and Ylvastrya froze, each with one foot into an unexpected clearing. A reptilian head reared from the underbrush of ferns, and it was unlike any dragon either of them had ever seen.

Dense, green-black scales blended perfectly with their surroundings, coarse as bark. Atop its head was a crown of horns, but most surprisingly, pointed ears, flattened back in alarm, which dragons of the north did not possess. Its body was plumper, its limbs and wings angular rather than sleek, but it was unmistakably a dragon.

"Speak to them," Lilja whispered. "And make sure they know we mean no harm."

There was an uncomfortable silence as the two dragons communicated. Gradually, the green dragon's ears lifted forward, and he, or she, drifted closer and made a low noise.

"He says to follow him. He will take us to the Fae."

The green dragon beat his wings, rippling the ferns in the clearing, before tucking them away.

"They are not far away," Ylvastrya added.

Indeed, it was not long before Lilja was walking under an archway of vines, very much a doorway of the forest. She blinked, finally realising what mortals who strayed into the Faery realm felt like. Ylvastrya shook her great head, coming out of a daze herself.

She couldn't quite fathom the scent before her, though the magic at play was similar to that of her homeland. Obscured doorways and windows emerged through the trees, curtains were fashioned from cobwebs and shadows, tapestries of moss with delicate illustrations decorated the forest court, and at her feet, an indistinct carpet of fallen leaves.

Gradually, shapes of the Fae began to emerge from the trees, some stepping quite literally from them, and others always there but only just noticeable. They were as one with the forest as she had once been with the sea. Tears prickled her eyes, and her wings fluttered a little in excitement. Lilja followed the green dragon as he walked the carpet of leaves, at the end of which stood the most elegant man she'd ever seen. The dragon halted by him, turning back to face her.

"This is the King of the Forest," Ylvastrya whispered.

Lilja could only gape as the king laid his hand on his dragon. He wore a crown of frosted nuts and berries over his long, auburn hair. His robes were the forest itself, glinting with shades of winter leaves, shadowy hollows and shafts of light. Unlike her thin, dragonfly-like wings, his were wide like a butterfly, all earthy tones.

"Welcome to my realm," his voice was the wind in the trees, "I hope you have not come to burn our home as you do the mortals?"

Lilja flushed and dropped to one knee. "No, Lord. I am Lilja, the Seasprite of the Northern Fae. I have come to beg for your help."

He raised a brow. "What is it you ask?"

"Our mists are gone," she continued. "While yours are thick and full. How do you keep it so? Is there a way to restore our mists?"

The chuckle which rippled around the courtly Fae was like the bubbling of a brook. Even the green dragon rumbled with amusement.

"Why should I share such a thing?" Said the king.

Lilja straightened to her full height, daring to look the king in the face, though she sensed he and his people were older than the forest itself. "Because if I do not find a way to restore my Faery realm, my people will take yours."

The laughter fell silent. The breeze died and the air vacated her lungs. Time was frozen. Then the king waved his hand, her breath rushed back to her, and all the courtly Fae vanished. Only he and the green dragon remained.

In a heartbeat, he stood right before her, abruptly more corporeal than a moment ago. His eyes were the same vivid green as the rest of the forest, as his dragon.

He tilted Lilja's chin up to face him. "Do you know what the mist is made of, child?"

She shook her head, or tried to.

"It is the breath of the dragon. Purifying and lifegiving."

Lilja frowned. "So, the mist forms purely from where dragons dwell?" It was well known that dragons' breath had healing properties. Surely it couldn't be that simple.

The king shook his head gracefully. "To be precise, it is the last breath of a dragon. Our realm is formed of the spirit of a mighty and ancient dragon who died long ago. Its bones are our hills, its veins our rivers and its scales the seeds of the forest. We keep our realm strong by sacrificing one additional dragon every century."

Ylvastrya tensed, her tail wrapping unconsciously around her stomach where the egg grew. Lilja placed a hand on her shoulder to calm her.

The king smiled coldly. "Fear not. In order to restore your realm, you should only need to sacrifice one dragon. It must be not only the largest but the most powerful one you have to ensure the mist will take."

Lilja chewed her lip. The Viperlord would not like it, let alone agree to it. Vardhr was a colossal dragon, not only radiating magical power but well known as gifted in healing. That was why The Viperlord chose him.

Then there was Ylvastrya to consider. Even now she was trembling at the thought of losing the sire of her egg.

"I hope you heed me," said the king. "I do not wish to be your enemy."

"Nor I, you," Lilja's voice was gravely as she spoke.

The King of the Forest took her hand in his and raised it to his lips. The gesture was not common amongst the warrior clans of the north and would repulse many. However, as Lilja looked into the dazzling forest-green eyes, she was touched. This was the serene and peaceful life she truly wanted.

You will always be welcome here, came a voice. She was not sure if it was the king or his dragon.

With a brisk wave of his hand, time fell away again. Gone were the moss tapestries, gone the spider silk decoration. Even the lustre of the leaves had dimmed. It was a normal forest, such as one any mortal would see.

"Let us leave," Lilja said quietly.

Ylvastrya turned without looking, waiting for her rider to mount. Lilja sighed and flew up to the ridge on her back. Ylvastrya's powerful wings were slow to move, taking to the skies with more care than usual. If she'd been in a mood before, it was nothing compared to now.

"What will you do?" Ylvastrya said unexpectedly.

"I don't know. I do not think I should tell the Viperlord."

Silence.

"I will speak with Vardhr," Ylvastrya's words came out in a rush, almost in relief.

Lilja startled. "No, you do not need to do that."

Ylvastrya shook her great head. "I must at least discuss it. For the sake of our child."

Lilja pressed her eyes shut, conflicted. "I do not wish to add further blood to my hands. I came here to avoid conflict, not create discord. Please, Ylvastrya-"

"It's too late, Lilja," Ylvastrya barked venomously, emitting a troubling whining noise in her throat that broke Lilja's heart. "You've done what you set out to do. You've found the solution to our problems. The Seasprite triumphs again. If not a warrior, you are still a leader. You cannot avoid bloodshed."

Lilja tried to swallow the lump in her throat. "This isn't what I wanted."

"This is war," Ylvastrya bit out.

They flew for a long while in complete silence, watching the misty green realm slip out from below them. Soon, the salt air caught in their noses again.

The rocky island on which Vardhr basked in the evening rays came into sight. A single tear rolled down Lilja's face.

"How shall we do this?"

Kathryn is a British YA fiction author with a passion for classical art, mythology and folklore all of which echo throughout her work. She has been writing stories since before she could hold a pencil correctly but started her publishing journey in 2022 with her upcoming debut novel *The Shadow of the Scholar*. She was born and raised in Southampton and holds a Bachelor of Art from the University of Southampton's Winchester School of Art. She later completed a Postgraduate degree in Art Gallery and Museum Studies at the University of Manchester. Kathryn now lives in Chester with her husband and, when she is not writing, works as a librarian.

Learn more about Kathryn at: Author Website | Instagram

Phantasm of Armor and Flesh

Chrystal J. Raven

The embers in his eyes flickered

and grew as he stepped into view.

Purposeful stride; tonal, like the drum

beat heavily and slow.

Claws curved to etch against

the compressed earthen scape,

Scrape at the rush of my heart in turn to

bring into view and behold this visual capture.

In awe and terror, I witness the ripple of time

upon his scales; pearlescent armor and cloak,

they move like muscle on his back.

This colossal-

made space for as the clouds move away upon

the spreading of one wing forth and then the other.

The shrinking skies rapture of

this draconian primal.

Chrystal J. Raven is a Canadian, tri-racial poet and artist. Canvasing sublime emotional landscapes and the inspired energy of nature through the written word and visual mixed media. Combining poetry and mystical philosophy, she shares her stories to connect to self and create a space for readers to explore both celebrated and difficult concepts and experiences.

Her work can be found in The Poetry Institute of Canada's Anthology volumes: Passages of the Heart and Island Shores; The Far-Shining One from Bibliotheca Alexandrina, and Colonialism and Music Therapy from Barcelona Publishers.

Learn more about Chrystal at:
Author Website | Instagram | Instagram | Facebook

K.T. Morley

Iron poisoned dragons. The prince knew it. He used it to subjugate. Always, the prince had an angle. Furthermore, the rusted chains holding Rhonkan captive in the prince's dungeon held firm. The ferrous grind of the steely bit rendered his teeth useless, staining every painful swallow. His dragonfire had failed long ago in the metallic tang swirling through him.

Three points of iron, then, to fasten a dragon and docile him, driven through his tail, a rear foot, and one front claw. They swept memory into whirlpools of indifference. Rhonkan had hoped to spare his nest, its bounty of dragon eggs, and mate by surrendering to the human prince.

He'd erred.

Now, his memories were buried in fog. Each labored breath of the past thirty years tasted of ash and all-encompassing despair. He clung to all he had left. He knew his children lay imprisoned in their eggs, trapped when his birthing-fire withered under iron's stain.

On the good days, Rhonkan could see his offspring's souls. They flited and floated in the between world of not-life and not-death, caught between sleep and wake.

He sang to them then; to little Rhisa, whose spirit soared with rippling golden scales, to fierce Khelohm, the fire of his breath a beacon to friends, a pyre to enemies. The dragon-father sang to Elikhen and her twin, Elakhan.

The jailor's gong echoed. Beyond the door, the precise measured steps of the prince heralded his imminent arrival. Rhonkan shook himself, his girth rattling the chains. Wall sconces around the room erupted in dancing firelight as the prince magicked them into life. Rhonkan understood the magic. The prince had stolen that, too.

The prince wore his armor today. And his sword. He also had a small pouch on his belt. It intrigued Rhonkan, but the iron in his blood convoluted every mental pathway. He bowed, "My Lord." The words grew easier with practice.

"Dragon, it seems you remember your place," the man paused, patting the hilt of his sword and sneering, "Good!"

He drew a small, silver dagger and drove it into Rhonkan's thigh, laughing, a rolling thing filled with joy and merriment. The blade stung. A reminder. It could have been steel.

The prince wasn't a bad fellow, Rhonkan thought. Not really, for all his keeping a dragon chained and staked in his dungeon. The prince fought for his people and sought a better world for them. Honorable traits if one could get past the genocide and imprisonment.

"Tell me, Dragon, what is in a name?"

Name-games again. "My Lord, to know a name is to own part of the owner's soul."

"And your name, Dragon? You haven't mentioned it."

"I have not."

"Funny thing about that, Dragon." The prince reached into the pouch at his side. He drew forth a white object.

Horror gripped Rhonkan. He tried to rear. He tried to swat his tail and bite, but the prince had him trapped and staked for a reason. His eyes betrayed his anger. They burned with the fire in his heart.

"I tire of our game," the prince scolded, replacing the dagger and drawing his sword, slashing the steel blade across Rhonkan's unspiked front leg.

The iron seared into him, and the prince placed the object on the floor. Rhonkan could taste the scent of the bone in the air as it replaced the bitter stench of steel. He could sense his children whirling in anger and fear in that in-between place. The bone was his mate's foreclaw. He salivated, the animal nature pushing aside the calculating dragon. His mate—broken—slaughtered before his eyes as he lay wrapped in chains with a hundred arrows in his hide.

"I have been patient, Dragon!" The prince paced, tantalizingly close and just as assuredly out of reach. "More than patient, even." Another slash.

Rhonkan answered angrily, nostrils flaring, "That is of concern to you, my Lord. Not me." He fought the stain in his blood as fiercely as he had that first day. If he could have, he would have showered the room with fire.

The prince stopped and waggled a finger. "See? You call me Lord, and yet you refuse my command." He sheathed the sword and drew the silver knife again. "It vexes me, Dragon," he said, throwing his arms wide, the dagger dangling from loosened fingertips.

"I am chained," Rhonkan replied, panting, eyes fixed on the silver dagger. "I am hammered into the bedrock of this fortress. My blood waters its stones and protects your kingdom. It is not done of fealty. It is not done of friendship."

"No," the prince said, resting the other hand on his sword and changing his tone to royal haughtiness, "it is not." Each consonant ended crisply. The prince paced again.

Rhonkan spoke, an edge of disdain slipping past his fogged mind. "My blood serves because I am forced to give it. A better gift is one freely given." He clenched down on the bit again, the steel's venom fogging his desire to burn the prince to ash.

Iron interrupted the natural flow of a dragon's life force and magic. Shortly after chaining Rhonkan, the prince had ruminated on a book he'd read as a youth about trapping a dragon with three points of steel. The prince and his book proved correct.

Somewhere, the prince had come across a second text extolling the persuasive tongue of dragons and their wisdom. The prince needed wisdom; the world was a dangerous place. He didn't need the corrosive efforts of the dragon's tongue to turn guard against guard and free itself, so he invented the dragon bit. How illuminating.

"Dragon, I fear if you do not relent soon, I will be forced to bring your eggs here and smash them before you."

Rhonkan roared as best he could. His children danced defiantly in the ether, begging to avenge this travesty. The prince didn't know of Foresight. He didn't realize Rhonkan spoke with his children. Rhonkan wouldn't tell him, either.

The prince turned to the door and waved to the guards. Two men, each pushing carts, entered the dungeon cell. In each cart sat three eggs. Rhonkan quieted his thrashing and closed his eyes, singing to his children. The soul-song reached out to them, stronger with the eggs so close. Their souls burst with joy and readiness. Once the promised bodies fought free, their souls would quicken in them.

In his mind's eye, he saw Rhisa's golden scales as they rippled in expectancy. Khelohm's bristled with inborn intensity, chafing at the delay. Rhonkan could almost feel the rumble of Khelohm's roar. The twins, their eggs on separate carts, spun in the air—their serpentine bodies coiled around one another in angst. Rhonkan could sense how the distance between their eggs in the carts bothered them. They hissed and bellowed for birth and togetherness.

Soon, my children.

Mihska, soft and quiet, purred, too. She was withdrawn and demure, her white scales hiding her among the clouds and ice in the between-world of the void. Gehna stalked the shadowy forms of trees, her ethereal presence eager to take its place in her body. She shook her head, and scales rippled down the length of her spirit-self in emerald beauty.

"Dragon, I will give you one night in the presence of your eggs to contemplate all meaning of the word *loss*." He thrust the poniard alongside the silver dagger. "If you do not help bring them into this world; if you do not help me learn their names and chain them in my other fortresses, I will shatter them before you."

Fear and pain raced through his body. He hid it from the prince, turning his head to speak. "Why would you slaughter children? They have done no wrong. They have—"

The prince cut him off with a slice of his hand. "They have power! That's what they have. I want it. I need it," the prince balled his hand into a fist and slammed it into his thigh. "I am but one castle on this border, and I need the other dragons to strengthen more forts against our enemies."

And that was why Rhonkan left his children free in the in-between. They could be themselves. Once birthed, they would be captured and enslaved. It was a significant risk. Alive, even as slaves, they had value. As unhatched eggs, their value was merited as potential. Slaughtering one egg to leverage the rest? Rhonkan had trouble with the notion. He was confident the animal in the room was not Dragonkind.

Rhonkan shook. A tremor that started with his snout and worked its way down his neck and along his body. It rolled across his weakened muscles. The chains around his head gave him enough leeway for marginal movement but nothing spectacular. The guards before him set the carts at appropriate distances. Mostly. The cart on the left, Mihska's cart, was closer than it should be. Rhonkan looked into the golden eyes of the soldier pushing the cart. For a heartbeat, the soldier's eyes burned with a familiar fire.

Rhonkan turned his head away. "You are a barbarian. To slay children in an attempt to gain leverage is unseemly."

The prince was sly. He had trapped and chained a mated dragon. Stolen a clutch of eggs, too. "It may be, Dragon, but you won't give me your name. Perhaps with the eggs present, you will be more conventional in your approach to cooperation."

Rhonkan bowed, appeasing human arrogance, tilting his head once while carefully avoiding a view of the eggs or guards. He then laid his massive head on the stone, facing away from the carts and their cargo. When he closed his eyes, golden eyes stared back at him through the dark.

He let his song take flight in the void. Thirty years of capture and now a wyvern, a youngling, a dragon not yet risen to adulthood, had come. He could sing of freedom.

Footsteps on the stairs roused him from slumber, and he turned toward the sound. Circumstances seemed to dictate the prince wanted another go at breaking him. He eyed the egg-laden carts. He could reach one if he wanted, but he didn't know the plan, and his mind couldn't stay on it with steel's fog in his blood. He'd wait; he'd been doing that for decades already and saw no need to rush into a mistake when help had finally managed to arrive.

The prince barreled through the door, three guards in tow, and the jailor rushing to strike the gong in announcement. The guard closest to the prince was the one who had flashed golden eyes. There was more to him, too, but Rhonkan couldn't free enough of his senses to sort it out. This morning, the guard's eyes were blue, causing Rhonkan a confusion his addled senses couldn't unravel.

The blue-eyed guard stood to the prince's right, sheathed sword standing tall above his shoulders. The other two guards stood behind him, one to either side in a small triangle of steel. The prince put a hand on his sword and pointed a finger at his captured dragon.

"I am through with polite discussions!"

It was a shout and a command. The room flowed into motion from there. The rear two guards rushed forward to grab the blue-eyed wyvern while the prince raced to the closer cart and grabbed one of the eggs. Lifting it from the cart, the prince stalked to Rhonkan's side and ripped the poniard free. Glaring malevolently, he rammed it into the egg. The pierced egg shuttered, a crack running its length. The prince slammed it into the stones of the dungeon floor.

Rhonkan's eyes flared wide in terror as the implications tumbled through him. He could do nothing as the hatchling spilled out onto the stones. He freed a rumble from his throat, a great and terrible sound, loosing dust and dirt from mortar. A handful of scurrying things raced from hiding places in a rush to be elsewhere. He set free his song to his children in the void, closing his eyes to see their souls.

They were livid, screeching, and screaming at the ignominy. Mihska bowed and leaped from her cloud, spiraling in the ethereal of between. She faded from the sky. When Rhonkan opened his eyes, she was staring at him from a broken body mewling on the stone floor at the prince's feet.

Her soft eyes caught his and held them. He lowered his head to try to nuzzle her and wish her well on her journey, but the chains, bit, and spikes forbade it. He kicked the claw bone from the prince's last visit to his daughter. She nestled her head against the bone, sniffing it daintily before her too-weak body gave up, and her spirit disappeared. He and Mihska wouldn't see each other again in this world.

The wyvern warrior spun to life in the same instant Rhonkan's daughter was birthed, lived, and died. Three feet of glistening silvered steel flashed free of the sheath on his back as the now golden-eyed warrior danced free of the encircling gauntlet and worked the sword in a blinding arc. For all the hope hisA presence engendered in Rhonkan, the reality collapsed under the weight of calamitous inexperience.

The sword's arc failed instantly as the wyvern had jumped too near Rhonkan. The sword clanged angrily off the steel bit in the dragon's mouth. The wyvern stumbled, retreated several paces, and flailed with spectacular inconsistency. The two guards stalking him spread out and began a methodical advance.

Rhonkan's heart sank. He couldn't turn to help and heard the sword slam into stone and chain, time and again. The other guards laughed and chided their quarry. Nothing the youngling tried delayed his pursuers. The wyvern was cut and bleeding in several places when they circled back to the front. Curiously, no blood dripped from the swords of the other guards. The fool cut himself!

In a last lunging effort, the youngling swung the glistening sword at the guard next to Rhonkan's hide. He missed and sliced through Rhonkan's scales instead. There was pain, sharp and fierce, but no sting, no poison. Then the inept swordsman stumbled against Rhonkan's bulk, collapsing into his side and pressing his head into the giant dragon while speaking in the dragon tongue.

The guards were on him in an instant, clubbing him senseless and dragging him from Rhonkan's side. The prince shook his head slowly, *tsk-tsking*.

"Ahh, Dragon. When will your kind learn? You cannot bribe us and play on our human sympathies. You cannot beat us. We are too many, too clever. Even for the likes of magical beasties like yourselves."

The prince grabbed a corner of the wyvern's cloak and cleaned his blade before sheathing the knife. Then he picked up the sword.

"This is a fine blade. It is so much more than the likes of this," he waved a disinterested hand at the captured man, "should ever own. I think I will keep it for myself."

The prince motioned for the guards to drag the man out of the dungeon before turning back to Rhonkan. He pointed to the dead hatchling. "See your folly, Dragon?"

Rhonkan wanted to avert his eyes from the scene but would not deny Mihska the honor of his gaze. He hadn't moved since his daughter had died, frozen in time and transfixed by both his failure and that of the wyvern.

He closed his eyes and sang to his children. It was all he had. His anger and shame wrestled, and both found voice through his song. His children came to hear. They bowed their heads and rumbled for their lost sister.

"I am sorry, my children."

Khelohm roared, fierce and bright. "It is as planned, Father. Aarik told us so."

"Aarik? Is that his name? I don't think his plan worked. He was taken."

Rhisa flared the golden scales along her neck. "He will be a cunning dragon, papa. I wonder if we will have a chance to mate. Our brood would be the fiercest dragons in an Age."

Rhonkan shook his head as he watched her spinning in the air, the sun sparkling off her golden scales. He spoke into the void. "He was less than adept."

Ghena spoke up next, her green scales washing back and forth like a forest in a gentle breeze, "Was he, Father? What did he say to you? The iron sickens you, and you miss things."

"Yes, Father," Elikhen said. "He spoke to you. Remember his words?"

Elikhan followed quickly, "He fought with a *mithril* blade. He sliced you with it, too, to let its power seep into you and fight the bite of steel. He used it on your chains and the bit in your mouth. And then he left you with us."

Rhonkan replayed the battle in his mind. He saw the first wild swing of the sword and the exactness with which the blade struck the chain of the bit. He saw the *mithril* hammer through the steel and leave it broken. He remembered the other times the blade had bitten into his chains. His mind had steel-stained holes, though. Ghena was right. He had missed things.

Rhisa continued, "He asked us if we would be willing to help. We said yes, of course. He told us it would be dangerous. Mihska knew, too. We all did."

A chorus of voices answered in ascent, "We all knew, Father. Mihska is a dragon. A true dragon, Father. So is Aarik. He is a youngling no more."

Rhisa leaped into the air and soared on golden wings. "And he will be a golden, papa. Like me!" She spun in the air and spread her wings to stop, turn, and glide back to the ground. "Free yourself. Breathe on us. We are ready."

Rhonkan opened his eyes. A rumble thundered from his chest. He struggled to contain it, daring to hope. Such a clever plan and ruse. Such a selfless act. Yes, Aarik will be, *is*, a golden. It could not be challenged. Rhonkan crouched low, tensing. He whipped his head to the side with sudden ferocity, snapping the bit's chain and forcing its surrender. The chain snaked through, and he spat the bit.

He opened and closed his mouth several times, free of steel's stain. Freedom's closeness coursed through him. He pried the spike in his front paw with his teeth, snapping its chain in the process, and freed his rear paw, too. Lastly, he turned to the spike in his tail and spat fire at it. It hurt as the steel melted and poured through the hole in his tail until it pooled on the ground underneath, dripping to the chamber below. He was free. Shaking himself, he spun in several careful circles, testing his limbs.

For the first time in decades, he shifted into human form. The steel had not permitted it. He gathered his eggs, setting them against the outer wall behind him. He settled Mihska's egg and body, too. When ready, he shifted back and breathed fire on the eggs. They warmed, thrumming in the heat. He gave a second, longer breath, raising their temperatures further and setting the rocks of the cliff a-glow. Finally, Rhonkan breathed the birthing fire he had held for so long.

Thin cracks and fractures appeared all over the eggs. The cracks became holes. The holes grew larger as the younglings clawed their way forth. As they left their eggs, their souls left the in-between. Rhonkan sang to them as the two meshed, body and soul united forever after decades of waiting.

A thunderous crash shook the room. Rhonkan spread his wings and cast his bulk between his young and the cell door. His children continued frolicking in the molten stone, wriggling on the ground, and then hopping and flapping their wings in glee. They chirped at each other and practiced little dragon roars. Rhisa stalked her siblings, wings spread wide and hopping from foot to foot in mock bravery. The room echoed with their sounds and glowed with the eerie red light of heated rock.

With a CRACK, the exterior wall faltered, and coolness rushed into the stale dungeon. Rhonkan breathed in long draughts of pine-scented air. He could taste the river, too, and fresh-cut hay. There was a gloriousness in all of it. He pawed at the wall to widen the hole, heedless of the burning stone's molten touch. The hatchlings were immune to the heat of birthing; it gave them life and vitality, without which they all would have perished as Mihska had. Rhonkan, though, wasn't.

The cell door blew apart, and a wave of super-heated air pummeled them. It had come from the far side of the castle, blasting through hallways and doors to rock their little cell. It blew dust and stone from still piles into whirling dervishes. An angry roar chased the super-heated wind.

Rhonkan turned toward the roar; he hadn't seen his brother in a very long time.

Rhonkan found the prison cell holding Aarik. Then, using what magic had found its way back to him following his freedom from the steel, burst the door inward. Limping, the pain from the knife wounds in his thigh still stinging, Rhonkan entered, strode to Aarik, and soundly slapped him.

"Why are you here?" Rhonkan asked.

"I came to free you."

"Is that all? To free me? I am a dragon. I don't need freeing."

"I came also for the eggs."

Rhonkan locked eyes with Aarik, noticing the fierce, golden fire deep within them. Disquiet slid across the youngling's face, though, anxiety building in his shoulders. Rhonkan said coldly, "You're too late."

The golden eyes flared wide, and he gasped, "Where are they? Certainly, the prince didn't do anything more before Bhethor attacked!"

When Aarik collapsed, Rhonkan rested a hand on the youngling's shoulder, "Perhaps my years in confinement have left me bereft of certain social norms, Aarik. My children speak highly of you."

"They are fighters. And yes, I am Aarik, son to Mhrassen, your mate's sister."

Rhonkan nodded, "I smell it. It is good to smell again. What I meant to imply is that my eggs have hatched. I've sent them down the cliff and toward the forest and river on that side of the castle."

The fortress shook in the tumult of too much dragon in too little a space playing out above. Both dragons steadied their human-form selves. Rhonkan considered Aarik before continuing, "You've earned your color, Aarik. Business here yet, though, join my brother above while I see to my children."

Aarik nodded, "We will be with you shortly."

"Beware their steel, Aarik. It is not something for which a dragon is ever ready."

Rhonkan turned through the raining dust and headed back to his former cell. Once there, he transformed and launched himself at the fractured wall. Stone collapsed with his impact, and he pummeled his way through. Below, he could see his children bounding down the slope in miniature hops and short flights. Their wings weren't yet ready for more.

He landed upslope, sending a torrent of rubble crashing into the tree line. Chirps and flaps answered back, and he trumpeted with gusto. No sooner had he landed than Aarik winged from the fortress above and landed next to him, an arrow in his shoulder and another in his hip. He had his sword, though. Together, they found and followed the baby dragons.

"Come forward, children. Let me look upon you under the light of the sun."

Rhisa bounded from behind a fallen tree, flapping into the sun and chirping. She raced straight past Rhonkan and bounced at Aarik's feet, exhorting him to stand and spread his wings. Rhonkan was going to chastise her, but children needed heroes, too, and the young dragon had proved himself such.

The twins slithered forward, laughing at Rhisa. Their form tended more snakelike than bulky dragon, and they wrapped themselves around each of their father's captivity-thinned legs. He folded his wings back to shade them from the sun's glare as they looked up at him.

They had barely settled before Khelohm rushed from the rocky trail farther down and came barreling into Rhonkan. He hopped quickly and managed enough wing-assisted lift to launch himself. The little dragon hit with a thud and a miniature bellow, coughing smoke as his tiny talons found purchase on thick scales.

Last came Ghena, her patience contrasting with the exuberance of her siblings. Rhonkan, belabored by the miniature weight of three of his offspring already, bent and picked her up, settling her on his shoulder where his wings joined. Looking out over the collection of dragonkind, her wings arched back and teeth-filled maw wide with her effort, she roared triumphantly.

Bhethor landed farther away and struggled to join them. The pain of his hurts and the stain of iron having an obvious and deleterious effect on the gold dragon. Rhonkan, thirty years a captive and slave, seemed to have the best shot at defending all of them with a brood of hatchlings and two wounded goldens.

"We need to move," he offered. "The prince will be here shortly, and he will come to enslave us all. The sooner we can get away, the better."

Aarik looked up and nodded, "I agree." He shook his head to clear it. "I don't know how you stood the iron stain for so long. It is tearing my soul apart."

"Pain helped me focus. And I had my children."

Rhisa raced around Aarik's legs, chirping excitedly as the bulk of Aarik's dragon form cast her in shade. Her siblings risked chortling at her, but she stopped and spun on them, back arched, wings half spread behind her. She hissed at them and stalked forward, ready to defend her honor and hero.

"Young Aarik," Bhethor added, "it looks as if you have a charge." He waded past a tree to join the group. "Rhonkan is right. We must move. Now. I will lead. Since the young can't fly, we will go on foot. I would prefer to stay in dragon form, but we will be slowed too much by the forest. We walk as our lesser selves." He looked at Aarik and Rhonkan before finishing, "Stay alert and keep the young between you."

Several hours later, Bhethor limped into a small clearing. Aarik brought up the rear, limping as well. Rhisa darted over, chirping at the youngling's hurts. Bhethor smiled, bemused, before gazing at an open skyline toward the river. "Brother, shall we leave this unholy place?"

Before Rhonkan could answer, the prince strode, uncaring and without fear, into the clearing. "No. I think not!"

Ghena looked up from where she sat before darting back into the bushes. Rhisa crouched at the feet of Aarik. Her roar was soft, barely a bark, but her eyes beamed with intensity. The others moved closer together.

The prince took it all in. "Dragon, you've done well. I figured the only way to get the eggs to hatch was to let you sniff freedom." He cast a beaming smile on the little ones, "I didn't count on their voracity."

The prince began an incantation. A shimmering dome coalesced over himself and Rhonkan. Aarik recognized the battle-ward and heaved the *mithril* sword through its gathering mist. Rhonkan caught it and began his half of the incantation. They would fight under a weave of the arcane; none would enter—none could enter—until one of them was dead. It was dragon magic, stolen by the prince over the decades.

The prince attacked immediately, slashing with his sword and hammering at Rhonkan with a steel shield. The shield hurt, and though he parried brilliantly and the *mithril* blade stung the prince several times, the brute force of a warrior in his prime against a weary recent captive began to take its toll. He would not be able to transform, either. The casting required both to fight in the form held when voiced.

Soon, the steel began robbing him of energy, fogging his mind. He slipped and bought a wicked cut across an exposed shoulder for the error. More poison. More fog. More pain.

Rhonkan fled to the opposite side of the dome and laid the *mithril* blade against his new shoulder wound. The cool blade slid across the angry cut, drawing forth the poison. No magic could be used in the dome. But properties of the elements would work. The steel and its counter, *mithril*, proving the point. *Mithril* gave more than steel took, though. It focused Rhonkan's mind, lent him strength, and wove itself into his mettle. He became the sword.

As one, they advanced.

"Come, Dragon," the prince taunted, "it is time to die."

Rhonkan obliged, feigning injury and confusion, "I concur."

Rhonkan's parries were sharp, and his *mithril*-fueled body raged against the prince. When the opening presented itself, Rhonkan slid sideways, parried harder than usual to turn the prince's body, and thrust the *mithril* blade through the gap in the armor under the prince's shoulder. The ward flickered and went out as the prince slid off the blade.

Rhonkan turned to Aarik, "Your sword is truly wonderful. What fine craftsmanship." He handed it back.

A sudden roar erupted from above the river. Aarik raised his sword to the sky and shifted form, "Mhressen, Dhaksana, to me."

The blues circled and landed, crushing a few small trees and bushes. The three dragons escorting the children transformed back as Rhisa chirped, "Oh, she's pretty."

Aarik felt the color rise in his cheeks but covered it with a rueful smile. He bowed to the larger dragon, "Mother." He turned to the one Rhisa spoke of, "Dhaksana."

Mhressen cast her eyes about the older dragons, "Can you fly?"

They nodded.

"Then we fly. One child apiece."

It took a moment to sort adult and child, but they took wing quickly. Rhonkan led. It had been a long while since he'd been home.

KT Morley is an Eastern Pennsylvanian author. He spent twenty years conspiring to teach the youth of America about Algebra and the plight of a hopelessly lost X before advancing to manage his school's Humanities department. He has published in several anthologies: Rogue Blades Entertainment's *Crossbones and* Crosses and *Death's Sting*, and the Dragon Soul Press Anthology *Coffins and Dragons*.His latest anthology work, *21 Futures: Tales from the Timechain* by Konsensus Network, released in the fall of 2023.

Learn more about KT at: Facebook | Instagram | Author Website

D.A. Schneider

I soared through the sky knowing I wouldn't be caught. Beneath me was my faithful companion over the past ten years, his massive wings cutting through the air, his green-black scales reflecting the light from the full moon overhead, his eyes gleaming with mischievous glee, the dragon called Slate.

On the ground below, several soldiers gave chase on horseback, futilely shooting arrows our way. With the dragon's speed, we were out of range just moments after liftoff.

Slung on the saddle around me were several bags of coin we'd procured from the king's stores, as well as a few extra items that caught my eye. Paranoid about losing his wealth and power, King Stephon had taken to hiding his money and treasures in several different "secure" locations around the country. Apparently, the vaults were not dragon-proof. It was the second one we'd hit.

Slate soared over the vast River of Ateon and toward the small island where we'd set up camp. There, he landed and lowered his neck so that I could slide down to the ground. "Well, another successful score, my friend," I called to the dragon. He shook his head and grunted, which I knew was his way of celebrating. "Sure, we're wanted by four of the seven kingdoms, but it's a small price to pay for all these riches."

The dragon dropped to his belly and rested his head on his front claws. It was a position I knew all too well. He was ready for a nap.

"Hey, buddy," I went on. "I grabbed something special. Do you want to see?" I lifted one of the bags from the saddle on Slate's neck, then reached inside and pulled a bottle of brown glass from within. "Rum," I called, triumphantly. The dragon raised his head to examine my prize. "And you know what's better than a bottle of rum?" I stuck my free hand in the bag and then pulled it out. "Two bottles of rum."

At this, I could swear the dragon shook his head and rolled his eyes. He dropped his head down once more and I left him to his rest, content to build a fire and enjoy my drink alone. I was halfway through the first bottle by the time I got the fire going. Slate was snoring away. He had no need for campfires or rum.

Within a couple of hours, I had the fire roaring, and I was fairly well blazed myself. My dragon friend stood suddenly and sniffed at the air. This was a fairly common occurrence and it meant that he smelled something tasty on the wind.

"Go on and get your dinner," I shouted, my words coming out slurry and stunted.

The dragon raised his wings and the downward thrust created a gust of wind that nearly bowled me off my feet. I only chuckled and tossed another log on the fire. Life was good. I had a faithful friend who was a dragon. And we had a connection. He couldn't speak, but I understood him well enough. His grunts and growls, his facial expressions, his mannerisms. What seemed like nothing to others was crystal clear to me.

By the time I cracked open the second bottle of rum, I had the flames of the fire as tall as a man, and Slate had yet to return from his hunt for supper. I sat (for the act of standing had grown far too difficult at that point) and pondered our next move, mesmerized by the crackling embers of the fire.

Then I caught movement on the other side. Men were emerging from the woods. Soldiers. They must have come ashore by boat. How had they found us?

"Your fire was a great beacon," the lead man said as if he had read my mind. "Thanks for showing us the way."

I reached for the hilt of my sword, unsheathed it, and with an enormous amount of difficulty, got to my feet. However, I was far more pissed than I realized and fell right back down on my ass.

The soldiers laughed at my drunkenness and the lead one spoke again. "Cort Sashi, you are under arrest and hereby charged with-"

Suddenly, the faces of all the men (I saw eight but there may have been only four) changed from glee to fear in an instant and I saw the large, clawed foot of Slate drop down just in front of me. A stream of fire engulfed the soldiers and that was the last thing I remembered, as I slumped sideways and let unconsciousness take me.

I came too only briefly and realized I was clutched limply in my dragon's foot as we flew through the sky. Then I returned to darkness.

When next I woke, it was to a blinding white pain ripping through my skull. I found it difficult to open my eyes. There was a fire nearby, of that much I was certain, for I could feel the heat as it cradled me like a baby. As much as I wanted to return to sleep, the pounding in my head refused to let me. Then my stomach lurched and I knew I was going to vomit.

"Oh no," said a female voice from nearby. A wooden pail was shoved into my hand. "Here you are."

The contents of my stomach (which mostly consisted of rum) splashed into the bucket. I heaved three more times, and once I was finished, I dropped back on the pillow, my head pounding even worse than before.

"Drink this," said the strange woman. "It will help."

I blindly took the cup and sipped its contents. It was water, but the texture told me it was mixed with some sort of powder. Or medicine perhaps. The pain did abate ever so slightly. Enough so that I could at least open my eyes and see who my savior was.

At first sight, I thought there were diamonds weaved into her hair. They sparkled in the firelight and gave her an almost angelic radiance. For one panicked moment, I was sure I was dead. Then my vision cleared a little more and I saw that there were ice crystals and not diamonds in her hair. Her dark, cocoa-colored skin clashed with a pair of eyes as blue as a summer sky. She was breathtaking.

"You're Mankish," I said, referring to the people of the north who had the ability to manipulate water and ice.

Her smile was indescribably beautiful. "That's right, I am."

"What are you doing *here*?" I asked.

Confusion set in now. "Well, I live here."

"No," I clarified, "I mean what are you doing so far south?"

Now she seemed somewhat guilty. "Oh…I um…that is to say…"

And then it dawned on me. My jaw went slack and my eyes wide. Forgetting my splitting headache for a moment, I clambered to my feet and stumble-walked to the front door of the little cabin. With hands that seemed as though they belonged to someone else, I twisted the knob and pulled the door open. That's when I saw the rolling, snow-covered hills and Mt. Sussick blotting out the sky like the spinal plate of a huffamoose. Slate was lying on the crest of one of the hills and at the sight of me, he raised his head and grunted. This translated to a sarcastic, *What?*

The girl gave a nervous little laugh behind me and said, "Welcome to Mank."

Mank was the farthest country north in the western hemisphere, and its frigid temperatures were only surpassed by the desolate and lifeless land mass at the south pole only known as "the country with no name". Imaginative, I know. I was aware Slate had brought us here, but I had no idea why. I was, in a word, bewildered.

I closed the door and turned to my host, attempting to snag one of the many questions tumbling around my aching head. Moving back toward the bed, light from the fire cast my shadow on the wall and I was made aware that my usually immaculate, dirty blonde mane was smooshed in on one side and sticking straight up in the air on the other. There I was in the presence of this gorgeous creature who was trying to nurse me back from a night of too much rum, and I was suffering from a serious case of bedhead.

"Please," said the Mankish girl, "get back in bed. You need to relax, and I will explain everything to you. All your questions will be answered."

"All of them?" I asked, raking my hands over my scalp in an effort to tame my wild hair.

"Every single one," she replied. "I promise."

I climbed back into bed and she pulled the blanket up to my chest, giving me a feeling of warmth and coziness that I hadn't experienced since I was a child. This, plus the heat from the fire, quickly thawed the bracing, frigid air I felt from the few minutes I had the door open.

"Let's begin with introductions," said the girl, dropping down on the chair beside the bed. "My name is Layla."

I nodded dreamily. "Layla. That's pretty. I'm Cort."

"Cort Sashi, yes I know." She said this as if she'd always wanted to meet me. "The cross-shaped scar on your cheek gave you away. That, and the giant, black dragon you call friend."

"Okay," I said, uncertain.

"Your story has become legend," Layla continued. "A former dragon knight who turned to a life of crime after the war ended and the dragon knights were disbanded. The stories have even made it all the way up here."

Although I found this fascinating, it wasn't my major concern at that moment. "Can you tell me why I'm three thousand miles away from home?"

"That started with Slate," Layla began. "As I'm sure you know, dragons can sense each other, even over vast distances. That's what brought Slate here originally. He returned twice after that."

I thought back to a couple of instances when Slate had gone off for a day or two. I never worried that he wouldn't return, he always returned. "So, there's another dragon nearby?"

"Yes," Layla answered. "But things are slightly more complicated than that."

"How do you mean?"

Layla looked down at her hands, folded in her lap, and the movement made the icicles in her hair tingle like wind chimes. "There's another dragon knight who has set up camp to the south of us along with a small army of monsters I'm not familiar with. He is a large man with a bushy black beard."

"He rides a red dragon," I finished.

She studied me, suddenly serious. "You know him."

I nodded. "His name is Rayker. We were dragon knights at the same time. He was…surly, cruel, power-hungry. An all-around jerk."

"Now, he torments my people," Layla said. "The town down in the valley is called Snowden. The people look to me for leadership. My father was their king but he's taken up a quest for an ancient object that legends say could make one immortal. He's been obsessed with it for more than a decade now. I have no idea if he's even still alive. In his absence, I have ruled and things have been peaceful and prosperous. Until this man arrived. He burns houses, pillages food stores, and I am desperate to be rid of him. I believe Slate has brought you here to help."

I barked laughter and her look of concern turned to one of surprise. "I'm not a knight any longer," I explained. "I'm a thief. I break into the vaults of lords and kings and relieve them of their coin. Then I run. Gods, I can't even remember the last time I crossed swords with someone."

Tears filled Layla's eyes, but when she spoke, her voice was infused with anger. "I'm a *damn* good fighter myself, but I cannot stand against a dragon. If I didn't need your help, I wouldn't ask. And if you aren't *willing* to help, Slate certainly is, or else you wouldn't be here. If you'll kindly loan me your dragon, I'll take care of this problem myself."

I let out a sigh and knew she would do just that. She was right, Slate had brought us all this way. It was clear he had a stake in this fight, even if I wanted no part. "Riding a dragon takes a little more than just hopping in the saddle. I will help you. With more of your medicine, and perhaps some coffee, I should be fit enough to scout Rayker's camp later tonight and see what we're up against."

This made her happy and I have to admit, I liked seeing her happy.

Layla came through on the medicine and coffee. She also fed me a thick sandwich stuffed with pork and lettuce. All this went a long way in restoring me to my normal self, even if my eyes were red and puffy from a morning spent bent over the wooden pale. As night fell, I climbed into the saddle at the base of Slate's neck, now protected against the cold with heavy furs supplied by our host.

"Another fine mess you've gotten us into," I said to the dragon.

He shook his head and gave a short chirp. He was laughing at me.

Layla handed up a bag. "This should help. There's a looking glass and a loaf of bread in there. The latter in case your stomach sours again."

"Thank you," I said. "We shall return soon."

We flew low and landed on a ledge just above Rayker's encampment. Then I dropped from the saddle to the snow and we crept to the edge to get a good look. The tents were lined up in rows, with the red dragon sleeping at the rear, and I could see several soldiers milling around near fire pits. I used the looking glass for a better look.

"Tenziers," I said. The monsters were similar to orcs, only they were shorter and more compatible with humans since they didn't crave human flesh. I looked up at Slate. "You know, Rayker is a wanted man. If we could capture or kill him, we could claim the bounty."

The dragon gave me a dubious look with one eyebrow raised.

"Okay, sure, the fact that I am also a wanted man would make it difficult to claim that bounty," I conceded. "However, Layla could claim the bounty. She could use it to rebuild the houses in town and recover from the attacks. And, if she sees fit to kick a little our way as a reward, so be it."

Slate nodded at this. He liked the idea.

"What do you think?" I asked. "Sneak attack at dawn?"

Slate gave a grunt and another nod. The plan sounded good to him. With that, we quietly moved away from the ridge and flew back to Layla's cabin under the cover of darkness.

After dropping me off, Slate went on the hunt for his dinner. Lyla opened the door to her cabin as I approached. "Well?" she asked. "What are our chances?"

I nodded. "Good," I replied. "Better than I expected, in fact."

As I warmed by the fire, I drew a crude map of Rayker's camp on a piece of parchment, then began to lay out our plan. "Does your town have warriors?"

"Just a handful," she answered, leaning over the map. "Most left with my father, but those who stayed behind are skilled."

"Good, they should be more than enough." I used a saltshaker on the map. "This will be your team. Lead them over the ridge and to this group of evergreens. Wait there until Slate and I make our first sweep. Once we lure Rayker and his dragon away, your team can go in and clean up the remaining soldiers."

"And Rayker?" she asked.

"Let us worry about Rayker." The fight wouldn't be easy. In fact, during training sessions, I had sparred with Rayker on several occasions and never won. I figured this information was better kept from Layla. "We attack at dawn, so have your team in place."

"I'll head to town now and gather them," she said. "Please, make yourself at home. Eat and drink but stay away from my rum."

I raised my hands. "Don't worry. I learned that lesson the hard way."

I spent the rest of the evening preparing for battle. Above all, I wanted to stay warm and knew a fight at high altitudes would mean even colder air. I helped myself to Layla's collection of furs and picked out a woolen cap that would cover my ears.

Layla returned with her team of Mankish ice warriors just as Slate returned from his hunt. They were five men and two women, all with similar dark skin and icy hair, but rather than Layla's brilliant blue eyes, they were either brown or black.

Once they were prepared, I wished them good luck. "I will give you an hour head start," I added. "By then, you should be in position."

They agreed and went on their way.

As I waited, I searched the upstairs bedrooms of the cabin and found an impressive array of weapons in a display cabinet. It looked as though Layla had loaded up, and I wondered if the others had similar armories in their own homes. Or perhaps they had a central collection that the town shared. I added a set of throwing knives to my belt and three powder bombs to the pouch inside my coat.

After an hour had passed, I walked up the snowy hill to Slate. The dragon's green-black scales bristled with anticipation. He was ready for a fight. It had been far too long. I climbed up into the saddle and spoke. "Let's show them what we can do, old friend."

His wings spread and he pushed off the ground. Soon, we were nearing the enemy camp.

The first light of the sun was creeping up on the horizon as Rayker's camp came into view. Slate glided on the frigid winds and awaited my command. I held tightly to the pommel and shouted, "Light it up!"

Slate pinned his wings back and dove. As we neared the ground, he leveled out and opened his mouth to spew a spray of flames as we passed over. The tents erupted and we turned for another pass. Fire rained down on the army of Tenziers and their screams of agony broke through the night. I was hopeful we'd taken out Rayker as well, but farther to the south, we caught sight of him mounting his dragon. It was time to take the fight to the skies.

"Up, Slate," I called. The dragon responded by climbing upward as Rayker chased after. Far below, I could see dark figures moving across the snow-covered ground and knew it was Layla and her team moving in to clean up the last of the Tenziers.

The sky had lightened, chasing the last bit of night away and giving us a better view of our enemies. The red dragon was larger, stronger than Slate, but my dragon had the advantages of speed and agility. Upward we climbed until I pulled on the reins.

Slate folded his wings in and we spun in mid-air to face our pursuers. We dropped fast, only pulling up as we drew nearer to Rayker and his beast. Slate expanded his wings to slow his descent and spit fire, the stream engulfed the red dragon, singeing its wings as it flipped to avoid any further damage.

The red dragon had a head covered in spiky horns (instead of the sleek fin that curved back from Slate's) and a ball at the tip of his tail with matching spikes. It opened its mouth wide and released a stream of fire that Slate barrel-rolled away from. We dodged the attack, but I felt the heat.

Then the dragon was on us, attacking with its clawed feet. Slate fought back and I pulled two of the throwing knives from beneath my furs. I let them both fly at once, catching the dragon in the neck with one, while the second hit home in Rayker's thigh.

The villain cried out in pain. "Blast it, Cort! Ye'll not walk away from this fight."

Slate managed to pull away from the red dragon's clutches and we dove back toward the ground. Rayker and his beast followed, spitting balls of fire as we went. I pulled the powder bombs from my pouch. I had an idea and hoped it would work. I knew it would take careful timing. Just as the red dragon spit another fireball, I let all three powder bombs go. They seemed to stand still as we fell away from them, and the red dragon approached. The creature spit another fireball just as the bombs neared its head. The powder balls exploded in a cloud of fire and smoke, and the concussion knocked the dragon unconscious.

Slate pulled up and the red dragon hit the ground, sending a wave of snow into the air and throwing Rayker from its back. Slate landed beside the man, and I pulled my sword, although there was no need. Rayker was as out of commission as his dragon.

Cheers from behind us. Layla and her team had the remaining monsters on the run and were celebrating the defeat of Rayker and the red dragon.

In the end, Layla collected the bounty on Rayker. The money went to rebuild the town as I'd guessed, and when she offered Slate and me a bag of coins for our help, we didn't turn it down. We didn't leave either. At least not right away.

Rather than turn the red dragon over to the authorities, who would have likely put her down, I had the town's folk help me chain her up in a nearby cave. It would take some time, but I wanted to retrain her to another rider. With Slate's help, I knew it was something we could manage.

"Who will you train as the new rider?" Layla asked over supper one evening. Things were finally getting back to normal in Snowden and Layla and I had grown to be close friends, although I must admit I was hopeful we'd become more, but that's a story for another time.

"Well," I replied, "I was thinking I could train you."

"Me?" said Layla, flabbergasted.

"Rayker is set to be executed for his crimes in less than a week," I explained. "When that happens, his connection to the dragon will be broken. She will be ready to connect with someone new. It should be you."

"Why me?"

I shrugged. "You are a great ruler. The people look to you for protection. A dragon at your command would be highly advantageous."

There was a pause as Layla pondered this. Finally, she nodded. "Okay. Let's do it."

With her in agreement, I smiled. I was sincere in my assessment, but what I didn't say (and what I suspected Layla already knew) was that I wanted an excuse to stick around and get to know her better. And there it was.

Outside, I climbed onto the saddle at the base of Slate's neck. He gave a shake of his head and looked back at me. "Feel like a flight, old friend."

Wearing what I could have sworn was a smile, the dragon lifted off the ground. It was the first of what would become a nightly scout of the town and the surrounding valley. Although it was cold and barren, a place where the sun seemed to be a stranger, Mank was growing on me. So too was the town of Snowden. More than any other place I'd been to in the world, I could see myself settling down in the snowy countryside. The fact that it was one of the last countries in the world where I *wasn't* a wanted man was certainly a bonus.

D.A. Schneider is an author of horror and mystery who lives in Indianapolis, IN. After trying for some time to break into the comic book industry with his artwork, D.A. decided to focus on writing instead. A former NFL and entertainment columnist, D.A.'s most recent books include the cozy murder mystery Death of a Scholar (Holly Reynolds Mysteries Book 1) and the horror/crime novel Salvation. D.A. also writes fantasy under the name G.R.V. Stone.

Learn more about D.A. at:
Author Website | Amazon | Barnes and Noble | Audible | Instagram

Curtis Moore

The most dangerous part of putting the first ride on a young dragon wasn't the teeth or the tail; the saddle sat just over the shoulder where neither of those parts could do any damage. It was the wings and the claws. The wings could knock a man senseless if he got too far over the dragon's shoulders when it jumped. A rider who fell off a twisting, plunging fledgling was liable to get caught by the scrabbling talons and torn to bits before he could get out from under the animal.

Bayard knew this. Those claws were at the front of his mind as he stepped into the round pen with the glittering red dragon, resting the heavy leather saddle against his hip. The danger was part of the job. He didn't necessarily relish it, but he didn't mind it so much. It kept a man honest, and required him to put the animal's needs before his own. Getting on a fledgling who wasn't ready could set her training back weeks, unraveling the work he'd done to build trust and teach her to give to pressure. That was enough to convince him to wait until the time was right, but the threat of getting thinly skived was a good incentive as well.

The buckles on the straps tinkled as he swung it over the top rail of the fence. The dragon's eyes followed the saddle, but she made no move to get away from the noise.

"Morning, sivax," he said softly. He didn't name the dragons. Their riders, properly known as the Knights of the Wyrm, would name them once they were assigned to their string of dragons. Until then he called them by sivax, if they were female, or velox, if they were male.

The dragon snuffed back at him, stepping forward and extending her nose toward the pouch on his belt, looking for treats. Bayard smiled. Fifteen years ago he'd have said he didn't believe in giving an animal treats just for doing what it was supposed to. Now, at thirty-five, he saw a certain value in making his job just a bit easier.

"You've got to do something for it first," he pulled a dried fish from the pouch and held it between his fingers. With his other hand he made a wide circle over his head. "Come by!"

The sivax launched herself into the air and spread her wings, gliding around the pen two full times before coming to rest across from him, her front feet extended so her shoulders were low to the ground. She waited, perfectly still, until he twitched his hand and she relaxed, snaking her head toward him to collect the fish. Her delicate nose tapered to a point about the size of the palm of his hand.

A dragon this age only stood about eighteen hands at the shoulder. Over the next two years she would shoot up to closer to thirty, her wings would extend to four times her height, and her body would lengthen to be nearly forty feet long. During that time her gas bladder would expand, giving her the ability to breathe fire with magical assistance, and her spiked tail would lengthen and narrow into a whip at the end, becoming a deadly weapon in its own right. The last three years of training had been focused on gaining the dragon's trust and confidence, leading up to this first ride. From here on out the focus would be on flying as she learned to maneuver with a rider on her back.

Bayard slipped the hackamore over her nose, fastened it behind her budding horns.

"There you go, love," he ran his hand along her jaw, scratching her favorite spot where the hard, sharp scales on her face gave way to the smooth horn of her nose.

Next he settled the saddle right behind her wings, and buckled the leather straps to keep it in place. Her nose followed him as he moved around her, waiting for the flap on the pouch to open so she could get another fish. When she pushed too hard he would push the nose away, talking to her in low, calm tones.

"Someone should make you into dragon bacon," he said in the same tone he used to call her "love." "Or maybe some kind of stew. You're too tough to make a good bacon."

She got another fish now that she was tacked up and he rubbed her neck, alternating between praising her and debating how she would taste. Finally, he touched the back of her leg, right above the wickedly hooked spur that jutted out right above her ankle, with his boot. The sivax cocked her head, and he touched the same spot again. Recognizing the command, she leaned forward and knelt, bringing her shoulder close enough to the ground that his hanging stirrup nearly touched the dirt.

"You're going to behave well enough that I'm going to have to go through with this, aren't you?"

The dragon slurped up another fish.

"You're awfully cocky today. Fine, try this. *Famel*!"

He pushed against her ribs with the stirrup as he spoke, and the dragon opened her mouth and released a huge belch. The gas from her internal bladder, poisonous in its own right, could be ignited with magic in battle. Releasing the lighter-than-air gas would also make her a little heavier, and keep her from flying quite so high during their first ride.

"You're pretty proud of yourself, aren't you?"

The sivax gulped down another fish.

Bayard led her to the fence and unbuckled the belt the pouch hung from and hung it outside the gate. He didn't need fish pouring out of his pouch while the sivax thrashed around. He had a feeling she might not even buck once he stepped up, but there was no way to know until he was fully committed and in the saddle. He led her back to the center of the round pen and touched her over the ankle with his boot. She knelt and he lifted his boot toward the stirrup.

Wings flapped overhead as a flight of knights appeared over the rim of the Hollow. Bayard stopped, watching them for a moment. Unable to access the magic that allowed them to ignite dragon's fire or to fight enemy wizards, Bayard had been denied the rank of a full Knight of the Wyrm. He made himself useful, riding and training young dragons. If he hadn't, they would have tossed him out of the Hollow years ago, culled like any scrub out of a cavvy. He'd accepted his lot a long time ago, but the sting of that denial still rose up sometimes as he watched the knights fly off in their enameled armor on some adventure or other while he remained in the round pen, flying low in endless circles to make sure there were plenty of remounts for new riders and retiring dragons.

He dropped his foot to wait for them to pass. He didn't need the little sivax's attention divided between him and the other dragons. But there was something wrong with the cerulean velox in the back. That was Johanes' dragon, and it was injured.

Bayard cursed. It happened sometimes. Arrows weren't much of a threat to an armored knight and grown dragon, but if enough of them hit a wing the dragon's weight could cause the wounds to rip if they weren't healed quickly enough. But that sort of mistake mostly happened to younger riders. Johanes was an experienced knight who knew how to heal minor wounds just fine.

It wasn't really his business. There was a whole team of healers who would get Johanes and his velox—was his name Gringolet?—all fixed up straight away. He watched the dragons pass overhead. Sylina was in the front, instantly recognizable on her orange velox and green armor. She would tell him what happened later. Except, there were deep gouges in the back of her armor. What in the world had happened?

Well, this red fledgling would keep for a few minutes. His curiosity got the best of him, and he took the hackamore off and hung it outside the gate as he left.

Even with the strange, asymmetric gait he'd acquired from breaking young dragons, his long legs ate up the ground between the fledgling stable and the Rookery, the huge circular building that housed the full-grown dragons and the riders' armor and barding. The wounded dragon disappeared through the hole in the middle of the Rookery's roof in a flash of bright blue before he was even a quarter of the way.

It wasn't surprising that the Rookery was in a flurry of activity when he stepped in. Squires and grooms raced back and forth, removing equipment from the dragons and their knights. He looked for Sylina, but heard her well before he saw her.

"Yes, it was an ambush. I don't know how they managed it, but they did it."

He heard another voice speaking in low, hurried tones.

"You don't think that us flying across the country with a bleeding dragon raised some questions? I think we're well beyond secrecy."

Bayard rounded the corner to see Sylina, holding her creased and dented armor, talking to a slight man wearing a clean, blue cloak. Fligond was the Information Minister, and he already had a pen and a roll of paper ready to make sure the Knights' angle of the story was the one that got told first and most.

"What did you do to my dragons?" Bayard asked, his sudden presence making Fligond jump.

"I was just getting that information, Childe Bayard," Fligond said, putting unnecessary emphasis on the word *Childe*. It was an old word for an uninitiated knight, and the highest title Bayard could ever achieve. "It will be available once I get a full..."

"We were ambushed," Sylina said, pushing the armor toward him.

Bayard took it, looking at the gouges in the backplate. He'd heard her mention an ambush, but he didn't want to let on he had overheard anything. "These weren't made by claws," he ran a thumb down the edges where they had started to tear. "Did you fall off and hit a rock?"

"You moron," she hissed at him. "What kind of rock do you think would make a mark like that?"

Fligond looked uncomfortable and shuffled toward the door. "I will want the rest of your story," he eyed her as she made to throw her enameled greave at Bayard. "Soon."

They watched him go, and Syl dropped the greave on a nearby table. "Thanks."

Bayard shrugged. "I'm just ambling around."

"Liar. You're being nosy as the rest of them."

Bayard studied the ceiling, suddenly interested in the grain of the lumber above them. "Looked like there might be an injured dragon."

"That we've got healers to take care of."

"Well, someone's dragon might need more training. I should do more quality control."

Syl smiled at him and hung her sword on a nearby peg. "Nosy nosy. Let's get you over there before they heal Gringolet up and you've got nothing to watch."

Bayard and Sylina were latecomers to the crowd gathering to gawk in the center of the Rookery. Some of the squires and grooms were making an effort to look like they were working, but most were now openly loafing in a loose ring. They were so focused on the dragon they didn't notice Bayard and Sylina moving through them. This was pretty normal for Bayard, but Sylina was a full knight and was used to people making more of an effort to get out of her way, and her impatience was starting to show just as they weaved through toward the middle.

They emerged near the nose of the blue dragon. Its breath came in rolling, ragged waves. He was only ten years old, and not even half as big as he would eventually get, but the rough oval made by his tail and nose was wide enough for a fencing piste.

A terrible retching sound sounded from his left, and he was surprised to see Johanes kneeling by the dragon's head. The knight's body jerked with heavy sobs as he whispered into the dragon's ear. Bayard looked away quickly. Knights typically didn't break down in front of the whole Hollow. They also didn't usually have a wounded, hemorrhaging dragon on the floor of the Rookery. There wasn't much precedent here.

He turned and walked along the tail, avoiding looking at the wounded wings until they were right in front of him. When he couldn't ignore them any longer he looked, and his stomach turned.

"What did this?" His question wasn't exactly addressed to anyone, but Sylina answered.

"They're called cannons."

"Are they magic?"

"Arctos insists they aren't. They fire a huge metal ball. They have smaller ones too. That's what made those dents in my armor."

"How?"

She didn't answer. But now he could see what happened. The ball had struck the dragon's wings at an angle, tearing an oblong hole through the membrane stretched between its bony supports. How had he flown anywhere?

"Gaheris' dragon helped him most of the way," Sylina spoke quietly in response to his unasked question. "I helped as much as I could, but his dragon is bigger than mine."

Bayard nodded.

"We wanted to land," the words poured out of her now, "but who knew if there were more of those things anywhere, and we needed the healers."

That was certainly true. The knights focused on offensive magic, and only knew a few minor healing spells. Other candidates who could access magic but who weren't martially inclined could learn healing. Bayard didn't understand why anyone would choose that. Access to magic was all that stood between his life here and getting to see the rest of the world, and they squandered it by spending a lifetime studying rank, dusty books in the Hollow's archives. Nothing about the graphic pictures of human or dragon anatomy appealed to him, and he was content to let these weedy scholars do their work.

As if on cue, three healers in their crisp, blue tunics rushed into the Rookery. One carried a long staff, while the other two clutched narrow wands.

There was nothing about this process Bayard understood. A job this big, on tissues as complex as a dragon wing, would probably take a few healers, but what they would do was entirely beyond him.

They spoke quickly to Johanes, then came to the back near where Bayard stood. The one with the staff said a few short words and then slammed the spiked end against the ground and leaned on it, panting. Really, it seemed like he was being a little dramatic. But his skin prickled as the flow of energy in the room bent toward the staff. The gush of blood slowed, then stopped. The dragon's breathing slowed and his eyes clouded over.

The other two healers, wands raised, murmured quietly while the spell pulled one of the massive wings to the side until it was fully extended. Then, standing with one on either side of the wing, they started down it with the tips of their wands nearly touching, the skin slowly sealing behind the crackling ball of energy they formed. The smell of hot metal and burning blood stung Bayard's nose. As devastating as the wound had been, it looked like there wasn't any danger to the dragon now.

Except, by unlucky chance, in the frenzied rush of a returning patrol, and the added complication of having a wounded dragon with them, some squire had dropped a rolled leather strap off a saddle. To a person walking along the level floor of the Rookery with no distractions, it would have posed no more inconvenience than the time it took to stoop and pick it up. But, to a healer whose entire attention was focused on the glowing tip of his wand, it proved an insurmountable obstacle.

He fell hard. Both healers were totally focused on their spells, and had no chance to stop their channeling before the glowing ball exploded, knocking all three healers sprawling. Johanes jumped, and the dragon jumped, and suddenly there was chaos.

A spasm ran through the dragon as the spell that kept him from feeling either the wound or the procedure broke. It started at his tail, which swept up in a wide arc and slammed down again, nearly skewering the squires who stood by on its spikes. The tremor continued up the dragon's spine and through the wings, sending Bayard and Sylina sprinting away to avoid getting thrown across the room. It ended at the head, where the sudden jerk caught Johanes mid-jump and sent him flying. The knight landed hard, and the screeching grate of his steel armor against the hard rock floor echoed through the Rookery. He skidded to a stop and lay still.

Neither the dragon nor Johanes moved. The healer lifted his staff again to try and regain some kind of control. But before he could finish his spell the dragon blinked, his eyes suddenly clear.

If Johanes had been up and moving, it probably would have been fine. Dragons put great trust in their riders, and even through the sudden return of the pain the dragon might have understood he was being helped. But as it was, coming out of the magical daze with a wound and seeing his knight unconscious on the ground, the dragon panicked.

A dragon in its right mind would have noticed the familiar surroundings, and even probably sought out Johanes' squire so he could be groomed and put away. This dragon only saw a circle of people, smelled his own flesh burning, and felt pain. So he tried to attack and escape all at the same time. He wheeled around and, seeing Bayard and Sylina near his wings, lunged at them. The saber-like teeth sheared through the sleeves on Bayard's coat as he jumped back. Spells ricocheted off the tough blue hide, and someone screamed as the writhing tail caught them with a spike. The dragon spun again and, with a huge effort, jumped into the sky to escape.

Bayard took a deep breath and cursed as he exhaled. There was blood all over the ground. Some was certainly Gringolet's, but some was human too. Johanes was still unconscious. Someone else moaned in pain. He heard a woosh and a groan from above, and saw the dragon climbing in jerking circles toward the rim of the Hollow.

He reached out and plucked at Sylina's sleeve. "We need your dragon."

"He's not saddled," she spoke in almost a whisper. "Gringolet will be gone by the time he's ready."

"He'll bleed out by the time he's ready. We'll have to wing it."

Sylina was faster than he was, a fact he blamed on fifteen years' worth of dragon-related injuries. But the fact remained that she was mounted by the time he reached her dragon's stall. The animal balked slightly when he was asked to kneel to allow a second rider on, but it was only a moment until he and Sylina were in the sky, speeding after the wounded dragon.

Bayard hoped that once he was in the sky and had a moment to think that Gringolet would have calmed down a little. But the wound throbbed with each flap of his wings and the pain was maddening. Sylina's dragon caught up to him easily, but the blue dragon turned and snapped directly at the riders on its back.

Sylina cursed. "I was hoping to get under him and help him home, the same way we got him here."

"Try it again."

The orange dragon came close again, this time from the side. Gringolet tried to glide away, but the extra pressure on his wing sent another wave of pain through him and he again snapped at the riders. This time the poisonous, flammable gases from his bladder flooded over them, and Sylina had to push her dragon away so they wouldn't faint.

Sylina turned and yelled over the wind. "We're going to have to follow him until he lands and bring a healer back."

Bayard frowned, watching the dragon as he climbed higher in his attempt to escape. "It's no good. He's going to tear through that wing and fall if he doesn't calm down and glide. And at this altitude he'll die."

"We can't really help that. It would take a dozen casters to subdue him with magic and let him down easy."

Sylina's velox pulled back, letting the blue dragon have his way. The wind whipped at Bayard's eyes, pushing a tear out and down his cheek.

"No. We need to help him."

"Help him how?"

"Get above him."

"And push him down? That's dangerous. He'll still fall."

"No, just get above him and close to him."

He thought Sylina could tell what he was planning, but she was a good enough friend she didn't ask. If she asked, he would have to answer. And if he answered, she would have to refuse.

The orange velox caught up in seconds, this time flying above Gringolet. Dragons have few defenses from above and have to rely on their riders to protect them. Having no rider, Gringolet could only snap side to side as his bright, pain-maddened eyes burned into them.

"I need to get up farther, closer to his shoulders." Bayard shouted in her ear. Flying kept the muscles around the dragon's neck tight enough that he would be safe once he got to the shoulders. Much farther back then that and he would be vulnerable to a bite.

Sylina touched a heel to her dragon. Bayard gauged the distance, unsure how the air currents would affect him as he tried to fall ten or so feet onto the moving dragon's back. He hesitated, looked at the widening tear in the dragon's wing, and then let go and fell.

Everything about this plan hurt. Rather than landing astride the dragon and locking his knees behind the shoulders, Bayard landed with his stomach perpendicular to the dragon's spine, about six feet farther back than he'd have liked to be. He wheezed as he tried to suck air back into his lungs, then jerked as he felt a tooth drag through his leather boot. He scrambled for traction as he tried to swing his leg over the dragon's back. This far down the spine it was like trying to ride a water snake on a rough sea, but eventually he was able to get astride. He wheezed again, and his head felt light.

The dragon's rough scales gouged him as he pulled himself forward against their grain, and he could feel blood dripping down his leg and into his boots. But eventually he was up near the shoulder where the tail and the teeth couldn't get to him. The dragon dove and he lurched forward, and if Gringolet's wound hadn't weakened him Bayard would have been knocked unconscious and fallen. Instead he leaned back, pushed his knees up against the shoulder, and ran his hand down along the dragon's neck. Another deep breath filled his nostrils with the hot-copper smell of dragon's blood, and he lifted his voice to speak.

"You know me, you worm-ridden sack of bones."

The dragon thrashed. Bayard curled his heel against the dragon's side, looking for any sign of release.

"Come on. You've got this. Easy. Easy."

He might have imagined it, but the dragon moved ever so slightly away from the pressure, and he released it entirely.

"See? You know this. Easy, you bloated lizard."

He applied pressure with his other heel, and the dragon moved the tiniest bit away from it.

"You had me doubting whether you were broke. That's it. Now glide, damn you. Just glide."

He put his legs forward, and the dragon straightened his wings and stopped flapping them. Bayard leaned to the side away from the wound, and soon the dragon was descending in slow, lazy circles.

A flash of orange below him told him Sylina and her dragon were still in the sky. He watched along the other side until she came into view. He smiled and waved at her, and she gave him the middle finger.

When they finally landed, Johanes' squires rushed to Gringolet's side. Johanes himself was leaning against a post nearby while a healer twitched his hand back and forth through his hair. He was wobbly, but he was upright.

Bayard stumbled away from the press of people. Sylina was putting her dragon away, and there would be plenty of time to get his own wounds looked at. Right now, Bayard just wanted a few minutes to himself.

Four days later, Bayard rose early and caught the little red velox and walked to the round corral. He put her through her paces and gave her more fish than was probably strictly necessary. He could have taken more time off. The healers would have liked him to, which is why he made sure to get up before them. Sylina would be cross, but she would understand.

The young dragon did everything he asked for, and more besides. She was ready to ride. He put her hackamore on and checked his cinch. Suddenly they heard the pop of wings, and a flight of a half dozen knights and their dragons rose into the sky. He watched them, wondering where they were off to. Really, it wasn't any of his business. All he needed to do was get this dragon rode. He lifted a foot to the stirrup, gathered the reins a little tighter in his fist, and swung up.

Curtis Moore grew up in Bishop, California, where he spent his summers packing mules in the Eastern Sierra. He has published articles on scientific mediation in Nevada Lawyer and the Rocky Mountain Mineral Law Journal, as well as articles on horsemanship in Nicker News, and was shortlisted for The Milk House's 2023 Best of Rural Writing contest for his essay Co-Parenting With Cormac McCarthy. In his spare time Curtis rides his horse, writes, and makes memes about underrated fantasy novels.

Learn more about Curtis at: Author Website | Instagram | Instagram

Peter Devonald

Remembers yearning

times when the heavens were filled

with majestic grace

a thousand dragons flying

catch sunlight brilliance unbound.

<u>*If We Dragons*</u>

Peter Devonald

People who deny the existence of dragons

are often eaten by dragons. From within.

Ursula K. Le Guin

There is nothing like witnessing a dragon in the morning

to see resplendent sunshine bright and glorious

reflect off magnificent dragon's wings

as it ascends with splendour and ease

across the mountains and the seas

wings glide effortless and free

with pleasure and wisdom just to be

an enchantment, a freedom,

bathing in the early morning light

the dragon soars so perfectly in flight.

Peter Devonal is widely published in magazines/anthologies including *London Grip, Door Is A Jar, Bluebird Word, Metachrosis, Vipers Tongue, Visual Verse, Voidspace,* and *the6ress*. He won the Waltham Forest Poetry Prize 2022, Heart Of Heatons Poetry Award 2023 & 2021, joint winner FofHCS Poetry Award 2023, Forward Prize nomination 2023, two Best Of The Net nominations and shortlisted Saveas 2023 & Allingham 2023. He is poet in residence at *Haus-a-rest*. Won 50+ film awards, former senior judge/ mentor Peter Ustinov Awards (iemmys) and Children's Bafta nominated.

Learn more about Peter at:
Author Website | Instagram | Facebook | X

The Beasts of Shadow: Dragon Rising

N.M. Lambert

I used to dream of flying. Of soaring high above the clouds without a care in the world. Of massive golden wings sprouting from my back as I take to the skies. Of the wind whipping my hair and the freedom of the whole world at my fingertips. I used to dream of riding on the backs of mighty dragons and the limitless possibilities of where to go.

Now, I've relegated myself to the fact these dreams were just childhood fantasies devoid of a semblance of truth. After all, dragons aren't real. Mythological beings in *general* aren't real.

Except…maybe perhaps they are.

Last year, I met a girl. She was beautiful with golden, sun-kissed skin and long, silky hair the color of fresh snow. Her eyes were two pools of honey brown, holding my own green ones captive in their mesmerizing stare. And her lips were plump, pink, and soft to the touch. I still dream about her sometimes, about the stolen night we had the first time I saw her.

I had just turned eighteen. My small village of Wrycrest was holding a coming-of-age celebration for me in the town square. There was dancing, alcohol, and an assortment of breads, meats, and cheeses. In Wrycrest, eighteen is an important age worth celebrating, for it marked the official threshold of adulthood. At eighteen, I could now do whatever I wanted without stipulations. I could study whatever I wanted, stay up as late as I wanted, and make my own decisions. It was something I had been looking forward to for years, and now that it was finally here, I could hardly contain my excitement.

"Alex, calm down!" my older brother, Edwin, joked, placing a single hand on my arm. "The celebration isn't going anywhere!"

I rolled my eyes, shrugging his touch off my skin. "Easy for you to say! You've been an adult now for…how many years? A hundred?"

Edwin scoffed. "Five."

"Practically a dinosaur!" I grinned, shoving him lightly in the shoulder.

"Edwin, let the girl have her moment," my dad said lightheartedly from behind. "At *your* ceremony, you were practically bouncing off the walls too!"

"And drank *way* too much wine," my mom chimed. "We had to practically carry you home!"

"Don't remind me," Edwin grumbled, but he was anything but hurt by their comments. Our family was constantly teasing each other, poking fun at the littlest of things. I loved that about them, since it was in direct contrast to the serious nature of my friends' parents. My family was my rock, and they always would be.

On my other side, my younger brother, Lukas, was his usual silent self. He never talked much, preferring instead to communicate through pictures and hand gestures. He was a brilliant artist, and his drawings never ceased to amaze me.

If only I had some sort of hidden talent. I groaned. Because next to him, I was just…ordinary. Basic, plain Alex who never once had a boyfriend. Not that I was particularly *looking* for one. I just genuinely didn't *like* any of the boys in my village, and whenever one would try to get close to me, it didn't feel right. My mom always told me that soon, the right boy would come along, and it would feel like fireworks, but I was doubtful. Because while I can appreciate a guy's attractive form, I never wanted anything *more* with any of them.

As we neared the town square, I could already see the lights from the party. The sun was making its final descent behind the Westfall Mountains in the distance, bathing the sky in a purple hue.

I shivered as I gazed at the mountain range in the distance that was a good day's journey away by foot. The Westfall Mountains were magnificent, tall peaks that were rumored to house a deadly beast. I wasn't sure I believed in that, but there was one thing I *was* sure of. Anyone who ever ventured there never returned.

I shivered just thinking about the stories people tell children about those mountains. And I've always hated how close we were to them. Someday, however, I would muster up enough courage to visit them myself, if only to prove the rumors false.

"What are you thinking about?" Edwin suddenly asked.

I shook my head, forcing all thoughts about the Westfall Mountains from my mind. "Nothing. Just the event," I lied.

Edwin pursed his lips together, and I could tell he didn't believe me. Yet thankfully, he didn't press the matter further, only giving me a small nod.

I turned away from them, my sights now on the party in the distance. Music thumped in tune to my own heartbeat as the violin quartet played a fast, upbeat song. Before I knew it, I found myself swaying my hips to the beat as I moved closer to the revelry, only pausing once to glance back at my family. "How are you guys *not* swaying?"

My dad chuckled. "Well, when you get to be as old as your mom and I, you will come to realize you risk breaking a hip at the slightest inkling of movement."

I scoffed at my dad's antics, because what he said was *really* code for, "I don't dance." "Old people are so boring," I joked, flashing them a smirk before turning around and focusing, once again, on the scene in front of me.

"We can't all be hip and cool like you younglings!" my mom said before she and my dad burst into laughter.

I rolled my eyes. By now, I was close enough to see the giant banners with my full name spelled out. There were people already milling about, as to be expected, and as we approached, a crowd was already forming, ready to congratulate me and wish me a happy birthday.

This was the part I was looking forward to the least. Because I was an introvert, too much social interaction tended to exhaust me. Still, I plastered on a fake smile and interacted with each and every one of them, thanking them for their time and generous words. For thirty minutes, we danced and laughed and exchanged these fake pleasantries. Even my best friends, Sasha and Felicity, joined in on the action, also tossing in a joke here and there at my expense.

Eventually, however, I was able to get away from them all and made a beeline towards the table of refreshments. My eyes instantly honed in on the prize: several bottles of expensive red wine situated next to disposable, white cups. *Jackpot!*

As I was pouring a generous amount of wine into one of the cups, there was a tap on my shoulder. Immediately, I spun around, wine sloshing up the edges of the cup, ready to give another preprogrammed reply to what would undoubtably be another birthday wish or congratulations. I could already feel the words on my tongue.

And then, my eyes finally landed on *her*, and my brain instantly turned to mush.

The stunning woman flashed me an elegant smile. "Sorry to bother you," she said, her voice rich like melted chocolate. "Alex, right? The one this entire party is for?"

Dumbly and still unbelievably *speechless*, I nodded.

The woman gave a nervous laugh. "I've been waiting to talk to you. Give my congratulations. Until now, you've been surrounded, and I…" She shook her head, a deep blush coating her cheeks. "Well, Happy Birthday, Alex Winchester. That *is* you, right? And I didn't just say that to the wrong Alex?"

I nodded again. I didn't recognize the woman, which was strange given how small our village was. "Who are you?" I asked, and then immediately cringed when I realized how rude that sounded. "Not to be rude. I just…don't recognize you?" *Shut up, Alex!*

The woman, however, seemed to not have taken offense to my question. "No, you wouldn't. I'm just visiting," she said. "I'm Reine. Prideaux. Reine Prideaux. And you're Alex Winchester." She shuddered. "I'm sorry. Crap, I'm *terrible* at this!"

I belted out a laugh. "Join the club. Introverts, am I right?"

Reine relaxed her shoulders and chuckled. "Introverts. Yeah." She sighed. "Well, I just came over here to wish you a happy birthday, so…Happy Birthday! Again! I think I'll go now." She awkwardly shifted from foot to foot, her blush only deepening.

I froze, because the last thing I wanted was for her to leave. And as she took one step back and then another one, my own body acted of its own accord. I reached out, securing her tiny wrist in my hand and halting her movements. "No, stay," I said. "Please? Please stay! Do you like dancing?"

Reine pursed her lips in thought. Her full, luscious, *seductive*—

"I do."

My eyes were still on her lips when she said that, and it took all my willpower to tear them away. "Do you want to dance? With me? Possibly?" I squeaked, actually *squeaked*. As if on cue, mortification flooded my veins. *There's no way she'll say yes. Not after—*

"I'd love to!" Reine's radiant smile returned.

I led her to the dance floor after that, the quartet playing upbeat melody after upbeat melody. Reine and I swayed and jumped and danced until our feet were sore, but we didn't care. At one point, I had ditched my wine in favor of her hands, her shoulders, her *everything*, as we moved closer to each other.

My entire body was on fire. And then, as if someone flicked a switch, the quartet started playing a slow song as if the members *knew* about the charged chemistry that existed between Reine and me.

For a beat, we just looked at each other. Then:

"I think we're supposed to slow dance," Reine said dumbly, her blush returning. "Is that okay?"

Yes! my entire body practically screamed, but all I said was, "If it's alright with you."

She bit her lip, her arms snaking around my neck. I reached down to pull her closer to me, and that was how we found ourselves lazily rocking to the music, couped up in each other's arms. Her warm breath fanned across my face, and my eyes were once again drawn to her lips. Were they as soft as they looked? How would they taste? Only one way to find out…

Before I could overthink what I was doing, I brushed my lips against hers, silently asking for her permission. She tilted her head to meet my invitation, and soon, we were full-on kissing in the middle of the dance floor without a care in the world. My tongue ran along the seam of her mouth, and she parted her lips as her own tongue darted out to meet mine. I felt her hands dig into the skin on my neck as she pulled me closer, both of us tasting, taunting, *prodding…*

Reine broke the kiss, gazing at me with an unreadable expression. Suddenly, a pit formed in my stomach. *Did I misread her?* I thought as my heart leapt into my throat. *Stupid Alex! Of course she doesn't want you! Why would she?*

But then, a smile broke out across her lips. "Well, that was unexpected," she joked. "As much as I enjoyed it, I feel like this isn't the place. Do you want to…go somewhere else?"

My heart nearly stopped, and I nodded before I had a chance to think about what I was doing. We stepped away from each other, and I took her hand in mine. The party was still in full swing, and I had never heard of someone leaving their own party early before, but I didn't care. Because for now, all that existed were Reine and I and endless possibilities.

I took her home and up to my bedroom, which was on the second floor. I barely managed to close the door before she practically pounced on me, hungrily devouring my lips as she walked us back towards my bed. My lower half immediately heated at the anticipation, and we broke apart once again, staring into each other's eyes for a few seconds.

"Is this okay?" Reine questioned. "We can slow down if this is too fast."

Immediately, I shook my head. "It's perfect," I said, reaching to pull her closer.

Clothes soon flew in all directions as we shed our barriers. My core was throbbing, begging to be touched, as our lips found each other's once again.

Her hand dipped low, slowly rubbing that sensitive spot over and over as we rocked against each other, savoring this one stolen moment. I let out a short moan, my own hand reaching out to return the favor, but she suddenly stopped me.

"Not tonight," was all she said. And then, she laid me down gently, assuming a position on top, still rubbing that same sensitive spot over and over again. Her gaze hungrily ran over every inch of me, and she licked her lips. "You *are* the birthday girl, after all."

My body trembled at her words, watching with bated breath as she lowered her mouth to my neck, the combination of tongue and teeth enough to make my head spin. She trailed kisses down my skin, lightly tugging at my collarbone with her teeth before continuing her descent.

I threw my head back, the sensations both too much and not enough at the same time. "More," I groaned, practically grinding against her hand as she undid me one stroke at a time.

And then, her mouth finally reached my left breast. And with a stroke of luck, she sucked my hardened nipple into her mouth, rolling the bead around with her tongue as she gently bit down.

And that was when I finally fully unraveled, letting out a scream as the orgasm ripped through me one delicious wave at a time. Reine picked up the pace, rubbing faster and faster, as she milked every last drop from me, as I was left to ride out the birthday gift she had given me.

And when it was all over, she collapsed next to me, wrapping her arms tightly around me as she gently stroked my hair. I fell asleep that night feeling more satisfied than I ever did in my entire eighteen years of existence.

I woke up the next morning in a daze, instinctively reaching out to the spot next to me. Where I expected to meet warm flesh, my hand instead swiped through empty air before landing softly on the bedsheets below. Panicked, I rolled over onto my other side, only to see…nothing. Absolutely nothing.

Reine was gone. And I was alone.

Hurt like I never knew before blossomed in my chest as I scampered out of bed, hands going right for my chest as my breaths came out in quick spurts. *Was she real? Or was it all a dream?*

In my heart that still beat her name, however, I knew she was real. I knew that our time together had been real and meaningful and that we were meant for more than just one night. But she wasn't there this morning. My heart fractured as I stared at where she had been, as I recalled each electrifying, purposeful touch of her hands on my skin. Apparently, I was a fool because last night had meant more to me than it apparently had meant to her.

But then, suddenly, a crash sounded from outside. The noise was enough to rattle my bones, was possibly enough to wake my whole *family*, who I knew would've returned last night, and I quickly threw on last night's clothes before tearing through the house and out the front door. For all I knew, I could be running directly into the arms of a dangerous intruder, but all I could think about was Reine and that she was somehow still here. That she didn't leave after all.

Please let it be her, I thought. Because she would be easier to explain to my parents, and I could finally show my mom that I found someone, that I finally understood *why* all the boys in Wrycrest felt inadequate, and we would celebrate again with Reine by my side.

And then, I finally saw her. Reine Prideaux was standing off to the side of my house, staring off into the forest. My back door was wide open, which marked her exit point, and as I approached, I noticed she was still completely naked.

The grass crunched beneath my feet, alerting the beautiful woman to my presence. She spun around, her hair glistening in the morning sun, and a genuine smile stretched across her lips. "I have to go now, Alex, but this isn't goodbye. We *will* see each other again. That's a promise," she said in that same sweet voice that sent chills down my spine. She turned back around, and the cracking of bones soon filled the otherwise quiet air. I watched in fascination as shimmery, golden scales broke out all along her body, her face elongating into a snout. Her limbs shifted as claws sprouted from her fingertips and toes, and a lengthy tail sprouted from her behind. Leathery, majestic wings soon sprung from her back in the same shimmering golden color as her scales, slowly flapping in the breeze as if warming up to take flight.

And when the transformation was finally over, when the girl's body stopped convulsing and changing before my very eyes, a massive, beautiful dragon stood where she once did. I blinked, sure my eyes were playing tricks on me, but each time I did, the dragon was still there in all its breathtaking glory.

Holy shit, I thought, completely mesmerized. *Dragons are real!*

Of course we're real, Alex Winchester, a voice suddenly said in my mind. I jumped, because it was *her* voice. Reine. The freaking *dragon! We've been around for thousands of years, ever since our goddess, Quintessa, first created us.*

I took a step back, bewildered. "You can *talk* in this form?"

In a sense. We can telecommunicate, Reine said. *All shifters can when in their animal forms.*

I opened my mouth, but nothing came out. I was speechless. Completely enamored by the creature in front of me. I knew I should be scared, should run back inside and lock all the doors, but for some reason, being here felt…right. As if I were *meant* to stay here with Reine.

Like I said, this isn't goodbye, Reine repeated, softer this time. *I'll come back for you, and then, we can have our happily ever after.* Just then, she took off into the sky, her wings flapping as she propelled herself in the direction of the Westfall Mountains. I watched as she flew farther and farther away from me before disappearing from sight, blipping out of my life.

That day, I became a firm believer in dragons, something I still carry with me to this day. Every day since, I glance up at the sky, hoping for a glimpse of her, but each time left me disappointed. It's been a year, and yet, her promise to me still sticks out. *We* will *see each other again.*

I'm in a small clearing in the forest by my village on my nineteenth birthday, once again staring up at the sky, when the moment I've been waiting for finally happens. For a moment, I hear nothing but a few cicadas and bees. Then, a thump suddenly sounds from behind me, followed by the familiar sound of cracking bones.

And that familiar melodic voice whispers in my subconscious, *I told you I'd come back for you.*

I spin around, and there is Reine in all her beautiful, naked glory. I run to her, my heart so full it feels like it will burst, and soon, her sweet scent envelops me as her arms tug me into her chest.

"I'm sorry it took so long," she coos softly into my ear. "Dragon prides can be very…demanding."

I chuckle as I gaze at her familiar, honeyed eyes. "I thought about you. Every single day since our last encounter."

"And I, you." She brushes her lips over my cheek, and goosebumps pepper my arms. Then, she seals her mouth over mine, and for the moment, our universes are perfectly aligned.

For one perfect moment, all that exists are me and her, now and forever.

N. M. Lambert is a part-time writer, editor, avid reader and gamer, and a heavy metal enthusiast. She graduated from Northern Arizona University with a bachelor's in both criminology and anthropology and with minors in both French and psychology. When not writing, she can be seen surfing the web, singing and sometimes trying to perfect her metal growls, and spending way too much time on Animal Crossing, Oblivion, and Skyrim. She currently lives in Pollock Pines, California with her family and a menagerie of dogs, birds, and a cat.

Learn more about N.M. at:
Instagram | Twitter | Threads | Facebook | TikTok | Author Website

Lloyd Britton

The Mountains

It has been three days since I dreamt of Nilda, and I dread going to sleep tonight fearing that I will not dream about her again.

The fire we are huddled around spits hot dancing sparks, crackling away into the chill night air. The smell of burning wood and fresh mountain air fills my senses as the dark becomes all pervasive. Shamgar, Nilda's father and my tutor says that although it is still summer, this high up into the mountains there is little warmth during the night. Luckily for us Galthrimar has a natural proclivity for projecting fire from strong glands in his maw. He says that his dragon's fire is the most searing of all his kin.

Galthrimar's long black and red body is curled around us and the fire, blocking the wind out and shielding us from predators that lurk in the mountains. His thick scaled body makes a perfect defense for us, there aren't many predators that would dare to take on a dragon the size of Galthrimar, meaning we can relax as much as we are able to when sleeping outdoors in the wild.

"You are not tired?" Shamgar's voice cuts through the air like a blade, splicing through my thoughts of Nilda and those who captured her.

I look across the fire at him, the swaying flames giving his features an eerie quality.
I reply. "I fear we won't see her tonight." My voice is strained, giving away my exhaustion from travelling through the mountains.

We have been flying for six days on the back of Galthrimar, searching for those that took Nilda; for the first three days we were comforted that she still lived as we three have talent for oneiromancy and can enter into each other's dreams. We used our talent in dream magic to stay in contact, Nilda directing us as best she could the way that they had taken her, but now with three nights without communication from her I am beginning to lose hope, something that I never wish to do.

As Shamgar says, wolves, bears, cave lions and giant eagles are all predators that could kill us but there are others. Tales of trolls lurking in these parts plague the people of our settlement; a band of orcs are also said to roam through this way. But it is not who is hunting us that concerns us; we have a hunt of our own, the most dangerous of all, the giant bat riding vampires of Maramora, the patron of darkness.

"We will find her." says Shamgar, a determination in his voice that inspires me to have faith.

"I know," I say and look to Galthrimar who is watching me with a gentle ease in his eye, that would seem uncharacteristic of a dragon if I was not a dracomancer.

I offer my thoughts to him to receive thinking, "My tutor's determination is as strong as his courage, but I must admit, that as inspiring as that is, I begin to have doubts."

Galthrimar's thoughts enter my mind, "You should not doubt. Doubting leads to error, which leads to failure."

"That is true," I think.

I see Shamgar watching the exchange from my periphery, ignorant of what we discuss.

"I am glad that this dragon has come to us," says Shamgar. "I am forever grateful that he arrived when he did, or the fatalities would have been worse."

I nod and feel my eyes go heavy and try to supress a yawn with little success.

"Get some sleep," says Shamgar. "I will take the first watch."

"It definitely would have been worse if it wasn't for Galthrimar," I say shutting my eyes.

As I drift into a swirling state of slumber I see the seventeen giant bat riding vampires that had descended upon our hometown, a small settlement in the middle of a valley in the far reaches of the land of Lusal. Why these creatures wish to plague the likes of us is beyond me. Maramora herself led the charge; there was no warning and we had little in the way of defenses against them. Needless to say, there were few survivors, and there would have been fewer if Galthrimar hadn't turned up when he did. This was the night that Nilda was taken by them. The Unwanted Arrival

Nilda and I watched the last light of twilight fade to black and the stars prick out into existence. We watched from the opening in the attic; the window, not being made of glass like the rest of the house, just an open hole that has creaky wooden shutters. Zelma, Nilda's mother and Shamgar's wife often remarks that these decrepit shutters are the reason why it's warm in winter and cool in summer. She was the head of the household, running a tight ship of the maintenance of the house and garden, she always made sure Nilda and I completed our chores promptly, even as we grew up into the early stages of adulthood; she made sure we were always with a job to do around the house.

"What do you think the stars are made from?" Nilda asks me as she sips her hot milky tea next to me.

"I don't know," I say. "I've never really thought about it."

"Well think about it now," she says.

We both look up to the night sky wandering what the stars could be made of when we see it…

Something dark against the starlight, wings, giant wings. We exchange a glance and know that we needn't vocally confirm what we've seen; we can see the recognition in each other's eyes.

"Get father?" says Nilda.

"What was it though?" I say.

"Look, another one," says Nilda a little too loud and pointing out the window.

As I look out, I see more, more wings, coming lower, coming towards the house. A sudden scream from down the road where the nearest house is.

"That sounded like Patti," says Nilda, referring to the woman who lives in the house nearest ours. Another cry from farther afield.

"They are attacking the town!" I say.

"What are they?" says Nilda getting to her feet.

"I don't know," I say joining her in a stand.

A clatter of sounds come from above. The scuttling, scratching sounds reverberate around the room. They are coming from the roof; something has landed on it.

We exchange another worried look. Hear a screech and run for the door to the downstairs. Before we reach the door, a giant bat has reared its head inside the window and a figure, just a blur has leapt in front of the door blocking our path. By the light of the oil lamp burning on the wall I see a face that I recognize from somewhere…

The figure, of masculine demeanor, stands grinning at us. His face is pale and hair long, fangs protrude from his mouth, and I know this is a vampire of legend. But I know that face that stares at me with malicious intent in his eye. But where do I know him from?

The Outlawed Oracles

As a child, I lived in the city of Omanassa in the land called Imago, across the desert from Lusal. King Omanassa had built this city around a great river which shared his name. I'm not sure which was named first, the river or the king, and growing up, no one I knew had a clear answer. It was assumed that the king gave his name to the city.

It is said that King Omanassa had elven heritage, that his father was half elf, and his grandfather was an elf from the land of Urzana, which is a land that lies far to the south. Because of this he lived an extraordinarily long life and was still an active man when I was a child, although he grew strange in his wits as he got older and would make public speeches that made little sense and confused people. However, his prowess as a warrior still held his reputation firmly in place so that no one dared to overthrow him.

King Omanassa was a strong believer in The Gravidity Deity as were we all. However, just about at the same time that my talent for magic began to manifest, a group of men and women began to preach in the streets about the emergence of a new deity, The Fulminous Deity. People were at first nonresponsive to these public lectures until King Omanassa took in the oracles of The Fulminous Deity and listened to what they had to say.

Later after people began to be intrigued by this new faith, the king had all sixteen oracles publicly executed, one by one, many of the oracles fled from the city but all were found and hanged for their crimes of propagating a false prophecy. This display shocked all the city. The king also declared that he was highly suspicious of magic and although he would not outlaw the practice, he would dissuade the population from using it. This too was strange since magic seemed not to be related to the oracle's activities, with people being uncertain that they were even practitioners of magic, so naturally people were confused at what the relation was. Stranger still was that after all the oracles had been executed, he began to commission the building of temples to The Fulminous Deity.

This was when my father, suspicious of the king's activities, sent me with enough gold and silver to the city of Umayassa in Lusal to find a teacher for my magical talent, hoping that the distance from the king's strange behavior and suspicion of magic would keep me safe.

I remember seeing the first oracle of the Fulminous Deity in the street, preaching his religion. He called himself Manthrasar. He was tall, dark haired, well-spoken and wore finely crafted clothing and shoes. We gathered around to listen to his words and people were inspired by the hope that they felt. I too was caught up in the sway of his oration and there was a moment when he looked me in the eye and smiled, his features soft and gentle, a benign look in his eyes. The next time I would see him, he would be hanging from a rope.

The Menacing Glare

As I see the man before me, standing in the way of our escape, Nilda recoiling back towards the window, I recognize his eyes, but they are not the benign eyes of the oracle I saw all those years ago; they are the malicious eyes of a vampire. Manthrasar, the first oracle of the Fulminous Deity.

Desperate Hopes

I travelled with a caravan across the desert and reached Umayassa in fifteen days. I stayed in an inn for three nights, going each day to the universities of higher learning to find the mage my father had told me to seek out, Shamgar. Each establishment was as uncooperative as the last, telling me that Shamgar had once taught as a mage, lecturer and scholar but was no longer apart of the faculty and would not give me any information on where he might be.

My gold and silver were quickly diminishing and so I used my initiative and went to a fortune teller in the marketplace, who told me that I should buy a gemstone from her, and it will help me find the one I was looking for. That night I slept on the streets of Umayassa not having enough gold or silver left to pay for a room, and with the ruby I purchased from the crone of a fortune teller, I hoped I could reach out in my dreams and find Shamgar.

I was flying, which I rarely do in dreams and so it took me a little longer than usual to realize that I was dreaming, but when I came into land upon a hill with an apple tree growing at its peak, I saw Shamgar stood as if waiting for me. Waiting for me to realize that I was dreaming.

"Where am I?" I ask him, starting to suspect that something about this place isn't quite right.

"It looks like you are in the valley of Varteres far from Umayassa were you lay your head," he says smiling.

"Then this is a dream?" I ask.

"Of course it's a dream!" he laughs. "I have to admit that I was expecting more from you."

"What do you mean?"

"I know you are looking for me," he says raising both eyebrows. "I was hoping your talent in oneiromancy would be further along, but no matter. I will train you in magic provided that you are capable of reaching the valley of Varteres where I live."

"How do I find this place?" I ask.

"I will show you," Shamgar says and waves his hand over the scene that lays before us. Instantly it changes, and I see myself asleep in the street. Then a golden pathway stretches out before me, a sparkling light prancing about near the ground.

"Just follow that," he says and I wake up.

When I open my eyes, I see the trail that Shamgar had showed me, and I know that all I need do is follow the light and it will lead me to where he is.

After another week of travelling, I finally made it to Shamgar's house. I was hungry and dehydrated, my skills of survival are minimal and had been put to the test in working my way through the land to get to the valley.

Zelma welcomed me with open arms, fed me and bid me to bathe. She told me that I was destined to be a part of her family for as long as she lived. These words would later take on another meaning when I saw Manthrasar's giant bat claw her to death.

Swift As Shadows

The door to the attic bursts open, flying off its hinges and hitting Manthrasar in the back, knocking him to the floor. Shamgar stands in the doorway, a lantern in one hand and a fierce look upon his face. A wobble of air about his other hand that shows that he had used a telekinetic blast to hit the door.

"Father!" calls Nilda and runs to him; I follow.

"Quickly," he says grabbing Nilda and looking her deadpan in the eye as she tries to embrace him. "We must get to the woods."

We run. Through the garden, pass the hedge at the end and across the field to the wooded area beyond. I lead the way with Nilda and Zelma behind me and Shamgar behind them.

"Why are we going to the woods?" asks Nilda.

"They are giant bats," says Zelma. "The trees are too dense for them to enter."

Delving Into Legends

There are many wonders in the valley of Varteres but my favorite of them all, aside from the amazing people that live here, is the sky kingdom. I used to watch it from the window of my bed chamber. I would look at it when out working the fields, when walking through the valley I would occasionally glance its way. Dreaming about the inhabitants of that place. It is a huge floating land high up in the sky. Shamgar always said it is farther away than I realize and higher up in the sky than I could imagine, not that it looked like that to me. He would often tell me about the things he knew about it, which he liked to do when the sun was setting, and the sky would be ablaze with magnificent colors and the backdrop of it against the image of the sky kingdom mesmerized me.

He told me that it was the twenty-first sky kingdom out of twenty-four. The people that live there are beings called sylphs and they live there with dragons. Sometimes it was possible to see a dragon flying towards the sky kingdom, a traveler from one of the other floating lands. I became enchanted with the idea of dragons, as if something deep within me knew I was a dracomancer. Shamgar told me the history of these majestic beasts and I lapped up all his stories.

He said the first dragons were despotic rulers that sought to fashion a world where they were the center of the cosmos. In that time the earth was a forest, giant trees dominated the landscape, and one tree was the biggest of all, the mother tree. The dragons desired to destroy these giant trees and build a world that was based on strength and power and bathed in fire. The fire of their breath was something that caused them to feel great pride and arrogance. They began to burn the mother tree, but something happened. The welkin opened, and the tree was ripped from the earth and elevated into another plane of existence, by the Welkin Wanderers. The age that followed was a time of great strife, with the dragons coercing the other beings of the earth to chop down the trees that they didn't burn and build a mighty maze where the mother tree had stood. This maze would stand as a testament to the power of the dragons, but it would also be their undoing. For war began, between the dragons and their minions and all others who opposed them.

During the war that followed these events some of the dragons sided with the beings who did not agree with the building of the dragon maze. And it is these dragons who the dragons today are descended from, meaning that dragons still exist in this realm of existence. For all the dragons that built the dragon maze and entered therein were sealed within by the guardian of creation and plunged into the vast waters below the surface of the earth. The wooden dragon maze then petrified into stone and there was no escape for those inside. Furthermore, other guardians banded together to ensure that the souls of the dragons would remain inside the maze. So that when they died, they would not advance into the afterlife but remain as phantoms forever. Since then, the remaining virtuous dragons live and work closely with the sylphs to preserve peace and unity.

Captivated by this story and many others like it, I had so many questions, so many that one day Shamgar gave me a quartz crystal telling me that this was the method that sylphs who are not dracomancers, communicate with dragons. Needless to say, I tucked the crystal under my pillow and that first night I saw a dragon in my dream.

A Brutal Strike

As we run, we have not yet reached the woods when I see Manthrasar's giant bat fly over our heads. It circles round and dives for us. Shamgar releases a telekinetic blast, but the bat deftly dodges it. It lands between myself, Nilda, and Zelma, blocking my view of what is happening.

I hear a scream, a blood curdling ululation that strikes fear within me. The bat rises again, and I see Shamgar knelt by Zelma who has been slashed by sharp claws across her torso and is bleeding out fast. I look up at the bat flying away and can hear Nilda screaming. They have taken her. Zelma has already left this plane of existence.

Visions of Fate

In my dream the dragon flies low across a blue sky that is cloudless and seems to stretch on forever. I stand by the apple tree on that hill I first spoke to Shamgar on. The valley is full of golden light, it shines on the distant gathering of houses that is my home and everything seems hyper real and alive. Even the trees seem to be moving in an animated fashion, glowing with some preternatural power.

The dragon, black and red scales covering his body, lands on the soft grass next to me.

"Young dracomancer," he thinks and I can hear his thoughts. "What is your name?"

"My name is Tikki," I say.

"And I am Galthrimar."

As I look at him, I start to see things in my mind's eye, flashes of scenes from my past; the first time I witnessed a public hanging, the first time I conjured a ball of light using photomancy, and other moments in time. Moments that haven't happened yet, moments still to come.

I see myself riding on the back of Galthrimar with Shamgar through the mountains, then flying alone towards the sky kingdom. I can see the land in the sky, a mountain in the distance, forests and rivers running through fields. The scene changes again and I see Galthrimar flying with who I assume is a sylph on his back, flying around a tall tower. The visions begin to fade.

"What was that?" I ask.

"When dragon and dracomancer meet, we see glimpses of our lives that are important to our personal relationship together."

A sense of wonder soaks into my mind and heart, and I feel an overwhelming sense of joy in that moment.

"You have come from the sky kingdom?" I ask.

His keen green eyes look at me with affection as he speaks, "I am still in the sky kingdom as you are still in this valley. This is a dream, a dream that has connected us to each other."

"I know," I say. "I can tell this is a dream, but I would love to see a dragon in real life too."

"And so, you shall," says Galthrimar. "You are a dracomancer yet you are young and untrained and so, I am inviting you to come to the sky kingdom and be formally trained in the art of magic with our mages."

My heart leaps with excitement. I am lost for words and so I just stare dumbly at the dragon.

"Do you accept this invitation?" he says after a long pause.

"Of course," I call out and laugh at myself.

The Moonlight Massacre

An intense rage overcomes Shamgar as his wife's body lays lifeless upon the ground and he marches back towards the house. For a moment I just stare at Zelma's body, horrified at what I am seeing; then not knowing what else to do, I follow Shamgar.

We don't speak as we head towards the cluster of houses that comprise the outskirts of our small settlement. There are more houses beyond these, and we can see that the giant bat riding vampires are killing people in the street. One of the vampires darts from house to house ripping the heavy wooden doors off with his bare hands and slaying all in his path.

Shamgar holds out a hand and casts what I deduce to be a chronomantic spell, as the vampire leaps and runs quick as a lightning bolt. The spell takes hold and his movements slow as he flings the body of a woman to the floor. His body is slowing in its motions but it appears that his mind is unaffected for he notices that he is moving in slow motion and turns to face Shamgar.

Other vampires swarm about the houses, leaping from the backs of their giant bats, killing whoever they please and bounding back onto them to fly off and do the same further along.

Shamgar releases a telekinetic blast that hits the slow-motion vampire in the chest and sends him hurtling backwards. The chronomantic spell has broken and as the vampire gets to his feet he charges at us.

Shamgar uses geomancy to cause the earth to rise up in uneven and jagged points so that when the vampire trips on the unsteady and undulating ground he is stabbed in the stomach by a razor-sharp edge of rock.

Another vampire a woman has spotted us and charges directly at us. I call upon my defensive magic skills in photomancy and release a blinding light from my palm, she screams and staggers back, then leaps so high I lose sight of her. Before I know what is happening, she has descended upon me and knocked me to the dirt. Looming over me, she grins a maleficent smirk and I know I'm going to die.

Before she tears me limb from limb, flames erupt from the sky, and fire showers down over the town. The vampire stands over me looks to the sky and calls out, "Dragon!"

She bounds away with supernatural agility and is upon her giant bat flying away. the vampire fighting Shamgar is on fire and rolling around on the floor trying to extinguish himself.

Shamgar takes a step towards him but is intercepted by a giant bat who picks up the smoldering vampire and carries him away.

I see Galthrimar flying in circles high above. I hear a screech and look to where it originates from, a rooftop. Then I see her, sat atop her giant bat, Maramora, the patroness of darkness.

The Sky

By morning I haven't dreamt of Nilda yet again, and we move through the mountains on the back of Galthrimar at a decent speed, continuing our search for those that took her. Searching every cave and crevice for the resting place of the vampires. We figure that if we attack them while they sleep, then we will have the advantage.

But night falls once again with no luck on finding anything. However, it is this night that those we hunt, find us…

We have not yet fallen asleep when we notice the darkness thicken; Galthrimar rears his head and I hear his thoughts, "They have us surrounded."

"Who?" I ask.

"The vampires of Maramora."

I look to Shamgar and I know he knows something is happening; he can see it on my face.

"What is it?" he whispers.

Before I can answer, Galthrimar has opened his wings and kicked off the ground in an ascent high above us. He spins around breathing fire, illuminating the night, revealing the places where the vampires are.

"They're here," says Shamgar. We are to our feet in a second, ready for the attack.

But one bat has already approached us, scaling the cliff edge a little way away and now moves on foot towards where we are.

"You will pay for what you have done!" shouts Shamgar and I can feel him drawing his power, readying for a mighty spell.

But this rider is different from the others that we see hiding in the cliffs above us. She looks young, pale and fierce like all vampires but somehow familiar. It is when she speaks that I realise what has happened.

"Father." Nilda says. "You should go home."

Shamgar opens his mouth to shout but something catches in his throat as he realizes who the vampire is.

"What have they done!?" I say my voice just a croak from shock. "I am a vampire of Maramora now," says Nilda. "There is nothing you can do. You should leave this place."

She looks up to the sky and watches Galthrimar swiftly descend, landing behind us breathing smoke from his nostrils. Then she looks up to the cliffside. My eyes follow hers and I see her again, Maramora.

Shamgar shouts up to her as she watches us in placid consideration, "You will pay! You will pay for what you have done! Do you hear me? All of you! You will all pay!"

No one says anything while the echoes of Shamgar's voice reverberate through the mountains. I look to Nilda who is looking back with a blank expression that I cannot read. But the darkness around her seems full of spite. Full of some awful hostility that exudes from her. The spiteful darkness belongs to her.

Shamgar builds his magical force up further. Then it explodes out of him. The sides of the cliffs shudder and give way; he has used a geomantic spell so strong that it is breaking away chunks of the mountain itself, a cascade of rock and stone plummets towards us. All the bat riders take flight, including Nilda.

The earth is shaking with Shamgar's power, the earth beneath our feet is cracking, I stumble backwards, prop myself up against the body of Galthrimar.

He beats his wings with such savagery that the bluster steals the air from my lungs and I hurriedly clamber onto his back whilst trying to catch my breath; we take flight. Then reaching down to grab Shamgar, in an attempt to save him. With claws extended, we maneuver through the vibrating air, but the distraught mage bashes back the dragon's claws with a telekinetic blast. Galthrimar roars in pain, recoiling his arms into his chest and flies higher, abandoning him to the quaking earth.

Looking down I see the mountain open up and Shamgar falls through the crevice he has created. The earth is still shaking as we fly away. Thunderous rock upon rock tumbling downwards.

As we glide further from all that's happened, to who knows where, I don't think to ask where he is taking me, too shocked by the devastating experience. Suddenly the magnitude of it all hits me like a rapid river crashing downstream, the waters of my emotions smashing against the rocks of my despair. I begin to cry. Tears flood my face and I sob and sob until I fall asleep.

When I dream, I dream of the sylphs and dragons, and when I awaken, still flying on the back of Galthrimar, I look down and I see it. The sky kingdom.

Usually describing himself as an artist and poet, Lloyd Britton pursues many creative endeavours and has a wide variety of interests that shows his versatility and uniqueness as an artist and intellectual. As a writer of fiction, he explores the genres of fantasy, surrealism, experimental prose and the blend between prose and poetry. He also explores ideas of existentialism, philosophy, religion, psychology, sociology, linguistics, interpersonal and intrapersonal dynamics of relationships and the symbiotic and emergent nature of reality.

In 2020 he started a series of fantasy stories under the main title of Tales from the Welkin Wanderers. In this series Lloyd applies an experimental approach to high fantasy storytelling, using a wide cast of characters with multiple narrators and story lines that cross over and link in a variety of ways. Each character tells their story from their unique perspective, allowing the reader to visualize their internal world, while having to figure out the wider reality of the realm they exist in. This creates a complex tapestry of beliefs and perceptions that just like in real life are sometimes contradictory, showing the innate eccentricities in the way every individual perceives the reality they are a part of.

The ideas and themes that are explored in the fantasy genre are particularly appealing to Lloyd, with a strong emphasis on world building and creation of lore being prevalent in his work.

Learn more about Lloyd at: Instagram

A Monster's Repentance

Ryan Askew

Deep in the darkest recesses of his scarred and scaly

   heart, the last of dragons roars with remorse.

His years of silent solitude have consumed

   the fire within, leaving him as a hallowed husk.

With whom can he now converse when a keen

thought or insight suddenly fuels his furnace?

   There is only his own mind and marrow to descry.

Reflecting on time spent among humanity outside the world

   of his Platonic cave, he has come to the ardent conclusion:

Each and every one of them is insufferably mad!

Driven senseless by ego and fear

to maim, slay, and commodify life,

and all they do not understand,

these creatures know nothing

of the dignified humility,

the true nobility, of dragons.

For all his time spent alone

   in quiet rumination,

of dreadful deeds past—

which ache beneath his armor—

of present guilt, shame, and compunction--

which threatens to immolate his soul—

and of a future so dreadfully charred and desolate

--the greatest of his fears--

he yearns to take flight once more

while confining himself to a beastly cell

of his own design, to safely hoard his gold,

for he knows it was acquired at precipitous cost;

As the treasure glistens in his bleak Mountain Hall,

this mighty mourning dragon rests beneath it all,

as if he the throne and those riches King,

placing little value on his stately self.

Such is the fate of this majestic monstrosity,

who shares no kinship with mankind,

yet laments their losses as his own;

he has lived long enough, fought valiantly enough,

grieved profoundly enough to feel within the folly

of perpetuating ceaseless cycles of savory ruination.

Thus, he continues to toil away as a temperate hermit,

hidden from sun and sky in his dim, disconsolate den.

Ryan has always been fascinated by fantasy and fiction from a young age. Though he loves all visual mediums of storytelling, he grew up reading everything he could get his hands on, and was fortunate to have many books given to him over the years as gifts from his grandmother, herself an aspiring author, who encouraged his natural curiosity and proclivity for the written word. He later in life studied English literature and creative writing at the University of California, Berkeley and hopes to one day share his passion for learning and reading by teaching literature with an emphasis on graphic novels. He is thrilled to have his first published poem featured in Dragon Dreams by Storm Dragon Publishing and looks forward to sharing more of his writing with the world. Ryan lives in San Diego, California and travels to Canada as often as he can to visit family.

Learn more about Ryan at:
Blog | LinkedIn | Threads | Instagram | Tumblr | X

Landfall

Ryan Blaney

The hum of a vibrating phone pulled Jared out of the best sleep he'd had in weeks. He squinted at the glowing LED screen and read the name of his best friend in block capitals, illuminating his dark bedroom. H reached onto his bedside table and reluctantly placed his phone next to his ear.

"Good morning sunshine!" said an overly-cheerful voice.

"Todd," said Jared, groggily "is it even morning yet?"

"It's always morning somewhere, J." replied Todd. "Get your game face on and meet me at O'Hare Street. We just got a hit."

Jared blinked twice, then sat bolt upright. "We got a hit?" he repeated.

"Scanners erupted three minutes ago. We just got confirmation. Pressure was building across the Southwest all night and it's moving faster and faster. Approximate landfall in three hours. You in?"

Jared was already out of bed and scrambling to put his jeans on by the time Todd said, "Faster and faster".

"O'Hare Street," he replied, holding his phone with one hand and spraying deodorant with the other. "See you there."

"Attaboy!" cheered Todd as he hung up.

Jared pulled a blue shirt over his head and slid into his red jacket. Todd was never wrong about these things, but nobody expected the season to begin for another month. The atmosphere would get heavier after a dry spell around early summer, seeding the perfect conditions for landfall.

Landfall in May is practically unheard of, thought Jared, tying his laces. If this is a prank, he would take Todd outside and beat him with a rusty pole.

He scrubbed his teeth and poured some coffee into a flask, then raced into the garage and leapt into his jeep. The clock on the dashboard read 03:35. The sky above Salt Lake City was still emblazoned with stars. At this rate, landfall would take place at sunrise. He double-checked his camera was in the pack by his side and reversed out of the driveway. This should be something to see, thought Jared, his excitement building.

Traffic was non-existent at this time of the morning, and Jared reached O'Hare Street with time to spare. He spotted Todd's tell-tale navy-blue pickup truck parked by the corner and pulled up right behind it. Todd stepped out to greet him, dressed in a green raincoat and faded baseball cap. He might have been up all night, but the exuberance on his face didn't show it. At this time of year, his inner child ran riot.

Jared rolled his window down as he approached. "I swear to God, Todd, if this is a joke…" he began to warn his best friend.

"No joke buddy," Todd assured him. "Public warnings have gone out and locals have been evacuated. Thunderbirds are go, bitch!"

Jared rubbed the stubble on his chin. "Alright, then. Lead the way, man."

Todd let out a gleeful chuckle and ran back into his trunk.

Before long, both vehicles were out of the city and cruising up the freeway. Jared switched his comm on and checked in with Todd.

"We still on track?" he asked.

"We are," answered Todd. "She's zig-zagging her way over the Wasatch Mountains and will make landfall just outside Bear River."

Jared sipped the last of his coffee. "If it starts moving erratically, will it still make landfall?" he asked.

"Of course, it will," replied Todd, with an aggrieved tone in his voice. "There might not be as long a window as you were hoping though, so keep your camera ready."

Jared touched the pack in the passenger seat for good luck. "Copy that, T," he said.

As the two friends raced up the highway, the edges of the night sky began to bleed in yellow light, igniting the peaks of the mountain range to their left. The countryside around them slowly began to take form, the cityscape became grassland became desert. Jared's coffee was now working at full capacity, and not a second too soon. The traffic began to build in the opposite direction as buses and cars ferried people into the city for another day's work.

Jared noticed an increasing number of trucks and vans and RVs joining their lane. The few cars remaining were quickly overtaken and left behind, until Jared and Todd found themselves part of a convoy.

"Looks like a big turnout." Jared couldn't help but remark.

"Well, J," said Todd. "I'm not the only guy with my ears to the ground, y'know? Or to the sky, I guess. First landfall of the year and before the seasons even really started? Gonna attract a crowd!"

"Who do you think we'll see there?" asked Jared.

"Ah, the regulars," replied Todd, wryly. "Frank, Steve, Conan…maybe even Caroline."

Jared rolled his eyes. "Knock it off, Romeo."

Todd erupted in laughter through the comm in Jared's right hand. "You're the Romeo, J!" he cried, between chuckles. "I'm just Romeo's pal who wants him to get some!"

"Okay, then," said Jared. "Knock it off, Mercutio."

"Hahahahaha! Young hearts run free, baby!"

Jared switched off the comm.

When the convoy reached its end, almost two hours later, the promise of sunrise was put on hold by the tell-tale black clouds. The wind whistled and screeched around every vehicle as they jostled for a spot to park on the grassy outcrop that had been designated the best vantage point.

Jared and Todd, the early birds of this congregation managed to park beside one another. Jared pulled on his coat, grabbed his camera and stepped out of his jeep. The wind was now so strong it almost shoved him into the side of the jeep. He righted himself and looked around.

Around fifty trucks, cars, RVs and vans had made their way onto the small rise, churning up dust and dried earth in every direction. Looking west there were flat, featureless fields where in better weather, livestock would graze. Ten miles from where Jared stood was a small-town Google Maps identified as Pencilbrook. If Todd was to be believed, its four hundred and twelve residents had been duly warned and evacuated.

Jared walked over to Todd, still sitting in the driver seat with his laptop now open across his knees. The screen showed a radar system encompassing a fifty-mile radius, with an angry swirling orange and red mass honing in on Pencilbrook's coordinates. Thunder boomed and growled over their heads. An excited cheer came up from the convoy in answer.

"How long?" asked Jared.

Todd stroked his bushy brown beard, as he was wont to do when working something out. "Five-ten minutes" he answered. "I'd get ready, all the same."

"You two are always ready!" called a familiar voice.

Jared turned (a little too eagerly) and saw a woman with short cropped red hair walking towards them, a sleeveless jacket over a white shirt. Her arms were bare to the breeze, with the left arm decorated with a tattoo that read "CHASER" on the inside of her forearm. "Might've known you pair would be the first to arrive." she said, with a knowing smile.

"Hi, Caroline," said Jared.

"Hey, Jared," said Caroline. "Hey, Todd. Hope you didn't drag us all the way out here just to stare at a sad little town."

Todd folded away his laptop and pulled out a well-worn pair of binoculars. He practically skipped out the door of his truck. "Hell no, girl," he assured her." We're in for a show."

Another burst of thunder overhead. Another cheer in response. Everyone seemed to have rushed out of their vehicles, cameras, telescopes and other assorted gear at the ready. Jared spotted a few excited kids among the crowd, some perched on their fathers' shoulders. He wondered if this would be their first landfall. The thought made him smile. Caroline noticed it too.

"It's nice to see families at these things," she said. "Makes it more…special, somehow. Plus, smiling helps disguise how tired you are."

Jared laughed and turned to look at her, smiling up at him.

A final burst of thunder rumbled across the sky until it reached a crescendo. This time, instead of the din of human voices, a great screech could be heard through the crowds.

"Here we go!" yelled Todd, as the wind picked up. Jared instinctively whipped out his camera and focused on the expanse between him and Pencilbrook.

Something could be seen struggling within the dark storm clouds. It let out another cry, and the atmosphere became hot and heavy. The soft flapping of a pair of massive wings could soon be heard.

Suddenly, in the sky above Pencilbrook, a great figure burst out of the clouds, wisps of black and gray mist trailing behind it as it fell to earth, roaring all the way.

Through the lens of his camera, Jared estimated it must be forty feet long. Its hide was bright red, like maple leaves in October, spikes like bony protrusions ran from the creature's wide, forked tail all the way up its back to its huge head. It sported a pair of yellow-white horns, wide as a truck, atop its skull, and when it opened its huge maw, two rows of fangs, each tooth longer than a man's arm.

It flapped its wings again, making the air dry and arid, as it slowed its descent. It landed on all fours in the farmland outside the town.

Jared snapped a photo as the beast reared up and sniffed around. "Landfall!" he yelled.

"Landfall!" the call went up in voices old and young, all along the hill.

"Landfall!" cried Caroline, beside him.

Jared turned his attention back to the creature, marveling at the size of it. It was stomping around, its serpentine neck twisting from side to side. Something appeared to have caught its eye, and Jared spied a herd of cattle fleeing the beast in a neighboring field.

With a flap of its mighty wings, the creature leapt into the air and soared over the herd with ease. It glided above them, like a giant bird of prey as the panicked steers below raced in all directions. It opened its maw and spewed forth a stream of flames hotter than gasoline; fire scorched the ground beneath it. The heatwave rolled across the fields, forcing those gathered on the hill to stagger and cover their eyes.

Fire raged there now, blackening the once yellow field. The creature settled into it as a bird to a nest. As far as Jared could make out, four of the cows were killed by the blast. The beast bent down and tore into their smoldering remains. Jared's camera clicked incessantly.

After five minutes, the beast finished its meal and bellowed. Thunder boomed above in response. Smoke issued from its nostrils, and for a moment Jared thought it would spit flame again. Instead the beast turned around and began to gallop in the direction of Pencilbrook. It unfurled its wings and took to the air, ripping telephone wires as it went. It rose higher and higher, until soon it was enveloped by the clouds that hung over the plains. It cried out one last time and was gone.

Atop the hill, those gathered began to stir, as if emerging from a trance. They started sharing their excitement, comparing footage of the first landfall of the season. Jared pulled his camera down from his face and turned to Todd and Caroline.

"Well," he said." Breakfast?"

They both nodded enthusiastically. After all, it would be a long drive home.

"Okay there's a place not far from here." he told them. "We'll take my jeep. Climb in."

The two of them entered the jeep, Caroline in the passenger seat, Todd smirking like a teenager in the back. Jared navigated his way through the other parked vehicles and down the hillside. A sign plastered onto the back of his jeep read:

Jared Walsh.
DRAGON CHASER.

Ryan Blaney finished secondary school with record high marks in English Language & Literature. Twenty years later he decided to actually put that skill to good use. A longtime reader of fantasy novels and comic books, Ryan has written a number of short stories beginning with works of fan fiction on sites like *Archive of Our Own & Deviantart* before testing the waters with his original pieces on platforms like *Novello*. In the past Ryan has also written articles for pop culture websites such as *Bad Haven* and *Comicbuzz,* including a thought piece on how the Northern Irish Troubles have been reflected in comic book media. He lives in a quiet village in County Down with his wife, three kids and writing companion/dog Molly.

Learn more about Ryan at: Instagram

Michael Betancourt

(1)
8amCST
San Antonio, Texas
Menagerie Holdings, LLC Corporate Building and Apartments
8th Floor Suite

Thank heavens it is raining. The steady drip upon the windows gilds the bars of my cage. Intricate, large windows to watch the storm, modern air conditioning, the ready availability of delicious foods - all provide lavish levels of comfort, even for someone of my prominence. I inhabit an entire floor of this building, save for my 'caretakers' that come on their own schedules. Days are marked by notifications from the calendar app on my cell phone rather than scratches upon a wall, and my captors, my wardens, the Knights of St. George, provide all the modern advancements in home security to deter intruders. Given the nature of things, I could have made out much worse. In short, it makes for a very cozy prison.

My front door buzzed, thumping loudly as locks disengaged systems to allow access to my home for my daily visit. My guest, as was the case most mornings, was a Knight named Joshua. He was a respectful young man, kind-faced and good natured, whose visits were much more enjoyable than those of my "handlers" in years past. I turned away from the window and drew my current form to its full six-foot frame, meeting Joshua eye to eye.

Perhaps I was overdressed for the day in a midnight blue suit, scarlet tie, black button down and steel toe cowboy boots, but the outfit, while trivial in the grand scheme of things, lent a sense of formality, of ritual, to the proceedings. Joshua understood this well. He went through the motions of our meeting with a dedication appropriate to one of my stature and station. My toothy smile was prominent as he approached. While most would find it frightening, Joshua merely smiled back warmly. He stopped the required ten feet before me and spoke as he bowed.

"Sir Joshua Martinez, 3rd Degree Saint Georgian Knight of the Order of Shields at your service, great one. If it would please you, I would like to begin our required tasks."

The boy was a study in contrasts as he straightened, wearing a formal suit jacket and tie with jeans and brown boots. A creature of habit, he wore what he enjoyed, not dissimilar to his father's style.

I bowed in response and began my part of the formalities.

"I, the Storm Dragon Kasteelanthros Ventru Alastores, bid you welcome. I offer you safety within my domicile as an honored guest, Sir Joshua. Let us sit, share wine, and discuss new business."

Protocol satisfied; I ushered him towards the common room, after taking seats, offering food, and drinks, my guest resumed the more familiar tone he had adopted with me, and I had grown fond of, over his brief pair of years as my warden.

"Kasteel, we have reports from the border of herds of cattle slaughtered and violence escalating to encampments of migrants traveling up from Mexico. You are to investigate the growing threat."

Joshua continued, explaining operation details – travel via an armed SUV escort to the outskirts of Rio Grande City, Texas, release at sundown with flight clearance, beacon lit missile tracking safety measures, and ground support from a contingent of Georgian Knights. All of this was standard procedure for a reconnaissance mission, but one important detail was missing.

"Joshua, my friend, what exactly am I hunting?"

He sighed, pulling his phone from his jacket pocket, and began showing me pictures of bloody ruin. Animals in shreds. Herds of cattle torn asunder, yet uneaten. Their skins were gray in color, corpses dried up and shriveled, though blood was everywhere. The mess was monstrous in nature - which is saying a lot as I know quite a few monsters, myself not least among them.

These images sufficed, the danger to the area was clear, but when the young Knight pulled up the images of what had been done to the people – I felt the hair on my face stiffen into spines. These were trophy displays, territorial markers. Humans impaled upon mesquite trees and so much worse. I knew then what my job was to be. Recon be damned - I would find it, destroy it, and earn the return to my comfortable enclosure.

Joshua's penultimate image displayed the devastated bodies of children, but he immediately swiped away from the grotesque tableau to a photo of two deep, three-toed depressions the thing left behind on the bank of the Rio Grande. Heavy footprints, with long claws and a wide stride – a creature of size that rivalled my own.

"Whatever's doing this is stealthy and powerful, no one's caught hide nor hair of it, the prints are all we've got. Kasteel, I have no idea what that thing is, but when you find it? You make it pay for what it's done."

(2)
3pm CST
Rio Grande City, Texas
City Hall
Conference Room

The Chief of Police was a large man, and in better circumstances probably a jovial one, who fit the stereotypical cowboy image one would expect from an officer in deep South Texas, just this side of the Mexican border.

As for myself, I kept the traditional look I have worn for decades now. A tall Latino man of around forty with broad shoulders, short black hair, a trimmed beard mimicking the frills of my true form, and storm-black eyes. Handsome enough to get the job done, but not pretty. Other dragons prefer an almost inhuman beauty. Vanity demands the looks of a super model, drawing all kinds of attention, making it impossible to blend in. I, on the other hand, prefer something more subtle. No reason to draw attention. No reason to be obvious when hunting.

Joshua, to his credit, oversaw most of the speaking. He identified us as an offshoot of Homeland Security, cooperating with Border Patrol to identify the threat and prevent an international incident. Though we were not worried Mexico would retaliate, no one needed cartels seeking revenge or 'patriots' turned vigilante.

The Chief spoke confidently about the facts of the case. His team ran initial forensics on the area and found little of substance. They identified over sixty bodies, ranging from children up to the elderly. Differing nationalities, but all healthy and strong, and all undocumented immigrants. Their working theory was a coordinated group of nationalists, motivated by hate for the idea of more immigrants in the area. It was plausible if you didn't know what we, the real monsters, did. This was a hunting pattern.

Fifty miles or so, spreading across both sides of the river. The mutilated cattle happened stateside, and the first set of immigrant deaths were reported by a sister city in Mexico after a leaked video from an officer there went viral. In my ancient opinion, human networks of communication are their most effective weapon. The video also alerted the Knights of St. George, leading to their rapid mobilization, and my current presence.

Thunder rumbled in the distance. The line of the encroaching storm drew across the sky like a heavy blanket. The Chief continued rambling details about the case, but my attention faded. His knowledge and perspective were incomplete at best, for he did not believe in monsters. Another roll of approaching thunder cut him short as he shook Joshua's hand. Ah, a perfect night to hunt!

"Agent Martinez, I appreciate everything you and yours are doing here. This all feels wrong. I wouldn't want to be in your shoes for this mess and honestly, I'm damn glad I don't have the jurisdiction on this one. There'll be a standby team at City Hall tonight if you need us. Please keep us informed of what you find. Good luck out there."

Our hotel was...adequate at best if one was feeling kind. Rio Grande City was far from home and would provide only a brief respite before my hunt began. Thus, I opted for a nap, as the air conditioning violently screeched out sixty-five-degree, ozone scented relief from the heat; I could still hear thunder echoing across the sky. Rain was not falling yet, but the Mistress of Storms sang her sweet lullabies to me all the same.

(3)
10pm CST
Rio Grande City – Camargo International Bridge
Georgian Knight Mobile Recon Center

The storm carried an urgency on the wind. Georgian Knights barked orders in their military-style uniforms and modern armor which I found utterly amazing - much lighter than the plate and mail worn by Knights of old, yet every bit as durable. Joshua commanded the ground troops monitoring me from our mobile headquarters. The vehicle meant little to me when the clunky thing was brought into service, but it was now the flagship of Menagerie Unit. Lovingly dubbed the Kennel, the Knights had it kitted out with a ground to air missile launching system, multiple heavy guns, increased troop capacity, and enough tech to make the actual military jealous, courtesy of their friends in the industry.

Lightning crashed overhead. This was perfect weather for a hunting excursion. I stretched my neck and back, impatient to shift form while the unit technician installed my Missile Tracking Unit. The MTU was my backup and their insurance policy - strapped to my wrist and eventually folded into a scale on my arm, it allowed second-to-second tracking, accurate within inches. The missiles themselves were modified Sidewinders resembling armor piercing rounds, built specifically to penetrate my scales and explode internally, inflicting potentially fatal damage. Members of the Menagerie field team were outfitted with the units, and I honestly understood the necessity. A rogue asset running amok on a mission was the last thing the Knights wanted.

While the Order of Saint George consisted of humans and included ex-military from various branches in their service, the Menagerie Unit stood apart in its use of monsters. We were the things that go bump in the night, subjects of folklore and myths come to life - with a sprinkle of military training. Captured creatures became troops to defend from beings who refused peaceful treaties with man's governments. It is my wish to see my fellows recognize and adapt to this changing world, sooner than later. Alas, my hopes are just that for the time being - dreams and aspirations, nothing more.

My technician completed the MTU installation and stepped away from me, leaving space for a forklift to begin unloading the crate which housed one of our smaller unit members – my preferred tracker on shared missions. The operator maneuvered the crate into position facing me, then two Knights wearing reflective goggles began the process of disengaging the locks and mechanisms holding the beast within at bay. My shoulders shook with silent laughter as the crate rattled and the creature within screeched loudly – he was really enjoying himself this evening. One last shriek echoed through the night before the door dropped, revealing a pair of glowing amber eyes. I felt the force of his gaze wash over me to absolutely no effect, as it always was.

"Come now, Calix, must you attempt this every time you see me?"

Calix stepped out of the crate and stretched languorously, and the unique creature made for an odd sight. He was the size of a Labrador, if less cuddly. His head and torso were white feathered, with a crimson comb upon his head and electric blue streaks throughout his plumage. Past his wings, feathers faded to scales over his hindquarters and long tail, though the blue streaks remained.

In Greek, his name – pronounced similar to chalice without the h - meant "very handsome," a fact which fit his stunning coloration and which he never let anyone forget. Decades ago, he was purchased by the Knights as an Easter egg, sure to bring luck and great fortune according to the crone who offered him up. In truth, he was meant to hatch and disable the family who took him home, leaving them helpless sacrifices for the witch's own gains. She was stopped, he was hatched safely as part of the Menagerie and had proven himself a loyal compatriot ever since.

My prior experience with his species was slim to none, but I learned quickly on our missions. Cockatrices are constantly confused with basilisks and Calix utterly despises it. While their abilities are similar, their differences are as great as those between wyverns and myself. Cockatrices are more bird than reptile, scaled only on their hind halves, and this cockatrice was all trickster. Using his glare attack was Calix's favorite tactic, and more than a few inexperienced Knights had fallen prey to the stunning effect of his amber eyes. Unlike basilisks' petrification, cockatrice attacks mimicked drunkenness - causing prey to stumble, fall, become incoherent for a time, and sometimes go blind. All this allows the cockatrice to sink its single fang, akin to an egg tooth, into the prone victim, injecting venom to simultaneously paralyze its quarry and begin drinking its blood.

The species' enmity was mutual, they tended to hunt each other - but between the two I preferred the smaller cockatrice as a companion. I found the bus-sized basilisks unreliable, temperamental, and flat out rude. Plus, being raised by the Knights meant this little beast that thought himself an extremely beautiful Velociraptor offshoot was one of the handful of Menagerie Unit charges not actively dangerous to humans.

"Kasteel, you overgrown old gecko! How's the lifestyle of the rich and imprisoned treating you these days?" He fluttered his wings and squawked the chortle that passed as his laughter. "I see you still haven't changed your look. You're never gonna find love looking like a telenovela villain straight off Univision."

"Calix, my little chupacabra, are you ready to begin our hunt?" I said as my laughter boomed over the camp in an echo of the storm above. Creatures double his size, leaders of nations, entire armies would not dare speak to me in such a way - but Calix cared little for my fearsome reputation. As Storm team members, what mattered was that I was a friend.

"You know damn well chupacabras aren't real, Kasteel! They're a stupid urban legend!" Calix rustled his feathers in annoyance and muttered half to himself, "Damn goat suckers get all the fame when it's my species they should be honoring."

My little friend was not the only one who enjoyed a bit of teasing, it was amusing to see him so flustered. If there was one thing cockatrices as a species hated, it was being confused with another monster. Normally, that was a basilisk, but here dear Calix was immediately subject to the legend of the chupacabra – a vile, dog-sized creature that drank the blood of goats and livestock, freezing witnesses in their tracks with their glowing red eyes. Calix was convinced they were pure superstition and in no way existed, which was ironic coming from a chicken snake speaking with a dragon.

"I know how you feel Calix, but the fact we have never seen one does not mean that they do not exist," I replied with a stifled smile.

Despite being issued through a beak, Calix's scoff was the clearest I had ever heard. We continued our banter as we waited for his MTU to be set up before Joshua made his way through the ranks towards us. His imposing black armor was highlighted with electric blue accents that designated us as the Menagerie Unit's Storm Team.

"Evening gentlemen. Let's get tonight's hunt underway with as little fuss as possible. We're cleared for twenty-four hours over a fifty-mile spread. We believe whatever's hurting these people is acting alone. Judging by the size and depth of its footprints, it's upwards of forty feet long and three - four tons."

Calix whistled in surprise, a ridiculous sound coming from a chicken snake. Joshua acknowledged the response with a nod before continuing:

"Calix, I want you on the ground. Sniff out anything you can find that's not normal for the area and flag Kasteel. Kasteel, scout from the air until we identify the threat, then you'll neutralize it. I'll follow in the new Argo XTV."

Joshua dismissed us, climbed into the eight-wheeled ATV and signaled the troops to provide me clearance. The soldiers edged away from me as my face grew scales and my teeth lengthened and sharpened. Shifting form is not pleasant to witness. A low-budget 1980's werewolf film is the closest visual comparison I could make. My body bulged disproportionately as I fell to all fours. My hands and feet ripped apart, shedding strips of dried skin to reveal expanding claws that gouged chunks of dirt from the ground. Crunching, snapping, and popping sounds exploded into the air as my joints realigned, my body grew, and my neck extended in length. Wings burst from my back with a sound akin to fabric being shredded, and blue lights sparked in the air as my scales grew into place.

The process takes moments and unlike those werewolf movies, feels like complete ecstasy. The team called this stage my 'magical girl moment' as static electricity built around me, then released in miniature arcs of lightning between myself and metallic surfaces nearby. Not one to disappoint my adoring onlookers, I spun around with a flourish of wings and a resounding tail slam. As the lightning burst from my frame, I roared a challenge into the night sky. Cheers and applause rose from the Knights of Storm Team as I launched myself into the air, and the Mistress of Storms gifted us her bounty as well. The rain began to fall as we departed.

(4)
11pm CST
Camargo Municipality
Tamaulipas, Mexico
Rio Grande River Border Area

Calix was on a trail Joshua and I could neither see nor sense. Driving along, Joshua was limited to what his eyes and the vehicle's sensors could tell him. Advanced tech notwithstanding, he was only human. I flew forty feet above, allowing the storm to moisten my scales. The freedom I felt was exhilarating. I kept a close eye on my small friend as he ran headlong through the brush, tail lashing in the wind, following the trail of emotion and death that only his delicate senses could detect. The MTU's speaker squawked as Calix reported his findings.

"Hey y'all, I'm picking up fear tinged with desperation. Someone out here is sweating bullets in the rain, a mile or so away. The whole area reeks of grief and loss - I don't know what we're running into, but it isn't gonna be a welcome party."

Joshua barked orders over the MTU as he was forced to backtrack and find an alternate route. The XTV didn't exactly match the maneuverability of chicken snake feet.

"Kasteel, please close half a mile and report back what you find. I don't want anything using the rain to catch us by surprise."

Even aggravated, he was always so polite. I hummed an acknowledgement and flew ahead. The terrain was hilly with patches of deep brush, broken by occasional ravines. Nothing should have been out here, so when I saw the circle of stones and the large campfire completely untouched by the rain, I knew I'd found our target. I updated Joshua and banked around the stones to reach ground level, shifting back to my human shell mid-landing. The chatter over the MTU was loud so I pulled the earpiece from its casing and placed it into my right ear. Storm Team's response unit was on standby based on what I found inside.

The area covered about fifty yards in diameter within a shimmering dome that would have been invisible in clearer weather. Most agents would have entered by stealth; in fact Calix announced just that through the MTU upon arriving. I had not sensed him - rain covered his scent, thunder drowned out any sounds, and lightning flashes hid his movement. So much the better.

I walked straight up to the barrier. I am a dragon, specifically a Storm Dragon, and we are not known for hiding. The barrier felt cool to the touch, giving no feeling of threat. A simple deterrent for vermin and a place of inviting warmth for anyone passing through, so I stepped through. I was slowed by the sensation of walking through slime, then stopped, astonished at what the dome contained. In the center of the illusionary bubble sat a small cottage of Eastern European build with eight young women chained by the neck to its front porch. There was nothing but static when I attempted to contact Joshua - unfortunate but unsurprising, as magic wreaks havoc with communication tech. I have seen spellcasters catch cell phones on fire with a mere touch, so I was on my own until Calix could sneak in to check on me. Hands raised peacefully, I approached the women.

"Ladies, I mean you no harm, I will get you to safety. Just give me..."

And several things happened at once. The women raised bound hands and cried out, speaking over one another – I could recognize Spanish, and something Slavic, but the words and other languages jumbled together so I could not understand what they were saying. I realized it was a warning only after a fist pounded into my right temple, sending me flying to slam hard into the ground.

Gritting my teeth, I looked up at my assailant, a young man appearing in his mid-twenties, heavily muscled, with European or perhaps Russian features. He stood unmoving, stark naked, muscles tense, staring at me with blood red eyes and a wide grin. He spoke to me, but it was no language with which I was familiar. It was sharp, something old but not of my species. From his speech patterns, muscled body, and excessively pretty face it was a safe bet he was draconic in nature – so I addressed him in my native tongue.

"You have made a grave mistake by striking me. I advise you to release the women and surrender. We will transport you to a safe location for questioning."

The pretty boy laughed a deep belly laugh that horrified the captives and began circling me like a predator. His eyes shone crimson now and his mouth stretched into an unnaturally wide smile as a forked tongue flicked out to taste the air. The display was meant to shock a lesser creature, but I knew he was searching for other potential threats in the area.

I stood slowly, dusting myself off in a show of nonchalance. A few rolls of the neck and I felt a pop that eased the pain from his punch. Facing him now, I pushed my presence forward. All monsters have a presence, a will they can extend to frighten lesser creatures, and I hoped to force this fool into submission. His rumbling laugh did not inspire confidence in that plan as he spoke to me again.

"You have made mistakes this evening, but you are young and brash. I acknowledge this, and so offer you mercy. You crossed my threshold, entered my domain, made claims on my wives, thought to threaten me with your presence, but you know not what I am or what I can do. Leave here, now."

I prepared a vicious combination of bravado and mockery to make Calix proud, but as I stepped forward, he blasted me with his presence, leaving me shaking from his will as he spoke again.

"Youngling, today you were granted the opportunity to leave my domain, yet you chose to remain. I applaud your bravery, misplaced as it may be. Long has it been since I faced an opponent capable of standing before me. Know I appreciate your determination and be glad in the knowledge that your end is no average draconic beast."

He roared as his head split into five, necks stretching from his torso. His body snapped and tore as it grew, taking on a sickly gray pallor accented by crimson stripes. He stood over forty feet tall and as long as a city bus with five dragon heads spewing flame into the air. Debris swirled around me as he flapped his wings and the heads roared in unison:

"Today you face the mightiest of Zmei!"

(5)
1am CST
Camargo Municipality
Tamaulipas Mexico
Rio Grande River Border Area

I turned, playing for space as I shifted, forcing my body out of its human shell as fast as possible, but one head grabbed me mid-shift, lifted and slammed me into the ground four times. My shell broke apart with each impact, revealing me crumpled on the ground. The Zmei laughed a throaty chortle as another head blasted me with flame. The pain was immediate as my scales dried up and cracked. My opponent was a unique creature I knew little of. Ancient Slavic myths, they kidnapped beautiful women to claim as brides. The flame of their breath did not burn, rather, it withered – as my torn shoulder could attest.

My immediate area charged with ozone as I rolled out of the flame and sparks fired across my body as I released a lightning blast, impacting his center-mass. He stumbled and I pressed my attack. First Rule of a fight: Never relent, strike fast. I dashed forward to pounce at him. His heads snapped forward, teeth finding only empty air as I pulled short to blast lightning point blank.

He shrieked as the other heads sprayed me with fire. The bastard's breath was making me feel like the cattle. I reeled back from pain, and he charged right over me, slamming me to the ground again and raking ribbons of flesh from my flank. I was bleeding and my healing ability was not enough to counter both flame and claws. This was it, ended by a creature far more ancient than I was. Perhaps this was best. It was bound to happen eventually. Perhaps there was something to be found in the sooner rather than the later.

"Smile for the camera, you fugly iguana-faced bastard!"

In true velociraptor form Calix charged the Zmei, hitting all five heads with his gaze. The heads screamed in frustration as Calix hopped onto me and shouted,

"Let's get the hell out of here! Now!"

I struggled to take a single step and almost fell. I flew straight up, pushing with everything I had as Calix gripped my dorsal spikes. About 100 feet up, we broke the barrier with an audible pop, entering the storm. Voices exploded from my earpiece as Storm Team tried to prevent the Kennel from firing on us. We had been out of contact for far too long. Joshua was shouting orders to delay, to give us more time.

A shriek from below followed the rumble of thunder as the Zmei pursued. Only two heads remained functional, the others hung successfully stunned. I swung my head and fired a blast of lightning. Now charged by the storm, it tore through the leftmost functional head. Again, Joshua screamed orders to delay, but Calix shouted back to let the shot come. My wings missed a beat, I could not believe what I had heard. I knew he must be scared, but this was simply giving up.

"Are you mad?" I roared through the storm's gale.

He mouthed off with a series of curses I have no desire to repeat and then ordered me to grab hold of the Zmei and just dodge when I was told. The order came, the missile launched, our MTU wailed to warn of its approach, and the Zmei gave me little choice in the matter. He slammed into me, grasping with his front claws, raking with his hind talons. It was all I could do not to be disemboweled and both our wings flapped furiously to keep us aloft. The pain was excruciating, yet I fought. I fought as hard as I could, biting wherever I could find an opening, blasting lighting as he tore flesh from my body. It went on for an eternity. Seconds felt like hours. The MTU was unbearably loud, the missile was right on top of us. I was prepared to lose this fight, but not my friend, so it was good that Calix was well versed in the Second Rule of a fight: There is no such thing as a fair fight.

Calix peeked over my shoulder, screeched his raptor screech, and blasted the Zmei with his gaze again, blinding the final head.

"Kasteel! Bank now with all you got!"

Instinct took over as the "within inches" advertised accuracy of the missile proved true. It buried itself in the Zmei's chest and exploded. I tumbled from the sky, deafened by the blast, attempting to keep Calix safe. I watched the Zmei fall burning and bleeding, watched him slam into the ground moments before we did. Sweet darkness took me as I saw Joshua and his team appear through the storm.

(6)
11am CST
San Antonio, Texas
Menagerie Holdings, LLC Corporate Building and Apartments
8th Floor Suite

Thank heavens it was raining. I had been confined to quarters for seven full days of recovery with multiple guards at my side. Joshua shared that the young women were freed from their captivity and would be assisted with seeking asylum in the United States. The paperwork for the mission also fell on his shoulders - explaining the missile being fired, our communication malfunction, and the capture of a very live Zmei, which I admit disturbed me.

I fought that thing with everything I had and only came out on top with the help of Calix. He ended up with nothing more than a few bruises and was being rewarded with a drive-in movie marathon of his favorite Jurassic themed films. I had a standing invitation to attend if I could heal fast enough, but I knew in this line of work I would be needed again. Something would be found in the sooner rather than the later.

Michael Betancourt is originally from the United States specifically the Rio Grande Valley in DEEP South Texas. When you reach San Antonio you still have 4 hours further South to drive before reaching the RGV. Which after that the only place to go is either the Gulf of Mexico or actual Mexico. Michael is a proud Geek that fell into writing by way of D&D, Saturday Morning Cartoons, and Comic Books. He currently creates events for a living when he is not talking to the voices in his head and writing down their misadventures. Michael holds a BA in Public Relations and Advertising, a MA in Communication from The University of Texas Rio Grande Valley and is pursuing a PHD in Mythological Studies and Folklore by way of Pacifica Graduate Institute.

Learn more about Michael at: Instagram | Threads

Of Dragons and Long Hair

Rachael Ikins

It has become ceremony, this hair.
Weaving my braids every morning,
Releasing their day's adventures at night
Some kind of wavy silk I forgot lived there for so many years.

Hair. That king who lost his strength when his wife shaved his head, a princess who wasted a lot of time dangling hers out a tower window hoping for a prince to come along when, in fact, she could've cut off her braid, tied it around the bed frame and lowered herself out the window.

Rappelling past bats and birds, little lizards creeping in crevices between stones. Yes, maybe a few strands might've ripped out-a momentary sting that last drop— but waiting around for a knight in shining armor can waste a whole lifetime.

Maybe a dragon will grab that dangling braid long after the shorn woman (now shockingly light) has vanished beneath tree skirts. Talons will carry it back to a distant cave to line her nest.

Dragons never wait for someone else to solve their problems. Some might say a dragon can be a hot head, frustration builds and then *poof* explosion. No matter where on the planet they roost, they murmur at all the ways humans have misinformed themselves about draconian folk. How can a wingless one understand? A non-fire-breather? Swoop low over the sea, scream joy, spray splashes a belly, instant steam,

yes, it is true, a dragon is a hot-blooded being. Like the Earth herself, they don't appreciate being ridden. Touch at your own risk.

Rachael Ikins is a 2016/18 Pushcart, 2013/18 CNY Book Award nominee, 2018 Independent Book Award winner, & 2019 Vinnie Ream & Faulkner poetry finalist. 2021 Best of the Net nominee, 2023 2nd place winner Northwind Writing Competition. A Syracuse University graduate. Author/illustrator of nine books in multiple genres. Her writing and artwork have appeared in journals worldwide from India, UK, Japan, Canada and US. She is associate editor for Clare Songbirds Publishing House.

Learn more about Rachael at:
Instagram | Facebook | Facebook | Clare Songbirds Publishing

Sophie St John

Water is heavier when there is less of it to go around. The fireproof sacks clipped to my saddle bulge as the liquid inside them sloshes to and fro in time with the steady beating of my wings. There are six of the sacks in total, split evenly on each side of my body to give the illusion of heightened balance and optimal mobility. In reality, my spine bows beneath the pressure, as if ready to snap at any moment.

I have grown accustomed to the strain of propelling myself forward with so much precious cargo on my back. I have trained my lungs to fill only halfway with each laboured breath, fearing that they would only burst within the suffocating confines of my ribs should they inflate to their full capacity. Discomfort digs its hooks deep into my flesh, but I have honed the ability to ignore its presence.

These are precisely the kind of behaviours which have allowed me to survive this long. My kind have been dead for millennia – I was dead myself once, buried deep beneath the sea – but we have always had good, strong bones. Healthy foundations, as the Sapiens have often proclaimed. Our flesh is thick, and our scales are capable of withstanding the hottest flames. These are formidable qualities that have, in so many of the ancient stories about us, painted our kind as devils: greedy hoarders of gold, vicious beasts hungering for innocent souls, or cruel sentries ensuring that the shackles around maidens' wrists remained intact. Other stories interpreted our strength differently, boasting instead of our godly prosperity and graciousness. Perhaps elements of the truth can be found in all of these legends. There is good and bad in all of us. The endings of our individual stories are dependent merely on which qualities we deign to share with those who admire and fear us.

Except that the Sapiens did not give us any choice when they pulled our corpses from the seas and stuffed life back beneath our scales. What mattered most to them as they pumped air into our lungs and blood through our veins once more was something entirely different from good and evil. It may have been the desire for a certain kind of balance that drove them to restore us to our glory before harnessing us like dogs. I can believe that they discovered a harmony in us, for we have always possessed the ability to exist between ice and fire; drowning and burning; life and death. A dragon plunging into an ocean possesses as much grace as one marching through shrouds of smoke and flames. This has long been our legacy, twisted and splintered and scattered unevenly throughout various legends, and there exists infinite value in it. Thus, the Sapiens pieced us together, filling in the cracks between languages and stories until we were whole again; and as we struggled to stand collectively on our trembling feet, shaking the stiffness from our undead wings, they gave us our new purpose.

By the time we understood what had transpired and what now awaited us, the Sapiens had already secured the saddles across our backs.

Tydakon. Yield to Gliese 581c.

The message crosses lightyears to zip through my head as if it were a thought of my own, thanks entirely to the twin devices lodged in the sides of my skull. Metal fingers reach down to tap at the corner of my left eye – an unnecessary signal from my pilot, but we are still learning the intricacies of each other's behaviours a year on from meeting. Perhaps I have yet to convince them that I always obey the Sapiens' orders. I dutifully adjust our course, and we plummet downwards.

Tydakon approaching Gliese 581c, comes the pilot's response. Their voice is hollower than that of the Sapiens who has been instructing us throughout this shift. There is a certain absence to it. An echo of something lost, or maybe stripped away. *Please specify quantity.*

Fifty-percent, the Sapiens says. As if the words don't strike like a physical blow and leave me winded. As if they are not the harbingers of unthinkable loss and pain. As if they mean nothing at all.

Fifty-percent. Half of the water freed from my back in one fell swoop.

So much for balance.

Our pilots have been a part of our routines since our second lives began. They are extensions of us; our names, crafted and distributed meticulously by the Sapiens, become theirs also. The pilots fit against the curves of our backs, tune into our thoughts and movements, and oversee the coming and going of water from our sacks. When it is time for us to rest, they are the ones to guide us back to our stables, searching all the while for any signs of weakness or injury. As we sleep, they step up into the nooks carved for them in the walls beside our stalls; they sink back into the bed of tendrils waiting there to wriggle through the lines in their armour, pumping waves of new energy through their wires in exchange for the information they've collected during jumps between galaxies; and, as their memories cross the channel between our planet and that of the Sapiens, they stand as still as a corpse awaiting proper burial. Yet, always, they shudder awake upon the dawn of a new shift to collect us from our stalls and start over from the beginning.

My current pilot is not my first, and they will likely not be my last. My first was inferior in every way, constructed from aluminium that dented too easily and creaked with every shift of their limbs during those last few weeks of their use. They malfunctioned in the saddle behind my head, their hands never loosening around my neck as they shuddered and groaned. I felt them cracking open for hours until they finally went limp against me, and still it was several hours more before my shift ended and I was granted permission to return to Red with the body.

The pilots have never been alive – not once have I seen them eat, nor have I ever felt their chests rise and fall with breath as they press against me – but something about my first pilot's deterioration resembled the most torturous of deaths. After the Sapiens detached the pilot's remains from my saddle and dragged their husk away to be melted down, I crept into my stall, curled into a ball to bury my face into the plush flesh of my own stomach, and mourned for something that never lived.

Companions are almost as rare as water in this universe. My current pilot may feel nothing for me – in fact, they feel nothing for anyone or anything at all – but they are still mine, and I cherish them as such. It is my name that is branded across their chest. They are humanoid enough that one can sometimes be convinced that they are made of real flesh, so long as one ignores the distinct lack of a protruding nose in the centre of the face and the absence of a slitted mouth. They do have eyes: two pinpricks of blue that see everything and nothing at all. It is through these eyes that the Sapiens track our journeys between worlds, bestowing the water they so desperately need upon barren landscapes that they hope, someday, might soften beneath their touch. And if they don't – if the planets they have selected remain stubbornly intact and hostile – then perhaps our frequent draining of nearby water-planets will reveal some concealed landmass beneath the surface that they can flock to instead, saving them so much toil. Either way, with enough movement, something is bound to give. Through our efforts, they will build something permanent again.

Do we not deserve something permanent too? But perhaps it is not a matter of deserving. We must merely find the thing that gives us strength and hold onto it. We are entirely responsible for making this second life worth something. If this fragile connection between my pilot and me is all that I can find purchase on to keep myself afloat, then so be it. It may not be much, but one companion, however stoic, is better than none at all.

It feels good to carry something worth so much.

The water we deliver depletes now at twice the rate it did when all of this began a decade ago. The small groups of Sapiens uprooted and scattered throughout the universe were once soldiers; their will was as strong as their bodies, and they stamped their footprints into the ground of each of their assigned planets with a smug air about them, as if they deserved to be there at the expense of so many other creatures lost to the rising tides of their home planet. In time, though, I have witnessed the decline of these soldiers. I have seen their bodies shrink, their smiles wane, and their skin turn grey. With each new delivery, they become more desperate for the water that was always intended to be a temporary relief – something to sustain them while they strove to build something permanent.

Ten years, and not one of their chosen planets has accepted them. None of these ex-soldiers have dug beneath soil and rock to discover some hidden spring. None have built anything that might wash the impurities from their old water and transform it into something safe again. Their new homes are not the same as the planet they once knew so intimately yet took for granted anyway. They live in the dark; they live in shells of airtight cloth and metal; they do not live at all. Only the richest and smartest of their kind have the privilege of still living the way they all once did, watching the rest of us through their screens and sending out orders from the few patches of land yet to be claimed by the seas back on Blue.

(They had a different name for their home planet once. In the last ten years, I have not heard the old name spoken. I remember it though. All of us dragons do. After all, Earth was also *our* home planet once.)

The settlement on Gliese 581c was once capable of making a sixteen-point-six-percent yield last a full week's rotation. All six of the other water-carriers whom I am stabled with could complete their own assigned deliveries before this planet signalled their need for more. Now they take half of my load, and I expect another dragon will be replenishing their stock as early as half a rotation from now.

I wonder: will the Sapiens stationed on Blue never learn to fear the lack of progress being made? Will they have us carry load after load of water until every other planet in the universe has been drained and all other members of their species have perished from their perpetual thirst?

Yet I know that it is not my duty to worry on their behalf. For now, I bear enough of their burden.

We soar through the empty space between worlds. It took us all some time to learn how to fly without air, but now we do it well. It is simply a matter of manipulating the fire that burns within our cores, sending the flames to the ends of our limbs and to the tips of our wings. The heat drives us forward in all this cold.

My left wing beats twice as hard as my right, cleaving through the darkness that surrounds us. I know that the limb will be aching and stiff when I tumble into sleep tonight, but the pain in my right wing leaves me no choice but to compensate.

We leave 581c with three sacks still full, and all are soon claimed by 581d. Then we hurtle through the debris disk and prepare for our jump back to Solar One through the Firing Zone. I slow the motion of my wings as we approach the structure of pure, eternally burning flames. Of course, this is merely the visible section of the Firing Zone; similar sections exist in every pocket of space claimed by the Sapiens, appearing as vast walls of golden fire with dozens of black holes poked into their surfaces. To pass through any of these holes is to enter the system of tunnels that twist and turn throughout the universe, constructed from fire so hot that, between each end, they become invisible to the naked eye. It is through these tunnels that we may travel from one galaxy to the next, blipping in and out of sight – of existence, it seems – in a matter of moments as the heat consumes our atoms, tears us apart, then hurls us back together again. Although the Sapiens invented this technology, the tunnels were made tangible only by the efforts of my brethren. Maybe that is why a sort of peace always washes over me as I tuck my wings close to my body and allow the heat to pull me in.

There is a little bit of magic in all this, I think. To be incinerated before being spat back out into space, intact and reinvigorated… It is not unlike being born again. And maybe that's exactly what it is. Maybe every trip we take through the Firing Zone is another death, another rebirth. If I were to tally up every jump I've ever made, where would that leave me? How many lives have I been granted? Where does this all end?

This is why the Sapiens chose us. It never mattered how long we dragons remained buried in caves beneath the ocean, curled around our own tails with our flesh cold and our hearts still. Our sorcery kept us alive in their stories. We have always been immortal where it matters. What better creatures to withstand all that they have thrown at us? Fire, water, time itself – we embrace it all.

Yes, there is magic in all of this. One only needs to know where to look, and to have enough courage to do so.

When we emerge from the fire, I open my eyes and unfurl my wings. Here, the Firing Zone is suspended between Blue and Red, pinned between two orbits. I linger for a moment longer than necessary, staring down at the water that has swallowed so much of the Sapiens' home. They're doing this all backwards, I think, starting at the end and working their way to a shaky beginning. But this has always been their way. Establishing life before the most basic foundations have been laid; securing the saddles before their steeds have even had the chance to find their feet.

If they would just focus on what's in front of them, then they might have better chances of survival. The only planet in need of draining is their own, yet they refuse to let us redistribute Blue's oceans. How much land might be recovered if we were each allowed to fill our sacks just once? How many tired, thirsty strangers might be granted access to the home they've lost? How many other planets might be saved from the Sapiens' cursed touch?

But opportunity and selfishness go hand in hand. Blue's floods were merely a spark. The Sapiens arranged our bones as kindling, stacked their aspirations atop us until we bowed beneath their weight, and then it was only a matter of fanning the flames. Their ash-coated fingers have now brushed the very edges of the universe. An empire is still an empire no matter how vulnerable, how corrupt, how unbalanced it is. Why would they ever wish to reunite their peoples and restore their home to its former glory when it would require disregarding everything they have already achieved, and everything they might yet build?

My pilot shifts against my back. Their fingers have been drumming at the corner of my right eye for so long now that the flesh has grown numb. I jerk my head to the left, savouring a morsel of satisfaction at the way they immediately lose balance and lurch forward. They flail for a handful of seconds before adjusting their position in the saddle and curling both arms around my neck. I have not jostled them enough to make them lose their grip entirely, but I still wait until I am sure they have found their balance again before I turn my head and take us swiftly down to Red.

There were more of us at the start. For three years, I shared my stall with a younger dragon who had been little more than a child at the time of her first death. She fancied me for an older brother who I had no doubt really existed once. I hoped, for his sake as well as ours, that the real brother was one of the few lucky ones to remain undiscovered before the oceans rose too high to allow access to his tomb.

In time, I came to care for the young dragon as if she were truly my kin. The Sapiens called her Droshan. Like me, she did not remember her real name. If this fact ever haunted her, she never let it show.

Droshan was too small to make trips beyond Solar One, but the Sapiens did not only require water-carriers. There was still a purpose for her, just like so many other dragons who were too old or too young or too weak to transport water. Red was a dry, empty place. There were mountains to split, tunnels to dig, and stables to build. What was left of Blue could not accommodate the Sapiens *and* their loyal mules. Red was to be our shelter – I have never quite been able to call it a home – and only we could make it so.

Droshan was one of many to burrow beneath the dirt and build us a place where we could curl into ourselves and press our noses against our tails, our muscles remembering the shapes we adopted in death and falling naturally back into them as if we'd never woken from that eternal sleep. It is the same shape that the Sapiens now stamp on everything they touch. The circle of our lives; the creature clamping down on the vulnerable parts of itself to become its own beginning and ending. A symbol stolen, used, and manipulated until it became something bigger than all of us.

But in the spaces built for us by Droshan and the others like her, we are the middle point of all things. We are the pause between breaths and the breaks between waves. In those dark, quiet stables, we are allowed to simply exist.

And there's the real magic. It isn't being able to live amongst both fire and water, but being able to survive in the space between them. In the driest and coldest of places, with nothing else to sustain us, we find each other and ourselves.

Even now, despite everything I've done and seen, I believe that this makes our existence worth something.

You tilt, she told me once.

I didn't understand until she showed me, bending her left legs and allowing her body to droop to one side. Off-balance, she couldn't stop herself from stumbling. I caught her with my wing before she could crash into the wall, nudged her until she clicked back into place on her internal axis, and suppressed the growl clawing up my throat as pain flickered through my joints.

You tilt, she repeated.

You echo, I said.

You tease.

You make it so easy.

You are hurting.

It was the only time I had ever wished to lie to her. She was too young to carry my pain. Yet, I could see in her eyes that she would never be convinced by anything but the truth.

I am hurting, I conceded.

Where?

I pulled my right wing – the one I'd caught her with, too quickly to give the movement enough consideration – back to my side and grunted as it folded against my body. She tracked the movement with her eyes. Her slitted pupils narrowed. She blinked slowly to show that she understood.

Why?

How best to explain? How to reveal the truth whilst preserving some of the hope and joy that naturally accompanied her youth? I wrestled with these questions as the smog of silence grew thicker between us. In the end, it was within that very silence that she found all those harsh realities I could not voice. The pain, the hopelessness, the anger – she identified them all.

Before my pilot returned, signalling the beginning of a new rotation, I spoke the only words I'd managed to pull together.

The weight we must carry is no longer solely ours, I told her. *I tilt because of their weaknesses, not my own. And yet it is their strength as much as my own that allows me to stand at all. We must accept this if we wish to make anything of the life that they have given us.*

I feared that even these words, chosen as they were with great care, would unsettle her too much. But the yellow of her eyes did not dim, and the almost-imperceptible lift of her head sent a ripple of pride through me. This was proof of her own unique strength, and of the bond we'd both worked hard to cultivate. I felt then that, regardless of how much she understood the life we led, she had begun to know me better. Her trust had become as vital to me as any other life-force. If she had decided that she did not like the creature I'd been shaped into by the expectations and orders that constantly tore through me like flames in a kiln, then this second life of mine might really be devoid of all hope.

I have never been more of a coward than I was at that moment. I did not confess to her how sharply I felt the relief of her acceptance coursing through my veins; I did not tell her how proud I was of who she had become under my wing. My pilot was impatient, my duties beckoned me beyond the safety of our stall, and I was more than happy to use these two facts as an excuse to flee. Only later, after my shift had passed and a new ache had bloomed beneath my scales, would I know the right words to say to her.

By then, it would be too late.

When I learned of what they had done while my spine was splitting beneath the weight of all that water, I understood that magic is not always good. The Sapiens' power had allowed them to strip Droshan of everything that she was, and everything that she could have been. What was so magical about that?

She had committed no errors, save for her inability to grow old in her first life. If she'd been just a little bigger, a little stronger, a little less naïve, then the Sapiens might have found some other use for her after the tunnels had been built and the stables had been reinforced. She occupied such little space, but it was nevertheless space that could be used for better, more necessary things. As long as Droshan lived – my Droshan, my sister – there would be one too many bodies to house and mouths to feed. There was only room for excess on one planet.

I tried then, and I still often find myself trying now, to think of her destruction as a kind of liberation. A life of being needed and used is surely not a good life at all. In that quiet place where she now exists for the second time, she can instead do and be whatever she wishes.

Magic is not always good. That is why I am still here, providing the things magic cannot ever provide and trying to restore balance one drop of water at a time.

My pilot walks me to my stall. At the entrance, I falter at the sight of another scaled body occupying the space. The other dragon lifts his head and stares, not at me, but at the metal figure by my side.

Freikon, the dragon says.

I assume that he is telling me his name. It is only right that I tell him mine in return, so I step forward and speak clearly: *Tydakon*.

No, he says. His body coils tighter, ready to spring forward at any moment. His eyes still bore into my pilot. *Freikon. He has not yet lost his scent. They were cruel to move me here.*

I am hardly able to make sense of his words. I creep closer, more bewildered than wary. We do not fight each other here. I do not foresee an attack. But his words have gnawed their way through my flesh and settled somewhere deep within me, and the added weight makes my head spin. There is some connection I have yet to make, I am sure. A new imbalance I have not yet noticed.

You are not Freikon? I ask.

Steam curls from his nostrils. He bares his teeth. *No. I am his brother.*

Why were you moved here? What caused the two of you to be separated?

You know less than you think, he says, and it is impossible to tell whether it is pity or hatred that drips from those words. Perhaps the two are inseparable.

Tell me, I say.

So, he does. He describes the day he returned to the stall he shared with his brother to find that the Sapiens had dragged Freikon away and stolen the life from him again. As he speaks, I think of Droshan. This stranger and I share the same story, and now we face each other as if we were destined to meet here, at this precise point in our lives.

Next, the dragon describes the accident in their stables: a crack in the wall that led to several collapsed stalls, the others now deemed unsafe for use.

They sent us wherever there was space, he tells me, pawing at the ground beneath us. *Apparently, they also sent us wherever there were ghosts.*

Behind me, I sense my pilot shifting. The fact that they have remained at the entrance to my stall all this time registers as odd. They should have returned by now to their hole in the wall. Those horrid tendrils should already be writhing inside them, greedily soaking up everything they have seen and heard during our shift. Might their prolonged presence be a sign of malfunction? Have I not already lost enough that I must now lose them too?

But I am being selfish. There is proof of this, at least, in the other dragon's curled lip and dulled eyes.

You are afraid.

I am furious, he bites back.

You are allowed to be both.

Something in him breaks; his body loosens, sinks, and settles in a heap on the ground.

I know it now, he says. *The missing piece. I know what they do to us. Our lives will never end while we are under their command.*

My pilot is stepping into the stall, moving past me, raising a hand. I am so taken aback by this chain of events that I can only watch as – with a tenderness that one could never imagine a machine to possess – they rest their hand upon the dragon's head.

Freikon, the dragon says once more.

The pilot's eyes flicker. A slow blink.

And then, for a long time, all is quiet.

We hover in the space between Blue and Red.

Here is everything I know:

I tilt, always, to the left. I exist in a universe of imbalance. I will never be able to carry as much water as the Sapiens need. I will face my second death sooner than I ever expected. I will hardly have the chance to rest before my third life begins.

Freikon drums two fingers above my left eye: *tap-tap-tap.* Somewhere out there, power surges through Droshan's synapses to pool in titanium limbs of her own. I wonder whose skull she taps, whose neck she clings to. I hope that we might cross paths soon, and that there will be enough of our scent left to recognise each other by.

In the meantime, I give in to the unnatural list of my body. I relinquish enough power to the aches in my wings to send me careening along an unfamiliar path. I am afraid. I am angry. I am allowed to be both.

The six empty sacks attached to my saddle flap against my sides as we bear down on Blue. We will not leave until every last one is filled to the brim.

Sophie St John is an author based in Perth, Western Australia. She primarily writes short fiction that tests the boundaries and definitions of various genres. In her free time, Sophie enjoys reading, listening to classic 80s heavy metal, and spending time with her four pet rabbits.

Learn more about Sophie at: Author Website | Instagram

Phillip Leavenworth

All Neema ever dreamed of was being a dragonrider. She grew up as a member of the nomadic Hartoo Clan, known for their death-defying performances for the nobility and for managing the thrilling races for the other clans. Neema was not one to shirk from a challenge. Her dragon, however, definitely was.

Today was the start of the Dragondash, an annual endurance race for the dragons of the Earth-like moon Drakel, located in an uninteresting part of the galaxy. This cycle, the Drakellian year, the Dragondash was to be held in the Maker's Gulch—an immense canyon cut through the northern continent of the moon. The arena stadium was seven thousand feet (a little over two thousand meters) above sea level. The canyon top reached as high as thirty-thousand feet (nine thousand meters), so high that every participant needed to wear basic pressure suits. It was only the third time the race had been held there in the last five hundred years.

High above Drakel's skies, the moon was home to flying lizards that the colonists slowly came to call dragons after their counterparts of Old Earth myth.

Her palms were sweaty as she laced up her gear, grabbed her saddle, and approached the glorious gargantuan beast. He had four legs and two large wings that jutted outward to the size of a large carriage. This one was named Zamin. He was one of the feisty ones who struggled with companionship, but he always came through after exhausting all other options. She fastened the saddle onto his back and checked the strength of the stirrups. Tight, solid. The barn doors opened out into the arena.

The arena was filled to the brim with thousands of people lining the bleacher seats that surrounded the stadium. The top ten best dragonriders in the world competed in this race. Her heart raced as she felt the cheers and stomps of the crowd in her chest. I can do this, she thought. She never wanted to face the three-time winner of the race, Grey Jax, and his rider, Colvax. His dragon was called a grey volt, known for its grey coat and yellow eyes. She guided Zamin into place and began putting on her helmet and fastening her flight gear.

Goggles, check.

Armor, check.

Shin and shoulder guards, check.

Zamin yawned as she did this and laid down on all fours, eliciting laughter from some of the crowd. Colvax walked over to Neema after patting Grey Jax down.

"Neema, long time no see," Colvax said.

She tried to look away from him and avoid his attention but realized it was unlikely to do anything.

"It has been a long time, hasn't it," Neema said.

"Look, after I beat you, maybe we can share a drink at the Officer's Lounge."

Zamin heard that and perked up.

"Beat me? You'll have to do much better than that to get a drink with me."

"Really? This is your first time here. You know how many riders have died trying to attempt this?"

Neema thought it over but had no idea.

"Well, it's a lot. I don't want you to be one of them. Up there, you'll deal with cold temperatures you've never felt anywhere else, and oxygen is low, too."

She knew all of this, but she'd ignored better patronizing.

"I just don't want you to get hurt," he continued.

"Well, that's the thing, Colvax. I want you to get hurt," she said.

Maybe that was a bit much, she thought. Zamin agreed. So, the psychic link between the two of them still worked. Colvax turned away in shock and walked over to his dragon.

Zamin had never experienced such intensity from two humans with palpable attraction before. After all, in dragon years, he was relatively young and inexperienced in his own kind's mating rituals. It would still be a few more years before all of that was explored for him. Neema grabbed onto the harness and set herself into the saddle.

The crowd went wild when a winner from over twenty or thirty years before was brought out to open the race. He was given a small green flag to initiate the festivities and declared loudly, "This race has now begun!"

When the signal was given, Neema, Zamin, and the nine other riders and dragons rose into the sky, their wings beating in perfect synchrony as they raced above the gulch's red sand. The wind whistled through their hair, and the arena below became but a small dot in the distance as they ascended farther into Drakel's grey skies.

The canyon looped around like a winding serpent, twisting and turning, challenging even the most experienced riders. Neema guided Zamin through some narrower spots, noting that Colvax and Grey Jax were farther ahead. But not by much. The thunderous beats of all the dragons echoed through the walls of the gulch.

As they circled back toward the arena, Neema saw that Colvax and Grey Jax maintained a solid lead over them. Neema felt the pangs of defeat fill her, but Zamin could only push himself harder and faster than he ever thought possible. He slid farther ahead, becoming more and more winded by each beat of his wings. But he knew that he couldn't let her down.

Colvax and Grey Jax surged ahead with a burst of speed, their forms growing smaller in the distance. Neema clenched her jaw, her hands gripping Zamin's reins tightly as she urged him to push harder. But they couldn't close the gap no matter how much she tried.

Neema felt her heart sink as they rounded the final bend. Her fingers started to lock up as he began losing her grip on the reins. Zamin felt the fire in her slowly dying, making him feel responsible. He sent a thought to her that he knew she'd appreciate. Don't give up. We're almost there, he told her through their psychic connection.

She nodded and reinvested herself. She thought it wasn't always the best rider or dragon that won the race. But it is always the one with more heart. For her, Grey Jax and Colvax were heartless, and they didn't deserve it. Victory wouldn't slip through her fingers once again. The fire of determination reignited in her.

Zamin, I know you can do it. I believe in you, she thought as she touched his shoulder.

Thank you, Neema. I won't let you down, he thought.

His wings flapped faster and powerfully, with Zamin gaining on Grey Jax and Colvax, closing the gap between them. He communicated to Grey Jax and told him that they'll win their fourth race next year. This made Grey Jax filled with fear.

What's the matter, Colvax told Grey Jax.

I've never seen Zamin like this. I'm scared, Grey Jax thought.

Don't let them get the better of you. They're only playing games. We're so close! Colvax thought.

Zamin and Neema shot ahead of them, with Colvax and Grey Jax looking on in shock as they crossed the finish line. The arena crowd was split between Colvax and Grey Jax fans and a new legion of Zamin and Neema's fans who erupted in thunderous applause. Her fellow Hartoo Clan gave a standing ovation and clapped with intense pride.

Zamin set foot on the arena floor as Neema undid the reins and removed her helmet. A referee crossed his arms while carrying the green flag, signaling their unforeseen victory. She couldn't help but smile and wave to her new fans. They'd won. Grey Jax and Colvax landed shortly after, second-best, at least this year. Colvax jumped off Grey Jax's back and stomped toward Neema with a look of displeasure. She turned to face him.

"Not bad, huh?" she asked.

He stood before her for a long moment before raising his hand.

"You did well, congratulations," he said. "Both of you."

Neema's eyes widened as she returned his handshake in earnest and turned to Zamin, who was patting him on the head. Colvax grabbed her hand and held it up with his in recognition of their victory. From then on, they all knew that their destiny was written in the skies of Drakel.

Phillip Leavenworth often says that he couldn't find the book he wanted on a shelf, so he wrote it instead! He is a former Los Angeles Times employee. He received his B.A. in English Rhetoric and Composition with a Professional Writing certificate from California State University Long Beach (CSULB) in 2023. He has three A.A. degrees in English, Journalism, and Creative Writing from Long Beach City College (LBCC), with designs to collect more. He has been a participant in the LBCC Creative Writing community since 2011. He was accepted into the MFA in Creative Writing program at San Diego State University and intends to explore a Ph.D. in English Literature… eventually. He lives in Los Angeles County with his fiancée.

Learn more about Phillip at: LinkTree

I Am Dragon

Draco Amethystus

I Am Dragon.
Born to a privileged place in the world.
Lies spouted like so many licking flames.

I Am Dragon.
The heat of truth was scorching, burning deep.
It seared through my scales like wood on embers.

I Am Dragon.
I learned to love the shadows of our cave.
But I couldn't live up to their lessons.

I Am Dragon.
Finally, I clawed and crawled my way out.
Biting and tearing till I ruined all.

I Am Dragon.
A sheer cliff stood barren before me there.
Wind and life called while death waited below.

I Am Dragon.
Flaming fears could not hold back my courage.
Leaping with flared wings I dove down the cliff.

I Am Dragon.
Cold spray from crashing waves stung my body.
The ocean waited, an impatient death.

I Am Dragon.
Death would have to learn patience with me though.
I pulled out of the death dive and soared on.

I Am Dragon.
Following the rising sun, I still live.
Mystery awaits and I will find it.

I Am Dragon.

Draco Amethystus

The alarm on my phone plays one of those harmless melodies intended to wake you up without annoying the hell out of you. Inevitably, it annoys the hell out of you. It's five am and sleep flees like sheep from a dragon. Draconic comparisons are one of my unapologetic, nerdy little eccentricities. They keep me close to that imaginary creature I've loved since I was a little boy.

Rolling over, I turn off the alarm and slide out of bed. The cats follow hoping that I'll feed them early. I won't. It's nice to pretend that they love my company though. The door to the writing lair squeaks a bit. Calling the room where you do the majority of your writing by a ridiculous name really makes you feel like more of an author. It also combats that nasty little monster, imposter syndrome.

The desk lamp light and open computer screen glow in two different shades, casting shadows in the gray predawn morning. The cats lay down nearby, eyes closed, tails twitching lightly. Opening my current work in progress, soon enough I'm lost in a stream of creativity. The Muses speak to me, filling my soul with pure joy. Time disappears and the typing rhythm lulls me further into the river that is flow, gently floating me along.

It's in this frame of mind that my world changes forever. The cats notice first. They always do. Both of them dart from the room as light fills the writing lair. It's not the light of the sun or that of a lightbulb. Well, technically speaking it must be the light of a sun, but not my sun.

My eyes widen at what I can only describe as a portal that has opened in the corner of the room. The wall behind it remains, but from within the oval of light there is a green meadow. A figure steps out of it, snatching up all my attention.

I drink in the person with all my concentration. In my mind's eye I describe him as I would in a story. He's taller than I am by at least a couple of inches. He wears a forest green cloak with the hood up. The cloak covers everything on his person, casting his angular face in shadow. The only other thing visible is a leather satchel crossed over his chest from his right shoulder. His hands reach up gracefully and pull the hood back so that it rests on his shoulders and his face is fully revealed. The pointed ears stand out almost immediately and then it's the almond-shaped eyes. He's an elf. The Lord of the Rings sort of elf. His long hair is tied back and even in the pathetic light of my desk lamp it glows faintly, softly. His face is without lines and he smiles just as gently. Bowing barely while keeping his eyes on me, he speaks, "Greetings."

I jump to my feet and bow in return, but deeper. Coming back up I return his greeting but don't know what his name is so my words, well, word, stumble off lost in the shadows stuffed into the corners of the room.

He smiles again and speaks once more, "Favaok."

Thankfully, my brain isn't completely worthless in the midst of this fever dream. "Greetings, Favaok."

His smile widens. "Your desire to be courteous is most appreciated, and welcome. It proves to me that I have chosen correctly."

My eyebrow rises high in question. He smiles again and explains, "I think you have an inkling of why I am here. I believe it is something that you have longed for and desired in a deep manner for some time. Can you guess what it might be? Can you speak the words, the wish, the deep desire out loud?"

There's nothing about this moment that isn't surreal. But it's also a dream come true and all I have to do is say it out loud. Gathering my breath, and my courage, I speak. "A-a dragon egg."

Favaok nods in agreement. Pulling back the cover of his satchel, his hands delve into the depths. Moments later that feel more like an eternity, his hands return cradling a large oval of deepest violet. It's so dark it would be black if not for the faint glow of lavender around it as if a halo or aura. I can't, and don't want to, take my eyes from it. Fear fills my whole body that if I were to look away, it would all disappear, melt back into my imagination.

Favaok appears to read minds, "This is real, I assure you." He walks toward me slowly. My knees shake, but I stay standing. I look him in the eyes as he continues to speak, "I present to you this dragon egg, the most precious of all gifts. If chosen by the dragonet inside, you will become a bonded dragon rider."

Somehow keeping my presence of mind, I wipe my sweating hands on my shorts. The last thing I want to do is drop the egg. To have this lifelong dream come true magically and then to drop the egg would be beyond mortifying. Favaok smiles in understanding.

I reach out and cup my hands. As he places it gently there and lets go, three things are apparent almost immediately. First, the egg is much heavier than I would have thought, but it makes sense given a dragonet is inside. Second, it's warm. It's a lovely warmth like a fireplace in a drafty house or an electric blanket or hot chocolate during a winter storm. I can't help the smile that spreads across my face. But it's the third realization that has my heart burning with joy. The egg is humming. Or rather, the dragonet inside is.

Looking back up in wonder at Favaok, I see his face mirrors my own. Tears of joy mist over my view for a moment, but as I blink them away, I see that he must do the same. "I see she has chosen well."

"She?" I ask.

Favaok nods his confirmation. "It sounds like she's ready right now."

I'm more awestruck than ever. Realizing I want her to be as comfortable as possible, I sit down cross legged on a blanket with the egg between my thighs to keep her warm while this happens. While the dragonet hatches. My dragonet.

I can barely believe my own thoughts. My dragonet. Is this really happening? They're like words on a page. Mental images of a story. Only imagination. But the egg begins to rock back and forth and before my eyes, cracks fissure up and down it. The shaking stops. A small, dark claw punches out of the front of the egg and I know my eyes are wide and my mouth lit up in a smile so genuine that I can't remember the last time I felt this happy.

The tiny claw grasps the eggshell and peels pieces off bit by bit. Slowly but surely the dragonet is exposed, curled up with wings around her little body and tail tucked up in her lap. Her eyes are a bit too large for her triangular face. But they glow with the slit pupils of a cat, a lavender marble of reflective beauty.

As the last remnants of the forsaken shell fall away, the hatchling unfurls her leathery wings, still shiny with the after birth of the egg. She looks straight at me and trills the way that a cat would when they're curious. I have to stop myself from melting from the adorableness. She's so beautiful.

Hesitantly, I reach out a hand toward her and she watches my hand with unblinking eyes. Before I can pull it back, she strikes like a snake, no other suggestion giving away her intent. Her needle-sharp fangs slide deep beneath my skin. A tooth remains behind, embedded in my flesh. Like the dragon, the tooth is much faster than I am, and I don't have time to remove it from my palm before it slips beneath the skin and blooming blood, the wound closes immediately. It was almost as if it didn't want to be taken out, like a giant splinter meant to stay on permanently. It begins to burn like a flame inside my hand. Looking up at Favaok for assistance, he only smiles serenely still.

I look back down at the hatchling as the flames burn their way through my entire body. It hurts, badly. I try not to scream out loud as the flames build, as they course their way through my veins and the entirety of my body. The hatchling watches on, as if waiting to see what will happen. For the briefest of moments I wonder if this has all been some kind of elaborate interdimensional joke, just to mess with me because they somehow knew that I love dragons so why not mess with me before killing me.

The pain grows unbearable. I almost lose consciousness, but out of sheer stubbornness I breathe through it and eventually it begins to subside little by little. With the pain fading, a new and unique sensation grows in my mind. And I realize after a moment's time what it is. It's my hatchling. She's speaking to me. Her crocodilian mouth doesn't move though. No, the words are coming to me in my mind. Surprise jolts through my entire body. We're bonded telepathically.

"Of course, we are, silly." Of all of the words I thought my dragon would say to me first, these were certainly not it. "I said what needed to be said," she continues. Clearly, I don't have any privacy from her. "Not yet," she teases. And she is a she. There's a feminine quality even to her mental voice. It's lyrical, musical. It's filled with colors, all bright and bold. "Thank you." Her voice seems to smile at my compliments. That is going to take some getting used to. "You'll adjust. I wouldn't have chosen you otherwise." Laughter escapes me.

Favaok smiles down at us. I'd almost forgotten he was there. "You have done well." His voice is filled with joy. I feel the same swell in my chest and stretch out through my entire body. "She needs a name."

My eyebrows rise. Of course, she does and I know exactly what I want to name her, but I can only hope that she will agree with it. I know she's listening to my thoughts and had already heard what I wanted to name her, but I want to say the word out loud. "Amethysta," I say. She sits for a moment more before she nuzzles me and curls up in a ball on my lap, a humming sound vibrating throughout her warm little body. I realize she's purring, or at least the dragon equivalent of it.

"I love it," she whispers sleepily into my mind. More warmth spreads through my heart.

Favaok speaks, "You have a decision to make now. The portal won't stay open for much longer. If you come through with Amethysta, you will be trained by other riders and meet more dragons who will school you in both war and wisdom. Amethysta will be with her kind. However, you will have to leave behind your own world, never to return. You will never see your wife, your children, or other loved ones again.

"If you stay, you risk Amethysta. This world is not for dragons. She will be alone, stranded without her kind. She will be adrift in a sea of humanity, her lone companion her rider, yes, but no other dragons with whom to live and love."

Words fail me, both verbally and telepathically. So many options and opportunities flash through my brain like lightning. They hurt nearly as much one way as another.

Amethysta waits patiently. She understands how difficult this is. She knows the repercussions with each choice. When I finally express my decision to her mind to mind, she trills softly in support. Speaking the words out loud, Favaok only nods in agreement once more. With a small smile he turns to walk back through the portal. I stand with Amethysta in my arms, prepared to make this impossible choice. A choice of dragons and dreams.

Alas, this isn't really happening. No, it's just me sitting here typing out each one of these words, a longing that will never be filled. A dream that will never turn into reality. A wish that will never come true.

My one comfort is my imagination. There I am a god of worlds without end and dragons without number. There I am both rider and dragon. There I am free. These are my dragon dreams.

Draco Amethystus is a published author of fiction and poetry. He has a deep and abiding love for reading and writing books. A self-proclaimed aficionado of dragons, Fae, and vampires, each often features in his work. When he isn't disciplined enough on his own to put in his daily writing, his cats sit on him to make certain he does.

When he isn't writing or reading, Draco travels as much as he can, mostly in forests or on the water…hiking, kayaking, and diving across the world. A polyglot, he loves to learn languages and collects university degrees mostly just for the fun of it.

Learn more about Draco here: Author Website

Acknowledgments

There are so many people to thank you. First, a huge thank you to each and every one of the wonderfully talented authors who were brave enough to allow me to publish their fantastic work in this inaugural anthology of the Muses of Mythology. Here's to many more to come!

A great big shout out to the Storm Dragon Publishing team. To Rowan and Persephone, thank you for all your kitty cat emotional support. No matter how down I might be, you always soothe me with your lovely purrs and sweet cat cuddles. To Crystal, you're always the first to read my work. Thank you so much for your honest and helpful feedback, no matter how bad the truth might hurt because it always makes my writing better than it would be without you. To Haven and Ty, the artisan power couple. Thank you both for all your support. To Jessie and Hope, I'll always be grateful for your beautiful art and that you've allowed SDP to use it.

No acknowledgement would be sufficient without a thank you to all you dear book dragons. Without readers, all authors would be lost. And not in the lovely Tolkien way.

www.ingramcontent.com/pod-product-compliance
Lightning Source LLC
Chambersburg PA
CBHW022115310726
48972CB00007B/2052